★

Think!

No one had noticed her come in. She had to get out as silently and unseen. But first she must cover herself, check what the man had on him, clean off any signs of her presence that might overlay the killer's traces; because clearly she'd been set up. She was meant to be caught here with the dead man, the only person in the building who could be proved to have any connection with him.

So he mustn't be identified.

Even while she planned, she was running her right hand, covered with a corner of her silk shawl, through the man's pockets.

And finding she'd been beaten to it.

——————————— ★ ———————————

"...the strength of her characterizations is exceptional."
—*Mystery News*

"...a tight, tricky whodunit plot..."
—*New York Times Book Review*

Also available from Worldwide Mystery by
CLARE CURZON

DEATH PRONE
FIRST WIFE, TWICE REMOVED
CAT'S CRADLE

Clare CURZON

PAST MISCHIEF

WORLDWIDE.

TORONTO • NEW YORK • LONDON
AMSTERDAM • PARIS • SYDNEY • HAMBURG
STOCKHOLM • ATHENS • TOKYO • MILAN
MADRID • WARSAW • BUDAPEST • AUCKLAND

If you purchased this book without a cover you should be aware
that this book is stolen property. It was reported as "unsold and
destroyed" to the publisher, and neither the author nor the
publisher has received any payment for this "stripped book."

PAST MISCHIEF

A Worldwide Mystery/November 1997

First published by St. Martin's Press, Incorporated.

ISBN 0-373-26256-6

Copyright © 1994 by Clare Curzon.
All rights reserved. No part of this book may be reproduced
or transmitted in any form or by any means, electronic or
mechanical, including photocopying, recording or by any
information storage and retrieval system, without permission
in writing from the publisher. For information, contact:
St. Martin's Press, Incorporated, 175 Fifth Avenue,
New York, NY 10010-7848 U.S.A.

All characters in this book are fictitious, and any resemblance to
actual persons, living or dead, is purely coincidental.

® and TM are trademarks of Harlequin Enterprises Limited.
Trademarks indicated with ® are registered in the United States
Patent and Trademark Office, the Canadian Trade Marks Office
and in other countries.

Printed in U.S.A.

To mourn a mischief that is past and gone
Is the next way to draw new mischief on.

—Othello

ONE

A BLACK CAB PULLED INTO the forecourt of Marylebone station and two women hurried across the precinct to scan the departure screens.

The flow of homebound commuters had thinned to a trickle. In parody of a Lowry tableau a few isolated figures were still scattered, briefcase by feet, waiting for the next computerized announcement of their train.

Sidestepping a youth popping the lid of a Sprite can, the younger woman saw the Wycombe screen blank out, backed by the sound of the turbo drawing away. 'Missed it! By the skin of our teeth.'

Her companion smoothed her cuff back over the face of a Cartier watch, smiled lazily and suggested, 'The next is in half an hour. So a coffee, I think.' She turned, not waiting for an answer, and headed for the buffet.

On the scarlet circular bench nearby, a lean man lowered his newspaper to watch her long-legged stride and the efforts of the younger woman to keep up.

Nothing changes, he thought wryly. Miranda, never short of someone to run after her.

ANNETTE BRIERS HEADED for the buffet counter while her boss stared around, selecting a table at the far end. She was seated there before Annette had found a tray and pushed it along the rails.

There was no one to take her order. Waiting, she debated whether she should have picked up some Danish or wrapped chocolate, but couldn't picture Miranda Gregory's fine white teeth embedded in anything so commonplace.

Shouting across the intervening tables to ask was definitely out.

And then what kind of coffee? Regular, cappuccino or espresso?

She consulted the wallboard opposite. Large or small were on offer. Were they expected to drink out of carton beakers? She didn't mind for herself, but Ms Gregory, well—she felt doubly maladroit.

Someone came from behind her and trailed round the end of the counter, a young Caribbean woman with a tired cotton cap and equally weary eyes. She seemed to have been crying.

Annette ordered, carefully carried the tray with the two coffees to the corner table, passing another where a large black woman sat with bulging carrier bags at her feet. A vacant swing-seat was pushed down alongside. It was here that the waitress must have perched, near the end of her day's work, for a welcome sit with Mum freshly come from a shopping spree. And then her company hadn't proved all that comforting.

Annette deposited her tray with the two coffees. 'I hope this is all right,' she offered, unloading.

Indifferent, Miranda Gregory looked at or through the offerings and laid two pound coins on the table. She reached for the nearer cup and saucer while Annette pushed back the money. 'Oh no, please let me...'

'Nonsense,' said Ms Gregory crisply. 'Of course not.'

'If you insist.' Annette scrabbled through her purse for the correct change. Behind her back the unhappy young Caribbean woman had returned to her mother's table and resumed a tragic low-voiced recital.

Miranda Gregory placed her handbag on the chair along-side, so the younger girl took the seat opposite, facing back towards the door. It gave her the first chance of their short journey together to look directly at her boss.

She was so elegant. Not just because of the smooth, ivory complexion, the delicate hollows under slanting cheekbones, nor the patrician carriage of her slender neck. Her immaculate body moved with assured fluency, as though she knew success was an award fate had primed her for, and she would willingly share her special gifts with the world. Small wonder that others' heads turned and eyes followed.

What could it be like to have such poise, such magnetism? Also the brains to go with them. Because Ms Miranda Gregory was by no means just a pretty face.

And the unique way she dressed. Today she wore a low-key slim suit of a peculiar smoky green, but over one shoulder and tucked through her fine lizard-skin belt was a heavy silk shawl with gold snakings over smudgy purple and the same muted green. Apart the two colours might have seemed drab, but together—and with her glossy hair, bluish-black, spilled over all—she was darkly splendid. Even a little scary.

I would do anything, Annette thought, to be like her. To please her.

Annette's home station was Wembley, and Ms Gregory lived further down the same line—in the stockbroker-showbiz belt, as Annette liked to think of it. Normally her boss drove to London in a blue BMW, but it was in dock, and this evening, after they'd stayed to work late, Ms Gregory had offered the girl a lift to the station in her taxi. It was then she discovered they would be taking the same train.

They both finished their coffee and Miranda opened her handbag for lipstick and mirror. Annette, furtively patting at her own mouth with a tissue, looked up at a suppressed exclamation. Ms Gregory had stiffened. She caught the girl's glance of open curiosity and started riffling through her handbag, searching.

'Oh, how stupid of me.' She snapped the bag shut. 'I'll have to go back.'

'Can't I do it for you? Is it something in the office? I could—'

The seat tipped as the older woman rose. 'Thank you. It's something I must see to myself. Go ahead, Annette. The train's probably in by now. I'll see you on Monday. It was good of you to stay late. I shan't forget.'

Outside, they parted abruptly. Annette watched her move quickly away towards the taxi rank before digging out her own ticket and passing through the barrier of the trains.

That last sight of the delicious Miranda Gregory was to remain forever imprinted on her mind.

The tall man on the scarlet bench half rose, put out a tentative hand, then sat back. As ever, he had missed his chance.

Knowing that today Miranda must take the train, he'd waited hoping to head her off. But couldn't with the other girl there. And now she'd gone haring off on her own. For a moment he was in two minds about following. Should he see what devilment she was up to this time, or give up and get over to Victoria for his own train?

Still undecided, he found himself stumbling after her, only to see her taxi disappear as he reached the station exit. There was only one other cab and that was already being taken by a small man in a tweed fishing-hat.

BALANCING GINGERLY, Detective-Superintendent Yeadings trod from beam to beam, ducking to avoid a rafter here, colliding with an invisible cobweb there, and distastefully flicking at his face to dislodge the silky stickiness on to his fingers where it continued clinging, rubbed into a fine elasticity.

He stumbled, one foot almost sliding into the fibre-glass insulation of the space between the beams. He had a brief vision of himself, more Laurel than Hardy, dangling with a leg through the plaster ceiling of the guest bedroom below, eventually rescued by the fire service and ever thereafter owing rounds at the Feathers on the strength of the humiliation.

Partially immobilized after breaking bones in three toes,

Nan called up to him from the foot of the ladder, 'It's more towards the kitchen corner. There must be quite a big hole. Can't you see daylight anywhere?'

Poor lass, frustrated at not being able to get to grips with it herself, Yeadings thought. 'I'm nearly there,' he rumbled back.

The house plan looked enormous viewed from the loft, with only isolated uprights and no room divisions. He felt his way along the waist-high boarding once fixed up as base for a model train track. The electric sockets were all laid on for transformer and signalling gear, but he'd stopped work on it when Sally preferred angora rabbits to Thomas the Tank Engine. Now that young Luke was getting steady on his feet he ought to complete the layout. But better have a solid floor put in first. Which could prove quite costly.

He rounded an upright timber and saw, as Nan had said, a patch of bright daylight, startlingly white against the biscuit gloom barely dispelled by the single bulb above the trapdoor.

There was some local mess where the squirrels had nibbled and stripped the coating from fibre suitcases and superannuated cane chairs. He wedged a torch to shine on the area, then took a tobacco tin of nails and a hammer from the back pocket of his jeans to begin closing the gap with the square of hardboard which he'd carried up.

That should keep the little beggars out. He'd had enough of their banging and bouncing overhead at night, like furniture-swapping neighbours in an upstairs flat. And, as Nan pointed out, before long the swallows would be building under the eaves. With squirrels as neighbours, their eggs could be at risk.

Interfering with nature's established cycle, he cautioned himself, dropping on to a convenient rattan stool precariously balanced on parallel beams. He surveyed his domain of cast-offs.

How had he ever supposed he'd find further use for this hoard of tatty junk? Had he miser instincts? Some of the stuff had been rubbish even years back, suitable Hallowe'en bonfire feed. Other pieces might yet give some needy person reasonable service, so why had he and Nan hung on to them? Was it fear that times would get hard again, harder even than his early days as a bachelor plod in rented rooms?

And then there were all those anonymous cartons stuffed with long-forgotten books, ornaments and photograph albums from the time when his parents were alive; relics from his childhood home; their old holiday brochures; even three hatboxes crammed with his dead mother's formidable millinery. Nan had once said they might some day do for party dressing-up, and that had been when they were still childless.

Things, objects: assembled witnesses to long-gone events. The boxed grey top-hat proudly bought for his wedding, resurrected since for lesser, shadowy occasions that echoed the original; the dismantled hanging-cot which recalled his numbing shock on learning that their longed-for baby had an irreversible defect.

His peaks and troughs. These objects had been a part of him, carried the mark of his formative tragedies and glories. He could almost believe them Dickensianly the Ghosts of Yeadings Past.

It seemed they had no future use, but in accumulating they had acquired a patina of history, therefore demanding some degree of respect. While they silently built up cenotaph significance, the guilt implied in abandoning them increased alongside. He half resented their slow emotional stranglehold. Recall of the past could shape one's future actions. One was, to some extent, possessed by what one hung on to.

Even now, uneasy at the extent of such senseless hoarding, he knew that on some dull day yet to come he would wallow pleasurably in opening up the dusty trunks and boxes, reliving their contents' glories and shames. Wraithlike as the cobwebs that festooned them, they were also as strangely unbreakable and clinging.

Nan called again from below. His hammering had sent her away satisfied, but the following silence betrayed his unproductive brooding. Downstairs, tea was poured and was cooling. Yeadings grunted, standing cautiously to avoid hitting his head on the sloping roof, dusted off the seat of his odd-job jeans, and made again for the ladder.

DUSK SETTLING ON THE outside world found Annette Briers also plunged in solemn considerations, facing up frankly to her image in the carriage window. Under a fuzz of gingery hair it was a pale-skinned squarish face with the normal number of features placed roughly where you'd expect. None of them was distinguished, perhaps with the exception of the widely spaced, round blue eyes which gave her a childlike owlishness at odds with her perceptive mind.

Below shoulder level the rest was better ignored. She knew she was rather dumpy and too plump. In fits and starts she had tried quite hard to remedy this, but high heels made her totter and she was frankly more gourmande than gourmet. When your impact on the world occasionally disappointed you, what better consolation was there than food?

At least she hadn't to wear specs. Her eyes were functional as well as reasonably—well, *un-ugly*. And her mental ability was surely confirmed when Ms Gregory chose her at twenty to be her personal secretary. The streetwise girls of the typing pool might despise her as old-fashioned and naïve, but she was long on loyalty, even a bit given to heroine-worship where her boss was concerned.

Staring past her own image into the darkening night, she resolved to make that asset indelibly her trademark. It was time to stop being negative. She must stress what qualities had helped her get as far as this. As Ms Gregory's assured progress continued, Annette would follow in her shadow, equally on the way up.

AS MIRANDA GREGORY went back through the station archway there had been two cabs waiting at the kerb. A man went striding past, brushed against her elbow, muttered an apology and made for the second, leaving her to tell the first cabbie, 'Longthorne House, Lowndes Street.'

They ran into the usual late shopping crowds milling on the pavements, spilling over and skipping out from under the cab's wheels as it crossed Oxford Street, and in due course a snarl of traffic turning into Knightsbridge. She tapped on the driver's partition and pushed the fare through. 'Drop me here. I'll be quicker walking.'

It was quite dark as she went in by the smoked glass entrance doors of Longthorne House. The porter on duty had his back turned at the night switchboard. If she used a lift the *swoosh* of closing doors would make him glance across. She turned towards the stairs and ran lightly up.

On the second floor the double doors engraved with *Matherson and Corby* stood open, the cleaners' keys on a ring in the lock. Inside, the corridor lights were on. From the typing pool area, as she passed, came the whine of a vacuum cleaner which cut suddenly to expose a reedy treble duet wailing 'Lerv, lerv. Lerv is all you need.'

Miranda Gregory continued to the door that bore her name, and the designation 'Expo & Merchandizing Manager'. She used her key to get in, walked through the darkened outer office to her own, into which sodium lamps from the street below threw up a garish glow, allowing her to skirt obstacles as she made for the window.

With the vertical blinds closed she switched on the standard lamp, observed that all was tidy and the waste bins cleared. There was a scent of air freshener. And something else. Anyway, the cleaners had finished here. There would be no interruptions while she sat waiting.

She rounded her swing leather chair and, startled, saw there was no need to wait. The man had arrived and made himself at home there in the dark. He lay back relaxed, his head in the shadow cast by the big chair's wings.

Cold anger at his insolence tightened inside like a coiling spring as she tilted the lamp that partially lit him.

Then saw the full horror. Part of the man's left temple and forehead were missing. And over the rest shone a drying mask of blackening blood.

SHE COULD HAVE LOST only a few seconds.

When the haze cleared she was still standing, bent forward, her fingers stiffly clutching at the desk edge, for an instant impossible to loosen.

She wanted to run. To run and go on running until everything stopped and she knew nothing. But a lifetime's hard-learnt caution took over. She forced back the nausea and made herself sit at Annette's smaller desk with a profile view of the dead man. Slowly the pulsing in her head and through her chest became less threatening. She was able to engage her mind to accept what she saw.

'Body,' she said aloud. It was only a body.

No, it was much more. Far worse. A message in itself: 'This could happen to you.'

The implications were awful. Not only the horror of a killer having been here, but someone had been close enough to know about the note in her handbag. That unknown person had stayed on in the building when everyone else left, had waited concealed and done this.

Could still be here!

Was she even sure that they were only cleaners along the corridor outside? Not a killer among them?

No, she must keep tight hold of herself. *Think!*

No one had noticed her come in. She had to get out as silently and unseen. But first she must cover herself, check what the man had on him, clean off any signs of her presence that might overlay the killer's traces; because clearly she'd been set up. She was meant to be caught here with the dead man, the only person in the building who could be proved to have any connection with him.

So he mustn't be identified.

Also Annette Briers had to be silenced, because inevitably when questions were asked she would blurt out that Miranda had left her at Marylebone, intending to return here.

Even while she planned, she was running her right hand, covered with a corner of the silk shawl, through the man's pockets.

And finding she'd been beaten to it.

He carried no ID, not so much as a handkerchief with a laundry mark. And there was no message for her. Everything had been removed, wiped out, the desktop left clear. Leaving nothing to work on, for her or anyone else.

A deadly chill invaded her body, with an echoing pulse of fear. She had a giddy sensation of being suspended weightless in space, with no future, no present, no such identity as Miranda Gregory.

She could hear the rhythmic functions of her own body, the pumping heartbeat and inside her head a rushing of blood, but it was as if she was outside, and these sounds came from the machinery of past actions relentlessly clanking on and threatening her world's destruction.

TWO

Even Annette Briers, who enjoyed her work, would have admitted that Mondays were not her favourite day. But nothing had prepared her for the grisly scene which she encountered after that weekend.

She had arrived at work early, the morning's post having brought a note from Ms Gregory to the effect that she was away visiting a client. Annette was asked to remove and reserve a file not picked up on Friday as intended. So she had collected the office key from reception desk, walked briskly in and was met by the obscene sight in Ms Gregory's chair, spotlit by the desk-lamp in an otherwise darkened room.

Sent home in shock, after a brief questioning by the police, she steeled herself to ring her boss, but couldn't reach her either at work or on her home number.

Tuesday brought a visit from a plain-clothes officer of Thames Valley Police with a copy of her initial statement to sign for the Met. She read it through, agreed the content and added her name. Next day the man came back accompanied by a woman colleague some six or seven years older than herself.

Again there were questions, some the same, some new. The stress now was not on her experience of Monday but on her parting with her boss at Marylebone railway station.

'Do you still have the note about picking up the file?' WDC Rosemary Zyczynski asked, closely watching the girl.

The question clearly upset her. It transpired that she had kept it, putting it carefully away before she left the house that Monday morning. It was the only time her boss had

written to her personally, and the little dumbo seemed quite
in awe of the older woman.

When asked, she produced the note and the envelope that
had held it. 'Posted Saturday in Beaconsfield,' Zyczynski
pointed out to her colleague.

'That's where she lives,' Annette offered.

'So has she been in touch with you since?'

Annette was embarrassed. 'No. I tried to telephone her
but she seems to be away. When it happened—I mean,
walking in and finding…I guess everything went out of my
head. It wasn't until they'd sent me home by taxi that I
remembered what I'd gone in early to do. So I rang one of
the girls in the general office and asked her to pull the file
out and lock it away until Ms Gregory came in. She said
she would, as soon as anyone could get into that office. The
police had sealed it off, and I thought that would be all I
could do. Didn't she get it?'

The two detectives exchanged a glance. 'Probably,' the
man said, 'if that's what she promised to do. What was the
file about?'

'It was just a forward booking. Matherson and Corby
arrange trade exhibitions and conferences. Ms Gregory
liaises on sites and merchandizing.'

The man's wooden face became even more expression-
less. 'Merchandizing?' he questioned, as if it were the name
of a mythical beast.

'She suggests extra ways of advertising and promoting
their products. The file she wanted put aside was actually
for a big charity organization. I expect she was working on
slogans for T-shirts, and overprinted freebies such as carrier
bags.'

'Ah.' He nodded, reminding her of one of those toy dogs
in car rear windows.

'Do they know yet who the dead man was?' she ventured. 'There's been no name mentioned on television
news.'

Again she was aware of the two exchanging glances.

'We're not actually concerned with that case. Do you take a local paper?' Zyczynski asked her.

'Yes, but I haven't seen this week's. Why? What—?'

'I'm afraid this is more bad news for you. There's the description of an unidentified hit-and-run victim, from an incident occurring on the Penn-Beaconsfield main road. We know now that it was Miranda Gregory, your senior at Matherson and Corby. One of her neighbours has identified her.'

'Oh, *no!*'

At one time it had annoyed Rosemary Zyczynski, this instant and instinctive refusal to accept the truth, but she knew it was a universal human need, to demand time's reversal and the unbearable not to have happened. She had cried out the same words herself, after a jewel robbery shoot-out, kneeling over a fellow-officer's body.

'I'm sorry,' she told the girl.

'Dead? She's not *dead?*'

'She's in coma, so there's hope yet. The accident must have happened on Saturday night or early Sunday morning.'

'Where is she? Can I go and see her?'

She was told that normally only close family were allowed in the Intensive Therapy Unit, but so far no one had been traced. If there was any chance that Annette's being there and talking to the unconscious woman could help bring her round she might be allowed in.

'I could run you there now,' Zyczynski offered, 'if you feel up to it.'

'If you think it could do any good.' The girl sounded willing but doubtful.

'Come on, then. I'll have a word with the doctor in charge when we get there.' She turned to the other detective. 'All right if I drop you off, Skip?'

He nodded again, and Annette was relieved. Something about the man's unmoving features disturbed her. She felt safer seeing a little of what other people were thinking. The woman detective was different, soft brown eyes full of sympathy, a moment's reassuring pressure on her arm. And yet competent; you could tell that from the clean-cut suit she wore, and the close cap of dark curls. Someone you could depend on.

ZYCZYNSKI WENT OFF to consult with authority, leaving Annette sitting in the corridor outside the IT Unit, looking almost comatose herself. A young nursing auxiliary passed twice, taking messages. The third time she stopped to speak.

Annette looked up as the other's shadow fell across the floor. Stiffly she unclasped the tense hands in her lap. 'I'm sorry. What did you say?'

'Tea. Universal remedy.'

It was kindly meant. The youngster handed over a polystyrene beaker and took the empty seat beside her, ready to give comfort. 'Are you a friend of the coma patient?'

'Not exactly. She's my boss. She hadn't come in to work this week, you see. And somehow—I was afraid... Oh, it doesn't matter.'

She tucked her head down. 'Thanks for the tea.' She clasped the beaker in both hands, as a lifeline.

The auxiliary nodded. 'I was helping in Casualty on Sunday when she was brought in, but I never heard who she was.'

'Miranda Gregory.' Annette muttered the name almost fiercely. 'Do you think she'll pull through?'

'I couldn't say. Not qualified enough. Sorry.' She watched the other warily.

'Has she had any visitors?'

'Just police, but I think they've given up.'

'I'm not sure I'll be allowed in to see her.'

The girl frowned, trying to remember Sister Tutor's lecture. 'She should have somebody sitting by, a familiar voice, music she's fond of, anything that links up with submerged memories. You could talk about your work maybe, or jokes you've shared. Nobody's sure just how deeply unconscious coma patients are, but it's likely they can hear and understand without showing any reaction. The past is still stored in their minds. It's just a matter of bringing it back.'

'I doubt if I'll be much use. We weren't that close.'

'So why do you want to see her?'

Why did she? Annette demanded of herself.

'She's a marvellous person. It seems so awful, what's happened: impossible. And at work they sent me home for a week, after the shock—of something else.' Annette's voice broke. 'And there's really no other place to go.'

The auxiliary grinned. 'I'm sure she'd enjoy being told she was so marvellous. That would wake me up fast enough. Look, your friend's coming back. Maybe it's good news. I'll push off now.'

Rosemary Zyczynski was smiling. 'We can go in together. You try talking to her. I'll just listen.'

At first it was hard. Annette had never been required to initiate a conversation with her boss and she was too aware of the difference in their age and experience. She was still learning the nitty-gritty of her new job which, after three years of straightforward shorthand-typing in an insurance company, covered diverse operations. On Ms Gregory's presentation and skilled liaising with clients hung much of the reputation of Matherson in the UK.

Of the six weeks Annette had been her secretary, for four of them she'd been separated from her boss by a middle-aged PA who without warning had either taken instant retirement or been unceremoniously sacked. Whichever way it was, one Thursday all was normal, but next morning Mrs Lodd had been missing from her desk, and a cab driver was sent to deliver to her everything cleared from it.

Annette knew there were whispers going round the firm, and several times she had been approached by the curious who imagined she might have been privy to the ins and outs of the affair. She'd been content to accept and pass on the official version, which was voluntary early retirement on health grounds. For herself it had meant wonderful and unexpected promotion, but it was clearly a delicate subject and one to be avoided now.

So what could she talk about, when apart from shared office files they were virtual strangers? Foremost in her mind loomed Monday's obsessive and totally forbidden topic of the dead man in her boss's office. How long must that horror crowd out all that was normal and reassuring?

While masked and gloved figures flitted silently between the bays, never stopping their checking, equipment renewal, notemaking, the still form in the white bed went on ticking into the machines it was connected to. The visible part of the face had little more colour than the gauze bandages supporting the mask over mouth and nose. Naked shoulders showed above the turned-down sheet and there were wires everywhere, monitor screens with a metronome bleep, and a ventilator sighing in the background.

Miranda Gregory was as inanimate, Annette thought with shaming irreverence, as an ice-shrouded side of beef in a freezer.

From the corridor beyond the slatted white blinds there came occasional voices and shadows of people hurrying by; once a sound of hopeless sobbing reached her. Annette looked desperately around for inspiration and willed her mind back into the office they'd shared since the departure of Mrs Lodd.

Oh God, no! Not the last time she'd been there—not Monday!—but all the other times.

She recalled the vase of hothouse flowers that were changed twice a week. She started to babble about roses and lilies; how lovely Mum's clematis had been this summer round the back door; what she'd do herself if she had a big garden and unlimited funds.

The silent white form on the bed went on ticking into its machines and slowly passing fluids in and out by transparent tubes. After about twelve minutes a nurse hovering in

the background nodded for Annette to release the pallid
hand and withdraw for the next set of intimate checks to
be made.

Behind her, Rosemary Zyczynski materialized again. Annette had forgotten her entirely, the silent watcher listening
to her babble. At the door they removed the caps that covered their hair and the disposable plastic aprons, binning
them in the anteroom.

Out again in the corridor Zyczynski's partner was waiting for her on the padded bench. Annette suddenly remembered what it was he reminded her of: the Pinocchio of
Disney's film, wooden-faced and round-eyed, with a mis-
matched sticking-out nose. 'I'm sorry,' she said, 'I've forgotten your name.'

'DS Beaumont.'

'DS?'

'Detective-Sergeant. Z, I've had a message from the
Boss. He wants you to get back sharpish. A patrol car will
pick you up out front. Shall I see you home now, miss?'

'No, I want to stay on. I'm going back in when the nurses
have finished their checks.' Annette looked regretfully after
Zyczynski hurrying away on recall.

Beaumont sat sideways, regarding Annette with something more than casual curiosity. 'So it was you who found
the man's body. At the office. Now this. Another near-
death. Anything to link them, do you think? Apart from
yourself and the firm you work for, of course.'

'How could there be?'

'The Met are investigating the murder in her office, and
needed Ms Gregory for a statement. That was before we
knew who our hit-and-run victim was. Since it seems
there's been an attempt to kill her too, there could be a
link. So now we've acquired an interest in the London
death as well.'

'But the man's was a shooting, deliberate. Ms Gregory
was knocked down by a car.'

'Which failed to stop. And that is criminal too. Or don't you think so?'

She looked at him wide-eyed, recognizing the new professional sharpness of tone, his alerted suspicion centred on her. Her stifled grief burst out in sudden anger. 'So now you're going to ask me what car *I* drive, aren't you? Well, I don't drive at all. I had some lessons once but I'd nothing to practise on so I never took my test.'

'That doesn't stop some people getting behind the wheel There's a lot of so-called joy-riding these days.'

'Not in the world I live in.' She stuck out her chin, then almost instantly her defiance crumbled. 'Still, I can't blame you for trying. I want whoever did this to be found. Have you anything to go on?'

He watched her coolly. 'There'll be certain traces on her clothing. But it takes time for the experts to get them analysed and then match them to the vehicle they came from. When we find it. Early days yet.'

'You just have to find it. Maybe...' Her voice trailed away.

'Maybe what?'

'Maybe telling her the driver has been found can help pull her out of coma.'

'You could be right. I've known that sort of thing happen.'

'Really. You're not just saying that—?'

'No.' Beaumont had finally dropped the accusatory tone. 'From personal experience: a man who came back from coma and quoted details he could only have heard when he was deep under. Genuine medically confirmed unconsciousness.'

But Annette's mind was more full of concern for the injured woman. 'I wonder if she had time to see the driver. Oh, it's awful to think that the information you need is locked away in her mind. Will you be talking to her as well, trying to get through?'

He picked up a note of reluctance in her voice. There could be alternative interpretations of it.

Alerted by a tap on the window opposite, he glanced up. A nurse was holding the blind slats apart and beckoning. 'It seems they're ready. Let's both go in.'

They seated themselves to either side of the silent woman, Beaumont backing on to the ventilator, Annette shyly taking the flaccid hand in her own. She was conscious again of the greenhouse build-up of heat in the confined space.

Before putting on the sterile plastic apron the detective had shed his anorak and loosened his tie. He didn't attempt to speak now, leaving it to Annette who plunged in about books. She was an avid library-user but had no idea what kind of reading Ms Gregory had favoured. It struck her that next time she came in she should bring a book and read out passages of description, or poems, maybe humorous writing. Anything was worth trying. Except horror fiction.

Ten minutes passed without any tremor disturbing the smooth face on the pillow. Beaumont was covertly looking at his watch. 'If you want to go...' she suggested.

'Let's both take a break. I think we should get something to eat. When was your last meal?'

He was right. He wasn't the company she'd choose, but she had missed lunch, and already the autumn evening was drawing in. They went out into dank chill made keener by a teasing wind, splashed across the car park's puddled black tarmac patterned with a collage of yellow chestnut leaves. The sweetly decaying scents of autumn were stronger here than the reek of stale fuel.

He showed her his warrant card before she took the passenger seat. 'You can't be too careful,' he warned.

'I'm not the sort of girl men snatch.'

The puppet face flickered briefly with humour. 'How do I answer that? "Some poor kidnapper's loss?" Or, "Not at all, I could gallop off with you any day"?'

She managed a weak smile. 'I guess you're a lot more

used to the real thing than I am. Vicious crime, I mean. I
don't know how you can still joke.'

He stopped abruptly, helping her to clip on her seat belt.
'I've been in the force a long time,' he admitted, 'and still
some things so turn my stomach that there's no way to
survive but make a daft remark. After years with the same
team I've grown a reputation for sick humour. So I live up
to the image I'm stuck with.'

She nodded slowly. 'I know what you mean. Role-play-
ing's a defence. It saves us from facing everything one
hundred per cent. Even now—' She stopped and slowly
shook her head.

'Even now—?'

Embarrassed, she laughed. 'I feel I'm dropping into a
role: the devoted employee. It blunts some of the hurt—the
fact that she never really saw me, not as a person—which
is what I wanted. The only time she ever took notice was
when I'd made some extra effort at work. I wasn't expecting much, but—'

'But, like cats, we all need stroking,' he said. 'And why
not?'

God, they'd never believe it back at the nick. He sounded
ponderous, like the Boss off on a philosophic tack. All because this girl was a novelty. How often in his work did
he meet up with such an innocent?

So he waited, encouraging her to talk in the steamy
warmth of the Tavola di Mama. The atmosphere was cosy
and close, a bright interior safe from the gathering darkness
beyond its plate-glass walls. At surrounding tables comfortable matrons checked over shopping lists and pondered
the size of tip to leave; school seniors loudly sucked the
last bubbly drops of lurid milk shakes in boastful compe-
tition, acting larger than life, not yet ready to shoulder their
way out into the dusk and complete the lone transition from
classroom herd to family bosom.

Annette Briers was remembering another place, another
table: the buffet at Marylebone station where she'd had

coffee with her boss before the nightmare had begun. When Beaumont again mentioned Miranda Gregory she was unaware of the change of subject.

'So you thought she'd gone back to the office on Friday evening, instead of catching the train with you?'

'Yes, until I had this note in Monday's post asking me to pick up the file she'd meant to go back for. You saw what it said. On the way there she'd seen someone from the cab and ended up going off for a meal with them.'

'Could you hazard a guess who this might have been?'

'Just a friend, she said.'

'No "he" or "she"?'

'Have another look. It's here in my bag.' She broke off to riffle through its packed contents and pass him the envelope.

'See? "…recognized a friend in the crowd near Harrods, and we went off for a meal together. As I'll not be in till late on Monday, would you make sure you hold on to the Berkeley Charities file until I can read it through again."'

'So you thought this implied that it was this file, or some part of it, that she'd suddenly remembered while you were in the buffet, and she'd intended to pick it up herself?'

'That's how it sounds. She was sitting opposite me, took out her lipstick, then starting rooting through her handbag in a rather panicky sort of way.'

'Panicky.' He said it thoughtfully, not as a question.

'Yes. Surprising, really. She was always so cool.'

'How big was this file she asked for?'

'A4. Not terribly full. It's correspondence mainly, dealing with a project she's setting up for next April.'

'Nothing particularly pressing, then?'

'No. The client may have phoned in with some query which Ms Gregory had intended working on at home. Any recent correspondence would have been passed through me, so I know there was no new request in writing.'

'But a file would have been too bulky for her handbag.'

'That's what I thought. So maybe just a précis she'd

made and meant to take home, but... Well, she seemed a
bit shaken. Since then I keep seeing her—'

'Describe it to me. You're sitting opposite each other.
Where in the buffet?'

'At the far end. There were only one or two other people
already in there, and she went for a table right away from
them while I fetched the coffees. She liked keeping to herself.'

'Sat with her back to everyone else?' He waited for her
nod. 'So you'd have had full view of the others?'

'Except for the waitress and a woman who could have
been her mother. They were off to the side a bit.'

Beaumont thoughtfully cleared the last mouthful of pizza
from his fork and considered the scene described. 'She was
starting to re-do her make-up, you said.'

'Just lipstick. She had one that fitted in a little gold case
with a mirror.' Her voice broke off as she saw his casual
glance harden. 'What's the matter?'

'I'm just picturing it. Close your eyes. Now, think back.
There she is, opening the lipstick, taking a glance in the
mirror to check. So what else could Miranda Gregory have
seen in it—behind her—that could be so upsetting? What,
or *who?*'

She stared at him. 'You think that's what scared her?
There really wasn't anything missing in her handbag? But
then why should she send me to the office early on Monday
to make sure I got hold of the file?'

'Because she was covering up. Perhaps she didn't want
you to know the real reason for her sudden panic. And she
wrote that note to make you believe she hadn't gone back
to the office after all.

'We've nothing but her word for it that she recognized
someone in the crowd near Harrods and went off for a meal
instead. Have you ever known her lie her way out of trouble
before? She sounds sophisticated enough to me.'

Annette hesitated, fighting back an automatic defence of

her admired boss. 'She could—well, if someone was being difficult, she'd...'

'Be economical with the truth? Aren't we all, at some time or another. But I think the truth *is* what we'll have to hunt up now, because your Ms Gregory may have had a fright, got herself into a very dangerous situation. Could be at further risk if someone meant her to go the same way as the unknown man found dead in her office.'

Annette sat gripping the edge of the table, appalled. 'You think she might have gone back to the office after all on Friday. But then she could have walked right in on the killer!'

'And simply walked out again? Before or after writing you the note and mailing it? Didn't you see what the postmark was?'

'Beaconsfield. And she lives there. It was dated Saturday, had a first-class stamp. So she was all right then.'

Unless she wrote the letter under duress at the office and someone else posted it afterwards, he thought, but he kept it to himself.

He signalled to the waitress that they were ready to leave. 'We'll have to pass all this back to the Met. I'm afraid it will mean more questioning for you, but I know you're anxious to help. By now they may have contacted the cab driver from Marylebone and got confirmation that Ms Gregory entered the building. We can't be sure the porter on duty was all that observant. It doesn't sound as though security check on visitors is all that good there. Unless the killer was a known member of the staff and was accepted going in and out in the normal way.'

Annette turned on him, chin jutting in defiance. 'You think she might be connected in some way with the shooting, don't you? Well, she wasn't. She wouldn't involve herself in anything criminal. Unless by accident.'

He sucked in his cheeks as though tasting a sharp lemon. 'So it's just coincidence that she's on life-support now?

'Think about it, Annette. Whatever she was up to on

Friday night, it's significant that somebody nearly killed her within a day or two of that man being shot dead in her office chair.'

THREE

'IT'S A BIT THIN, Ms Gregory's story of a forgotten file which she wanted Annette to secure on the Monday,' Beaumont reported to DI Angus Mott. 'I know women carry everything but the kitchen sink in their handbags but she can't really have intended to cram an A4 file in. And she didn't have a briefcase with her.'

'A single letter from the file? She could have meant to fold that up to take home. Or a photocopy?'

'Yes, we considered that possibility. But would forgetting it matter so much? This secretary bird of hers may be young and innocent, but she's observant and doesn't exaggerate for effect. She says her boss was visibly shaken. A sophisticated woman who's normally cool.

'My guess is that either she saw something unnerving in her handbag when it was open—something that shouldn't have been there—or else she glimpsed something, or somebody, in her make-up mirror which frightened the daylight out of her. On the spur of the moment she invented this line about having to go back to the office to pick up some papers she'd forgotten. The point is, did she actually go there, or was it merely an excuse to get rid of Annette and do something else she didn't care to have observed?'

'Like contacting someone who followed her out of the buffet?'

'That's a possibility which hadn't struck Annette until I suggested it, but then she's not the suspicious kind. Really sharp in some ways, observant but naïve. She gave a detailed description of a man who was sitting by the door as they went in. He might have shown up in the other woman's mirror, but he could hardly have known in advance that she would miss her train and use the buffet.'

'So he was there by chance. Have the Met traced any cab she could have taken back to the office?'

'They're still inquiring. The ground-floor porter at the Matherson and Corby building never saw one arrive. He's adamant she never came back after leaving with Annette. Not that you can trust anyone to have total concentration with a job like that. He did remember their original departure together because Ms Gregory wasn't one to fraternize with her juniors. Then again, she normally left by lift to the underground garage for her car.'

'Which was genuinely in dock?'

'With an electrical fault. Due back that evening.'

'How about the file the secretary was told to hang on to?'

'She went in half an hour early on the Monday, used Reception's key to open the office suite she shared with her boss, found a corpse in possession. Blinds drawn, desk-lamp on. She was scared half to death, but kept her head and avoided using the phone. Went for the daytime security man who'd just come on duty, and put off the screaming habdabs until she'd reported the corpse. Flaked out briefly, came to and reported to Met CID when they arrived, then was sent home by the MD to take sick leave.

'It's not surprising that with all that happening she forgot to pick up the file as instructed. Doubtless the Met will have given it a read through in view of her statement. Do you want me to ring them for info?'

'Let's stick to our end of it for the present: the hit-and-run case. Are we any nearer a precise time for when it happened?'

'No witnesses, Guv. Ambulance crew thought she'd been lying there for some time. Hours of darkness, Saturday to Sunday.'

'Which wasn't good enough. It may prove to have been a run-of-the-mill accident as we first thought, but in view

of her erratic behaviour of Friday evening—not to mention
a murder committed in her office—we have to query something more sinister. I'll see the Boss about a local radio
appeal. We need witnesses to her leaving Marylebone Friday evening and for the intervening hours until discovery
Sunday morning. Get hold of a recent photograph and have
copies made. You know the usual. Have a look yourself at
where she lived, maybe take Zyczynski along. Get the
woman's-eye view on the way this Ms Gregory lived.'

He picked the top sheet off a stack of papers on his desk.
'What's this?'

'Annette Briers' description of the man who left the buffet just after them on Friday evening.'

Rapidly Mott scanned the typewritten page, then went
through it a second time, frowning. 'This is good. Too
damn good. If he was following them, how did she get such
a detailed sight of his face?'

'Because this was the chap sitting by the door when they
went in. Just right to have shown up in Ms Gregory's mirror
when she held it up to put on her lipstick. And Annette
was facing him throughout.'

'Well, either she's unusually observant or she'd a special
interest in him. Did you get the impression she'd seen him
before?'

'I told you, she's sharp. When I'd taken this down I
asked for descriptions of the other people there, to check.
She gave just as much detail. A little dumpling of a girl,
not travelled far since secretarial college, but she's a
wide-awakey.'

'Right, then. Fax it through to the Met's Chief Inspector
Meredith. With a copy of your report. If we give them
maximum cooperation they may do the same for us.
There's always a chance this man from the buffet did follow the Gregory woman back to her firm. In which case
he may turn out to be their corpse. If he'd some of his face
missing on the Monday occasion, you might not expect the
girl to recognize him. We've nothing material to go on yet,

but I've a gut feeling there's a link between the two cases. Meanwhile I'll trot along and wise up the Boss.'

BEYOND THE DOOR MARKED *Superintendent M. Yeadings CID*, there was a comfortable subdued chortling and the aroma of perking coffee. Mike Yeadings swung round from contemplating the windswept waste of the station yard and greeted his inspector with a grunt. 'Come to heap more litter on my desk, Angus? Fetch your mug from the cupboard.'

With such priorities sorted and a steaming brew apiece, they passed to constabulary matters. 'We can't make any move on the Samways business, dammit,' complained Yeadings, 'because Drugs and Customs have an undercover operation on hand and it cuts across our case. When they finally move in we must hope to pick up something useful during searches. The good news is that it leaves us more manpower for surveillance on the money-with-menaces trio in Windsor. I'd like that set up at once. What's Beaumont on at present?'

'The B474 hit-and-run. He's querying a link with a murder in west London.'

'Which one?'

'Monday's shot male at a West End agency that organizes expos and conferences. The body's unidentified as yet, turned up inexplicably in the office of our hit-and-run victim. A total unknown.'

'Whatsit and Corby,' Yeadings murmured, scrabbling for his copy of the *Daily Mail* already consigned to the waste bin. 'Seems the press haven't made any connection as yet.'

'No. We have to be thankful that hit-and-run cases don't merit more than a few lines. But once the newshounds are on to where the injured woman worked, there's bound to be more interest shown. Beaumont had a word with her secretary and warned her to keep a still tongue as long as she could.'

'She wasn't unduly alarmed that her boss wasn't in on the Monday?'

'She had her reasons,' and Mott outlined Annette's story. 'Walking in on a corpse at work shook her somewhat. And it seems Ms Gregory was a high-powered law unto herself, came and went without informing the lower orders. It was assumed she was out contacting clients. On Friday there was no corpse when the cleaners did the office, and Ms Gregory had already left when they arrived. Later the Met were annoyed that they couldn't contact her at once, but not unduly suspicious. The identification of our traffic accident case was the first they knew of her whereabouts.'

'And to date there's nothing but a slight pong to indicate she suffered anything more than an accident. All the same, Angus, while waiting for whatever the forensic scientists may turn up, we'd better just check on her movements from Friday night onwards.'

'Beaumont has photocopied this description the girl gave of the man who might have followed Ms Gregory on Friday evening. It's been passed to the Collator to check Criminal Records, results to be rung through to you here.'

'That's my copy? Right. Let's see it, then.'

Yeadings sat rubbing his chin, humming quietly between pursed lips while Mott watched for the reactions of his eyebrows. 'Beaumont stressed that this Briers girl has all her buttons done up.'

'Apparently.' The superintendent began to read out aloud from the description. '"Early to middle thirties; small frame, fine-boned, about five seven in height. Neat grey suit under open Burberry-type raincoat, blue tie with darker spots. Pasty complexion, hair hidden by tweed fishing-hat but probably fairish. No obvious five o'clock shadow. Small skull, sparsely fleshed, short nose slightly uptilted, metal-rimmed spectacles, rather screwed-up eyes. His whole face looked pinched, like plasticine drawn up towards the bridge of the nose. Small mouth. An impression of rather wry intelligence."'

Yeadings laid the page down. 'What a formidable young woman. She's missed a vocation in TV casting.'

'Made me wonder how she would have described Beaumont.'

'M'm. A tweed fishing-hat in the metropolis. Either we'll get a trace on him immediately or he's a pretty piece of fiction.

'Get an artist in, Angus. When the girl okays his impression, circulate it locally. Let the Met know we'd like staff at Marylebone station to see it. But it's more likely that as a commuter he'd buy a season ticket from a station down the line here. Someone may previously have spotted Gregory and the man travelling together. Don't overlook the train's refreshment stewards.'

'She didn't commute by train. Normally drove daily up to London from Beaconsfield. Has a blue BMW, being serviced at the time.'

'But both probably living somewhere down the Chiltern Line. They could have known each other as neighbours.' Yeadings sighed. 'Don't spend too much time on it, Angus. If all we've got here is a genuine traffic accident, the murder end remains entirely the Met's affair.'

'Right, sir. About the council corruption inquiry at Aylesbury, I'd like to put a WPC in as a qualified typist. Someone personable with a head for figures.'

'That'll invite union trouble. A temp from outside when they're cutting staff to meet their budget?' The superintendent grunted. 'Well, you can try it. It'll have to be a girl from uniform branch. I'll see Inspector Grant about it. Anything else?'

'Not at present.'

'Nothing worth luring me from the office?'

'Afraid not.'

'Nevertheless... Well, try not to cover my desk in paper while I'm out.' Yeadings lumbered to his feet and reached to the hanger for his charcoal overcoat. 'I fancy a breath of air.'

He waved Mott out of the office, glanced back and snatched the top sheet from the pile on his desk, to fold it and thrust it into a pocket. Such a shrewd bit of observation—or talented fiction—by the Briers girl deserved his closer attention. He'd get a personal impression of her. It was good to stay in touch with mainstream police work, keep the experienced jack's hand in. But first he had another call to make, at the hospital where Ms Gregory had been taken.

'ALLO, ALLO, ALLO,' the pathologist greeted him mockingly. 'And what brings the brass here? I've nothing particularly choice on the menu, not for such a jaded vulture as yourself.'

Mike Yeadings stayed just inside the morgue anteroom, hands in pockets, one swing door propped against his foot. Nan always swore she could smell Dr Littlejohn's occupation on him whenever they'd been together, so he wouldn't risk touching things.

'Today I've an interest in the living,' he announced. 'The just-living. I'd like you to use your influence upstairs to pass me some info regarding a patient in Intensive Therapy.'

'They might take it badly: suspect I'm pushing for custom like an undertaker. But we'll risk it,' Littlejohn said briskly. 'So whom have we in mind?' He was removing his plastic apron. The latex gloves came off with a pair of liquid plops.

Yeadings told him.

'Hadn't heard about that,' the pathologist commented. 'But then I don't read newspapers, even the local ones. Too many unpleasant things in 'em. I'm easily upset.'

Still grinning fiercely, he darted the superintendent a shrewd glance. 'So what's your interest?'

Yeadings smiled blandly. 'Someone has to look into hit-and-run statistics. One can't always be sure they're as accidental as at first they seem. This lady's in coma, so she

can't tell us anything yet,' he said, voicing the obvious.
'I'm double-checking on the nature of her injuries.'

The pathologist ran a freshly scrubbed hand over his bald
dome and hummed with disbelief. 'Keeping umpteen dogs
and doing the barking yourself, eh? Or been reduced to the
ranks? Your disreputable double life been uncovered at
last?'

'Nan complains about the shine on the seat of my pants.
I was never built to drive a heavy-goods desk.'

'Any excuse to play truant,' Littlejohn marvelled. 'Well,
I admit to that myself. Let's go and take a look at your
lady's paperwork. I hope she proves worthy of my sticking
my nose into other medicos' business.'

AT HOME ANNETTE BRIERS sat thinking, staring into the
swirling pattern atop the mug of hot chocolate clasped between her fingers.

From the kitchen came sounds of Mum's suede mocca-
sins scuffing across the floor, her tuneless singing, the chink
of plates as she stacked washed crockery in the cupboard.

Poor old Mum, she had never been anywhere, couldn't
understand. When Annette had at last managed to get the
awful news out about her boss, she'd said, 'Well, that's a
chance for you then, isn't it? I mean, someone's got to get
her job.'

Living in another world.

Elsewhere Ms Gregory's mother would be bravely facing
up to her agony, because in the background there had surely
been a caring family. By now the police would have been
in touch, which was Annette's reason for not visiting the
hospital today. Close relatives wouldn't want any outsiders
hanging around.

'Annette, love,' her mother called from the kitchen, 'just
pop up and fetch my hot water bottle. I'm going for my
afternoon snooze now. I'll hafta put on a kettle; water's
running cold again.'

Annette went up to the bathroom, and on her way down

resolved that tomorrow she would return to work. The ice had to be broken, and when better than Friday, exactly a week after everything started to go wrong? A chilling plunge in at the deep end.

She made her mother comfortable on the old kitchen settee, her legs covered in a travelling rug, and went out closing the door quietly.

Outside, a car drew up and the driver sat on for a while, seeming deep in thought. When eventually he got out, burly and teddy-bearlike in a dark overcoat, he turned to look at the Briers' house, unlatched the gate and walked up the short path.

As he raised his hand towards the bell, Annette, alerted by the gate's familiar squeak, ran to whip the front door open, ready to repel all salesmen. Superintendent Yeadings met her fierce frown with innocent surprise.

He wasn't selling double-glazing or hawking religion, the girl realized. Perhaps he was lost.

'Miss Briers?' he asked mildly.

'Yes.' Suspiciously, because how could this stranger have got hold of her name?

'Thames Valley CID, Miss Briers. Superintendent Yeadings. You've already met one of my sergeants, I believe?'

'Sergeant Beaumont, yes. We were at the hospital together. There was a woman detective too.'

'I thought I'd like to meet you myself.'

Like Sergeant Beaumont—though utterly unalike—on second glance he wasn't all that alarming. In plain clothes too, but older, middle forties. He had a creased, good-humoured face with dark hair and eyes, and brows like furry black caterpillars, reminding her of that humorous Welsh baritone who sang about a hippopotamus.

'You'd better come in. My mother's taking a nap,' she explained, 'so perhaps you wouldn't mind being rather quiet? I suppose you've come about Ms Gregory. How is she?'

Yeadings eased round the door and seemed to fill the

hallway. He answered barely above a whisper. 'About the same, I'm told. I saw the doctor who's looking after her. He didn't like to commit himself.'

'Oh, I'd hoped— Still, if she's no worse...'

'You didn't visit her today?'

'I was leaving it to her family.'

He looked at her. 'What family? We haven't been able to trace anyone.'

'What, nobody?'

'She has a flat in Beaconsfield. Lives alone. No close friends.' The sergeant who looked through her desk there had found no personal letters. There wasn't even an address book. Neighbours could give no help about regular visitors. Round there they behaved distantly, priding themselves on respecting each other's privacy. But in Ms Gregory's case it seemed she'd had nothing to be secretive about.

'I can't believe that. I mean, I'm not doubting you. It's just that she was so—so attractive.'

He said nothing, watching her puzzled face.

'I always imagined... It's strange.' Annette thought for a moment. 'But she had a personal address book. I've seen her use it. She kept it in her handbag.'

'Which wasn't with her when she was found. Maybe you could describe it, also the clothes she was wearing when she left you on Friday.'

Again Annette Briers displayed keen observation. Every detail was listed, down to the cufflinks on the green silk blouse and the design of Ms Gregory's gold earstuds.

She had worn no jewellery when the ambulance brought her in injured. Over a mustard-coloured fine wool dress she was wearing a black belted raincoat with a circular skirt. These, and the silk underwear, had come from Harvey Nichols in Knightsbridge.

Aware of his silence while he considered the different outfits, Annette asked for a description of the later one. Yeadings obliged. 'I've never seen her dressed like that at work,' she told him.

'Weekend gear, probably. It was Sunday morning they discovered her. We need to find someone who saw her the previous day.'

'It started raining at lunchtime on Saturday,' the girl reminded him, 'but earlier weather forecasts had mentioned a frontal system on the way. She might have put on a raincoat in the morning, to be ready for it. So that's no help as a time check.'

He nodded. 'Unfortunately black's not a particularly striking colour, even if Ms Gregory herself was well worth a second glance. However, we'll hope someone comes up with a sighting of her when we show the outfit on TV. Thank you, Miss Briers. You've been most helpful.'

At the door, as she showed him out, he hesitated. 'I'm sorry to take you back to such an unpleasant experience, but could the dead man in your office have been the one you described from the buffet on Friday?'

She leaned against the jamb, frowning. 'He wasn't. They were about the same age, but the dead man was stocky. He wore a suit, but it was—'

'Shabby?'

'No. It was fairly new, I think. But it wasn't a very good one.'

'Cheap. What colour?'

'I'm not sure. It could have been navy blue. Something dark, anyway.'

Not quite so observant when the object was obscene, then. That was natural enough. One quick glance at a body with a shot wound to the head would be enough for anyone.

Annette went back to the front room and watched through the curtains as the big detective rounded his car, unlocked the driver's door and got in. He sat a moment drumming slowly with his fingertips on the steering wheel, switched on, and waited for the wipers to clear his windscreen.

Before he pulled away he turned and looked back at the house. She shouldn't have been visible through the heavy

lace curtains, but he knew she was there. He raised his hand
in farewell as she drew back in the shadows.

WHAT HE HADN'T MENTIONED was the folded paper found
in the box with Ms Gregory's passport and banking particulars at her flat. It intrigued him. Not that in these days a
change of name by deed poll was all that unusual for a
woman. It was often socially more acceptable to adopt the
same surname as the man you shared a roof with.

But Ms Gregory appeared to live alone. And why had
she chosen to change her forename as well? Christened the
pedestrian Annie, she had picked on the vastly more exotic
Miranda. In his experience sophisticated young women
liked to call themselves by the plainest of names—Jane, Jo,
Liz, or even use initials. In her search for some upmarket
label, hadn't she gone rather over the top? Or was she a
latinist, intending the literal meaning—she who should be
wondered at? The *admirable* Ms Gregory: a role she appeared to fulfil at least for her impressionable young secretary at Whatsit and Corby.

But she had made the change at a date (over ten years
back) when—if the passport details were correct—she
would just have reached her majority. So perhaps he was
making too much of what was merely a late teenage gesture
of defiance which she found herself stuck with until circumstances should suggest another change.

Anyway, they had a second name now from which to try
and trace her background, and any remaining family. Originally Lodd: Annie Lodd. Not all that common. So an un-
demanding job for Mott's little team.

FOUR

IF ANNETTE HAD EXPECTED gratitude for returning to work earlier than instructed she would have been disappointed. She found the place in a turmoil, the police still in occupation, nerves jittery. The double office she had shared with Ms Gregory had remained sealed during extensive examination, and as a result much of the work emanating from it had suffered a paralysis as total as that of her immediate boss.

Again she was besieged by colleagues demanding information. All she could tell them was that she had seen the injured woman, had sat with her, and despite all modern hospital aids available had observed no reaction. They responded with shrill or hoarse complaints of personal indignities suffered during interrogation, and of pressure building from clients to show some progress on projects necessarily suspended.

No opinion was voiced to connect Ms Gregory's 'accident' with events within the firm, apart from the universal observation that it never rained but it poured. There was much insistence on the irony of the coincidence.

As the only one of them to have actually viewed the dead body, Annette had temporarily achieved a new status. Her sudden—to others of the typing pool, undeserved—promotion over older and more experienced workers had caused a certain amount of resentment. She had been amazed herself at being selected by Ms Gregory, but attributed it to still being fairly new and not accepted into any clique. Ms Gregory had a thing about girlish gossip, insisting that client information required total discretion inside and outside the firm. Now, for the first time, Annette found herself in demand, a centre of interest and the recipient of fears that the shadow of scandal hanging over the firm might discourage clients from offering further work.

She was summoned to the office of the General Manager and questioned minutely on the new statement she had made to Thames Valley Police.

Upon defensively venturing a few questions of her own about the murder investigation, she was airily informed that all findings of the Scenes of Crime team had been forwarded to the Metropolitan forensic laboratories at Lambeth. Her fingerprints (taken while she was still in a state of shock on discovery of the dead man) had caused her to be provisionally eliminated from direct connection with the crime, and they would certainly be destroyed at the conclusion of the inquiry.

Everyone at Matherson and Corby, it seemed to her, was now an instant expert on police procedures and fluent in CIDspeak.

Having cleared these formalities, as he saw them, the General Manager moved to matters of greater weight. Forward Planning was complaining of a log-jam due to suspended workflow from the Gregory department. It was essential, since the office was today to be reopened for use, that Miss Briers should get in there and make things move.

Which was fine as regards completing tasks already assigned, but as a mere secretary—and one of quite recent appointment—Annette was in no position to guess what Ms Gregory had envisaged next, nor precisely how—even if she had access to her boss's planning diary—such future projects should be set in motion.

There followed some awkward exchanges, the GM assuming at first that Annette was of equal rank and experience to the retired PA. 'Well, surely you can manage to keep things afloat until Ms Gregory can return?' he demanded impatiently.

Ironically, Annette thought, Mum's ignorant forecast was

threatening to become fact: truly some did have greatness thrust upon them. But not herself. Abandoning all hope of miraculous intervention, she confessed herself unequal to the task.

'Ms Gregory's former PA hasn't been retired long,' she reminded him. 'I know the reason was ill-health, but she might be well enough by now to come back for a while. She'd be familiar with most of the urgent projects, and she'd know how to set up the new ones.'

The man faced her with the baffled expression of a taunted bull at fiesta. 'Well, under the circumstances, I don't see any alternative.'

He knew he shouldn't have let that department get into this state, all responsibility left in Gregory's hands and only this chit of a girl to fall back on when she wasn't available. But Miranda had been so confident, and the PA's transfer from salary to pension rate had come as welcome financial saving.

'Very well, I'll see that Personnel makes some arrangement.'

With that Annette was dismissed from the presence. She returned to her office. The police had already examined the files there and unsealed the murder room. Left alone in it, she tried tackling memos and correspondence which had accumulated in her in-tray. Her replies were copies of similar previous acknowledgements, assurances to potential clients and special offers couched in general terms. She took care to omit specific figures or guaranteed dates.

Without firm instructions to follow, she felt herself like a pauper drunkenly promising largesse.

At a little after four o'clock she received an incoming call. A low, controlled voice identified itself as that of the once-retired PA. She informed Annette that she would take over the office on Monday at 9.00 a.m. and would be glad if Miss Briers could spare her two hours tomorrow—Saturday—morning so that they might make any necessary preparations before starting up at full throttle.

Throttle, Annette considered. She supposed the woman had used the imagery of the combustion engine, but for her it had a murderous ring. All day she had been doggedly wiping from her mind the bloody ghost in Ms Gregory's big leather chair. The man hadn't been strangled: he'd been shot. Yet the term she'd chosen to use was unfortunate. In their short time spent together, her future boss had never struck her as particularly sensitive.

Nor were the police, of course. They hadn't taken away the murder chair, nor removed its terrible dark stains. These were still there, caked black on the pierced green leather, with grey powder dusted round the edges to remind her that killer hands must have touched it.

She walked all round the chair now and saw for the first time the neat hole at the rear where the single bullet had gone in, and the explosion of padding at the exit point in front. Much as the man's face had exploded in blood and bone.

She felt ill, remembering. She would never be able to work at ease here again. What she had achieved today at her own smaller desk was unauthorized gobbledegook. In a way she had made the effort for Ms Gregory. But Ms Gregory might never fill that chair, use this office, again.

Need she herself?

If she failed to turn up tomorrow her new boss might just think she refused to surrender free time, but it wasn't that. No; there was no choice really. She would have to force herself to meet the woman and see how they got on together without direction from the real boss. And perhaps by Monday another office suite could be made free for their use.

One thing she could do now was ring through to Building Maintenance and have that ghastly chair replaced.

MIKE YEADINGS WAS presuming on an old friendship in
contacting Chief Inspector Meredith at the Yard. They had
been divisional contemporaries on the beat in their twenties
although working in separate reliefs. A common interest in
youth centres had brought them together in their free hours
and by coincidence both had found wives at the old Westminster Hospital, Mike a sister in Casualty and Charlie a
physiotherapist.

Even since Mike's transfer to Thames Valley the four
had kept up a loose connection, meeting two or three times
a year to enjoy late supper after a theatre visit. As a result
both men maintained an interest in affairs on the other's
patch. Now, with Littlejohn's detailed report on Ms Gregory in his hand, Mike rang to give an opinion that their
two cases must be linked.

Overlooked on first admission to hospital because of
more urgent considerations, faint traces of chafing on the
upper arms and one wrist were still discernible, indicating
that at some time Miranda Gregory could have been se-
cured by ropes before the incident with a car.

If she'd been a bondage enthusiast the case might still
be one of a routine traffic accident. And even if held against
her will she could have escaped, to run blindly into the
road. Nevertheless the most likely option was that the hit-
and-run was some other party's attempt finally to obliterate
all traces of her having been held captive. Nasty, Yeadings
suggested; and Meredith agreed.

'Any sexual interference?' the Met man inquired.

'Apparently not. No recent activity of that kind, voluntary or otherwise, although she was experienced.' (Littlejohn had been pushing his prerogative there somewhat.)

Meredith was silent. Yeadings could picture his thin
frame drooped over the desk, phone hunched between
shoulder and chin, one hand absently rubbing at the mousey
moustache.

'Humph. Could be she chose a bad time to go back to the office, and ran into the feller who provided our corpse.'

'She'd changed her clothes from the Friday ones, so we think she'd been home. What's the alternative scenario?'

'Your guess is as good as mine, Mike. We've traced the taxi she took from Marylebone. Just as she wrote to the girl, she skipped from it in Knightsbridge. But no lead to any old friend recognized on the pavement there. She paid off the driver, saying it would be quicker to walk. Which it might have been. At that hour there was still a lot of home-going traffic clogging the streets.

'The porter at the office block sticks to his story that she never came back there, but he sounds a lot less certain than he did. There were desk jobs waiting for him and he was night staff, not been on duty for long. The street doors hadn't been locked, and cleaners at the Matherson and Corby level admitted they'd left the outer door on the second floor ajar "to let some of the heat out". They claim it's impossible to work properly until the temperature's dropped.'

'And close to powerful vacuum cleaners, they'd have heard little else.'

'M'm. The M and C layout is a sort of horseshoe shape with reception joining the outer ends, like a keeper across a magnet. They start cleaning at the far end and work back out, completing the rooms off one corridor first. Normally the murder office would have been done towards the start, but they had to leave it until Ms Gregory and her secretary had finished, say forty minutes later than usual. Then they went back to it before starting on the typing pool which always needs a pretty thorough turnout, finally the reception area, locking up at about 7.35 p.m.'

'So if Miss Briers is right about leaving the building at 6.10 p.m., Miranda Gregory had time enough to reach Marylebone station, drink her coffee, turn round and get back while the outer office door was still open?'

'Yes. The two cleaners divide a four-hour shift between that floor and the one above, spending roughly two hours in each. Which leaves ample opportunity for both killer and victim to get in unobserved before Ms Gregory returned. I'm assuming they left it until the staff, including our two women, had all gone home.'

'Unless one or both of them were staff themselves and therefore already on the spot.'

'Well, the dead body wasn't staff, and got in unobserved. No one owns to knowing him. And so far we haven't anything to go on. No ID, pockets emptied. Nothing discarded in the waste bin, no files obviously disarranged or missing.'

'How about the one Miss Briers got the note about?'

'The Berkeley Charities file. It was in place. In the shock of finding the dead man, the girl forgot to pull it out. I understand she's back at work today. Might be an idea to make her go through it again, see whether there's a whiff of something fishy. If so, my guess is it's pure red herring.'

It was Yeadings' turn to grunt and ponder a moment. 'Maybe,' he said at length, 'the dead man was the only outsider. Ms Gregory could have done the shooting herself if she had access to a gun. Suppose she came across him in her office, an intruder going through her things. Or could he be the one she claimed she saw from the cab on her way back? Then instead of going out to supper they went together to her office?'

'Yup, a puzzler, that. What we badly need is a name for our body. Which isn't likely until we get him a whole face. Shot at such close range, quite a bit of bone has been lost. Replica construction takes time. Meanwhile, without two complete eyes and nose to help, how many of the public would recognize each other by their lower back teeth?'

'Something's come up on Ms Gregory's identity,' Yeadings said, and told him of the change of name. 'She has an expensively furnished flat, but there's little that's personal in it, nothing that points to the past. And while she stays in coma, we've no help from the lady herself.'

'Count yourselves lucky,' said Meredith heavily, 'while she still breathes. Our man has a damaged face, is dead and anonymous. Your victim has *two* names. That should be plenty to work on, even in the sticks.'

Grinning wolfishly that he'd had the last, if only, laugh, Meredith said goodbye and rang off. He searched among the papers on his desk, pulled out the plan of Ms Gregory's office, and pored over it again.

Backing on to the window was a semicircle representing the big leather chair; in front of it a rectangle for the larger of the two desks. There was a bank of filing cabinets to the right, and the secretary's smaller desk to the left, diagonally across one corner of the room. A single door led to the anteroom which, furnished with more filing cabinets and a third desk, gave on to the corridor.

The close-up shot which killed the unknown man had come from behind, and through, the chair back. But it was a swivel chair, so it didn't mean the killer had to be standing by the window. The victim could have turned it to sit contemplating the evening sky, while the gunman quietly came in behind.

So how would he know the chair was occupied? Or the identity of the person in it? He couldn't, unless he'd come up close and looked round the side—and been seen himself. Or herself.

No, dammit. Later, when the Briers girl walked in on Monday morning, all unsuspecting and using Reception's key to the double office, the lights had been on in the further one and the vertical blinds drawn. No one would have sat there gazing at their cream linen slats. So (unless the blinds had been interfered with), as the killer came in by the door, the victim had faced him, saw him/her, was unfazed, allowed him—possibly during conversation—to go past and stand behind. Didn't feel vulnerable, although he was himself an intruder. Had known, and didn't fear, his killer.

Had even arranged this meeting with him? Him/her? Blimey O'Reilly, could the Gregory woman actually have found some message in her handbag that caused her to come back and confront the man?

She was pretty shaken by something, according to Annette Briers' statement. Well, Ms Gregory would be, surely, if she suddenly received instructions to rendezvous with someone threatening enough to need killing! And then where had she got the gun from?

He ran a hand over his face, consulted his watch, growled through the open door to the next office that he hadn't had his tea. When it came there were papers with it: a complete list of firms and employees for the entire building shared with Matherson and Corby, together with names of official visitors entering the building from noon until lock-up last Friday. With luck, somewhere among them could be the name of the dead man.

Meredith grinned savagely. His minions would have their work cut out interviewing this crowd.

FIRMLY RESOLVED TO AVOID any repetition of the previous week's actions, Annette left work strictly on time, joining the rush-hour jostling for the tube, at Marylebone catching her normal Chiltern Line train. It would be a long time before she cared to use the station buffet again.

Only as the turbo drew smoothly out did it occur to her to look for the man in the fishing-hat. At least he wasn't in her compartment. Well, this would be too early a connection, if he'd normally caught one after six thirty.

She wondered whether among the throng in the precinct any of the ordinary-seeming passengers were really plainclothes detectives on the lookout for the man. In television crime series, apart from the ultra-scruffy ones on undercover drugs work, they were recognizably solid types.

Householders would open their doors to them during an inquiry and guess at once what they were.

Her own brief experience was different. Apart from those on Monday when she'd been too shocked to take in their appearance, she'd met three. One was a pretty, dark-haired young woman, another had a puppet's face like Pinocchio, and the third reminded her of a Welsh baritone. None was pushy, nor dressed in a way that would suggest they were anything official.

Arriving at Wembley station, she experienced the usual faint reluctance to go home. Mum would want to know the far end of every detail of her day. At another time she might have given in graciously, but it all took so long because Mum frequently got hold of the wrong end of the stick. Then there had to be interminable explanations which she'd forget as soon as she was told. With all that, little evening would be left for going out again.

It would save time now if Annette rang Mrs Martin next door and explained she was visiting the hospital first and so would be late back. Mrs Martin wasn't averse to popping in to deliver messages just once in a while. Annette had had a telephone installed in her own room when she started work, but the first few bills had been enormous because her mother had begun ringing up numbers at random and sometimes chanced on people as lonely as herself. It had been cruel to cut it off, but on a junior typist's pay she couldn't afford to indulge poor old Mum. So, to provide alternative occupation, she'd traded in their small monochrome television for a larger colour one.

Annette caught the next westbound train, and still it seemed rather early to visit the hospital. The patients would be served their evening meal about now. Although Ms Gregory would still be on saline drip, the hospital system was geared to later visiting hours and she didn't want to upset anyone.

In the town she found a little café and drank tea while

they made her a mushroom omelette. By the time she left and was starting up the hill it had grown dark and a steady drizzle had come on. She tied a plastic hood over her hair, shaking it off her gingery frizz as she entered the lift, bound for Intensive Therapy.

They had moved Ms Gregory into a small ward with two beds, which must surely mean she was improving, but she still lay inert, ticking away through her machines. Across the room a mound of bedclothes covered an equally un-moving body, the head swathed in even more dressings than Miranda's.

The nurse who showed Annette in left her there, required on duty elsewhere. That too seemed to be a sign that Ms Gregory was progressing. Annette brought a chair to sit beside her bed, and opened a paperback book to read aloud. At first glad to have no audience, after a few pages she felt foolish at the lack of response, a voice in a void.

Above Ms Gregory's head green numbers lazily flickered on a display screen, changing from second to second within a narrow limit. Pulse-count? she wondered. She tried vary-ing the level of her voice, adding stresses, but there seemed no correlation between her reading and the figures.

It was a waste of time. She knew coma victims could go on like this for months, even years. Perhaps Ms Gregory had been moved here in despair of any improvement. They could be letting her gently slide away.

Annette went to ask why nobody from ITU was in at-tendance any more. Over the twenty minutes she had been there no one had come.

A passing nurse stopped long enough to point to the sister's desk where monitors showed heart-rates for the two side-ward patients.

'There's been a multiple pile-up on the motorway,' the nurse said, 'and ITU's full. Your friend's stable. We're keeping an eye on her from here. You mustn't worry. She's getting all she needs at present.'

Annette went back to the side ward to sit in silence a while longer. Neither patient moved. She went across and peered through the bandages of the other woman, middle-aged and yellowed. She seemed barely to be breathing. As she stood there she was conscious of someone coming to stand behind her.

It was a constable, his head tilted as he surveyed her. 'Are you a relation, miss?' he asked.

'No. A friend. That is, I'm a friend of the other one, Ms Gregory.'

'In that case, miss, perhaps you'll give me your name.'

It seemed to be what she'd been doing for days. They asked and she told them and they wrote it all down, and none of it was any use, because before long another one of them came along and asked all over again. She said as much, and heard her voice rising in pitch till it verged on hysteria.

'Right, miss. So your name is?' he ploughed on unmoved.

She gave in and watched him write it down, add her address, her connection with the unconscious woman.

'Shouldn't you have been sitting with her?' she accused, unable to steady her voice completely.

'Call of nature,' he gave back, almost smugly. 'Only one of me here to cover things. Can't spare more. And any change in her condition would sound an alarm in the main ward.'

Still needled, she collected her things, gave a last look at the woman she'd vainly tried to rouse, and left. Outside the ward she must have turned in the wrong direction, got lost and tried to find her way out by way of the ITU signs.

Passing the closed blinds of the unit, she was aware of people standing about outside, dismayed. She kept her head down and walked on. She had almost reached the lifts when she heard someone calling. She looked back. A tall, lean man reached out a hand in her direction. 'Miss, wait! Please!'

She didn't know him, didn't want to get involved. She entered the lift, and the doors closed before he could reach her.

Outside, the drizzle had turned to pelting rain. On the hospital approach lane she stood back as an ambulance *hooh-hahed* past, splashing her legs and the skirt of her raincoat. She re-tied the plastic hood over her hair and hurried off towards the station.

FIVE

ANNETTE ARRIVED AT THE office on Saturday to find Ms Gregory's replacement already installed in the new green leather chair.

'You'd better call me Gwen,' she told Annette briskly, having been reminded of the girl's name. 'Let's waste no time. There's quite a bit to catch up on since you've been off all week.'

'I was in yesterday. You'll find some correspondence ready for signing. It's all follow-through stuff.'

'I'll start with that, then, while you look out the list of approved schedules. Then I'll dictate some letters to confirm the new contracts. We don't want clients withdrawing because they assume we're at a standstill. I'll allocate your duties for next week so that it leaves me free for meetings.'

While her new boss read through the letters, Annette watched her covertly. Quite a number of clients were going to be disappointed when they met Ms Gregory's substitute. Not that she didn't appear efficient. She was rather grimly so, lacking the younger one's polished charm. Selling an expo concept involved selling your own personality at all stages. By her very presence Miranda Gregory had promised a magic world of sophisticated glamour. This woman projected nothing but the grey zone of contracts and sales charts. What clients would want to wine and dine her for creative ideas and the flattery of a charm offensive?

She had a narrow skull with a bulging brow which made her lower face appear insignificant, the chin weak. But her mouth was a straight line, determined enough. Her skin was unblemished but sallow, her eyes a washed-out blue. She wore her greying hair straight, almost to shoulder level, and a sparse fringe nearly met the top of her dark-rimmed spectacles in a vain attempt to distract from the gleaming brow. The dark grey tailored suit and white blouse did nothing for her complexion. She was some five inches taller than Annette, even in her flat walking shoes. And scraggy. Hadn't some famous Frenchman once said, 'Fat women are comic, but thin ones, *ah mon dieu*, that is sad!'

Precisely on the completion of the proposed two hours, Annette was dismissed. She gathered that the other woman would be staying on a while. At the door she hesitated, and said, 'Do we have to keep on with *this* office?'

The woman looked up. 'Surely the police have finished with it?'

'Just the same... They've been offered an empty office down the corridor. I wondered if we could swap. After all, this one...' She grimaced.

The washed-out eyes held her own a moment and almost seemed to glint with humour before returning to scan the papers on her desk. 'With the police, I think it's much the same as with sleeping dogs, Annette.'

'Let them lie?'

'Cause as little disturbance as possible. Thank you for coming in. Make sure the outer office door locks as you go out.'

At a few minutes after eleven on a Saturday morning Annette faced the choice of return to Wembley or a leisurely bout of window-shopping in the West End. The thought of Harrods and Harvey Nichols was a lure, but she still had Ms Gregory on her mind. She compromised with coffee and a cream slice in the Peter Jones restaurant and then ringing through to the number Sergeant Beaumont had given her.

His answering voice had nothing of Pinocchio. It was abrupt, with a south London accent she hadn't noticed when they were face to face.

'It's Annette Briers, the one you met—'

'At the hospital. Yes. Howdo. Something fresh you have to tell me?'

'No. I'm sorry. I don't want to waste your time, but I just thought you might have some news. About Ms Gregory's accident. Whether the car's been traced, or anything.'

In the short silence before he answered she regretted the move. The man must think her a simpleton and a nuisance.

'Miss Briers, where are you phoning from?'

'I'm in London. I had to come in to work for a while.'

'So are you free now? Coming back?'

'Yes, on my way to Marylebone.'

'How about staying on the train a bit longer, as far as Wycombe? I'm at Amersham. If you arrive first, wait for me, would you?'

'All right.' She'd let herself be hustled into it. But the suddenness of his invitation had taken her off balance. It *was* an invitation, wasn't it? Not police instructions? Well, she'd see. At least it would fill the next hour or so on a Saturday already outside routine.

HE WASN'T ON THE platform waiting. She went through the station and saw someone sitting in a blue Ford Escort halfway up the hill to the main road. He must have been watching for her in his driving mirror, because a hand came out of the window in vague salute. She walked up and slid into the passenger seat as he leaned across and pushed the door open.

'Hi,' she said, hoping it was appropriate to sound casual and relaxed.

'Had lunch?'

She hadn't intended to eat again until evening. 'No, I haven't.'

'Good. Pub grub suit you?'

'Fine. Thanks, but we'll go Dutch if you don't mind.'

Beaumont gave a lopsided grin. 'If you insist.'

He had turned right, heading again for Amersham. It was

instant country, a rolling Chiltern road between open fields edged with the black lace of distant bare trees. After a heavy shower fitful sunlight lit great castle shapes of cumulus, gold-tipped whipped egg-white. The sky looked huge over a rain-washed landscape.

They drove past a sizeable inn with a sign depicting magpies, and at a high point turned left. 'Coleshill,' he told her when she ducked to read a fingerpost. 'Nice little village. One of my favourite pubs.'

Behind a broad forecourt the Black Lion offered a snug Christmas-card welcome. Already there was a crush inside, but Beaumont was obviously known. They were nodded through to a back room where a young waitress cheerfully greeted the detective and cleared two settings from a table laid for four.

'Now,' he said, when they were halfway through their ploughman's lunch, 'I've something to ask you.'

'More questions?' She made it sound glum, masking her eagerness.

'Only one this time. And for the moment I'd like you to keep under your hat what I'm going to tell you.'

'About Ms Gregory?'

'Yo.' The puppet eyes became slits as he considered his information. 'It seems that isn't her name after all.' He darted Annette a hard glance, fork raised. 'Did she give you any inkling of that?'

'Ab-so-lute-ly none. Was she married, then?'

'Had changed to Miranda Gregory by deed poll.'

'But then it *was* her name legally.'

'Oh yes. I should have said it wasn't her *original* name.'

'So I've been trying to get her to respond to the wrong one. I mean, earliest memories are the deepest, they say. What *was* the name I should have used?'

He hesitated, then allowed, 'Annie.'

'That's what my mother sometimes calls me, sort of short for Annette.'

'But your boss was registered Annie at birth.'

'It's strange, that we should share a name when we couldn't be more different. Is that all you've learned? Nothing about the car that knocked her down? No witness to her movements between leaving me at Marylebone on Friday and being found unconscious in a ditch on Sunday?'

He shrugged. 'We know that she went back to her flat.'

Annette nodded. 'Your boss said she was wearing different clothes. A mustard yellow dress and a black raincoat.'

She saw a flicker of surprise cross his wooden features. 'My boss? Who? When?'

'Mr—Yeadings, I think he said.'

'The super. How did you come across him?'

She told him, and Beaumont listened po-faced. Sly old devil, he was thinking: can't keep his finger out of the pie when he scents something spicy. It was gratifying to know he'd shared the same suspicion as Beaumont and abandoned his desk to check on the only witness they had so far in the case. When the Boss smelled skulduggery, you could bet most times he was right.

'I'm going on to the hospital next,' Annette decided. 'I don't need a lift. I can get a bus. You must have a lot to do.'

He had: like tracing the man who'd turned up yesterday at the woman's bedside, taken one look and fled. One of the nurses had challenged him but couldn't give a good description, except that he was tall and thin.

They had paid for their meal and were leaving when a man came in from the car park. He brushed past, making for the back room they had come from. Something about him disturbed Annette but she couldn't put a name to the face. She glanced at the car he had just left, a tan Toyota with the current year's licence plate, the radiator gently steaming in the brief sunshine.

Sitting beside Beaumont as he ran her to the bus stop,

she puzzled over where she had seen the man before. He wasn't the tall one who'd called after her yesterday in the hospital corridor. If only he hadn't gone by in such a rush. All she was left with was an impression of haste and a red mark slanted across his forehead.

'Mind how you go,' Beaumont warned as he dropped her. 'I'm not sure you ought to get too deeply involved in Ms Gregory's affairs.'

'Don't worry, I'm going to be pretty busy at work. There's lost time to catch up on. Thanks for the lift and the talk.'

He watched her join two women at the bus stop, waited for a tan Toyota to slide past and made a U-turn in the street. A nice kid, he thought.

EARLY AFTERNOON ON Saturday wasn't a rush hour for visiting. Thanks to football on TV, even if the local pitches were too waterlogged, Annette decided. The wards were almost empty, patients tidied and dozing, a cluster of nurses seated round Sister's desk for instruction. One of them came into the side ward with Annette, checked on Ms Gregory's saline drip and tapped with a fingernail at the plastic tubing to accelerate the flow. 'No change,' she said, gave a small neutral smile and went away.

'Annie,' the girl said experimentally, 'hallo.' There was no response. Annette took out her paperback again—it was John Mortimer's *A Summer's Lease*. Maybe at some time Ms Gregory had gone on holiday to Tuscany and something of the setting would get through to her.

But perhaps she hadn't been Ms Gregory then, simply Annie someone.

She laid down the book and reached for the flaccid hand. 'What sort of little girl were you, Annie? Do you remember your first home, the other children you played with, your mummy and daddy? Did you have a bedroom of your own with dolls and teddy bears, a rocking horse?

'Annie? Tell me, Annie.'

'OH ANNIE, HUSH. Hush love, don't upset him more.'

She was pulled into the soft darkness of her mother's arms but she could still hear them: the two frightening sets of footsteps mounting the stairs, growing fainter, going right up to the attics. Heard the back room's door firmly shut, the dented little brass knob rattle on its shank.

For a moment there were no voices, only a terrible silence. She lifted her head out of the stifling folds of the old red cardigan, straining her ears for reassurance, willing the silence to go on.

And then the screams came, sharp and high, spaced as she seemed to see the man's arm rise, the whistle as the cruel, thin cane sliced down. Scream after scream. They went on and on.

Her fingers were buried in her mother's flesh as she agonized with him. 'No! No, no, no!'

'Oh Annie, my love. Hush.'

She tore herself away and looked up with sudden fury. Why did her mother do nothing? How could she? It was her flesh under torment, Annie's flesh. They belonged together all three, and that man was a devil. Why didn't she stop him punishing the boy?

'No,' the woman whispered. 'There's nothing can be done.' Her face looked swollen, suffused with blood.

Failing her, failing them all.

The child turned her face stubbornly away, thrust herself from the enfolding arms, stumbled off to less shameful darkness. Seeking somewhere to hide away.

BECAUSE THE DIGITAL display was silent, Annette missed seeing the racing figures, but she thought that momentary shadows passed over the comatose face.

Yet the individual features stayed unmoving. She

couldn't be sure, but she thought that for a second or so there had been contact.

She peered at the saline drip. It appeared to be feeding perfectly, no bubbles.

A nurse hurried in, put a hand on the comatose woman's throat, studied the flickering figures on the screen. 'Did she move at all?' she asked.

'No. Is she all right?'

'Fine. Just a momentary blip.'

There was nothing more for Annette to do now. She had read aloud, she had tried out the new name. She would come back tomorrow, and next night and the next, until some positive sign of life showed.

She should have asked the detective-sergeant what chance there'd be of tracing any family, now that Ms Gregory's former name was known. They were the ones who could do most good, helping to recall shared memories from childhood.

'LODD'S NOT A COMMON surname,' Rosemary Zyczynski murmured, running through her list, 'but there are still too many of them for my taste.'

Inspector Mott didn't look up from his report. 'We can't all be as exclusive as you. How many have you now?'

'From the Reading phone book alone, twelve. I haven't looked at Aylesbury or West Middlesex yet. And even then we can't be sure she came from these parts. Or that any family, if still existing, has a telephone registered in that name.'

'Start phoning the ones you've got. It covers the central southern area, and the woman must have had some reason for settling round here.'

'Has Silver come up with anything yet on "Gregory"?'

'Plenty of rebuffs. A prolific lot, apparently. Like Evanses in Wales.'

Zyczynski looked pensive. 'It's not normal, the way she lived so detached.'

'No more than you or I. We've both cut ourselves off from our roots.'

'But remember her apartment, Guv. It was impersonal, a show-place, yet neighbours said she'd been there for four years. Books, yes, and some CDs, but they hardly looked used. I guess we'd find plenty of clues to your tastes and habits if we turned over your flat. I know my rooms are a dead give-away.

'She'd kept no letters or mementos. Not so much as a holiday photograph. Her passport with the deed of poll certificate and her bank statements were the only personal touch at all.'

Mott pushed the pile of papers from him and planted his elbows on the desk. 'Is this leading somewhere? Tell on.'

'Well, to me it suggests a pied-à-terre, as if her real life went on elsewhere.'

'You think she shacked up with someone and just kept the flat on as a lifeline? So why hasn't that person come forward to say she's missing, even if they've not seen any of the publicity we put out? Her neighbours in that block say she was coming and going pretty regularly. Had no staying-over visitors; was never seen to bring a man home. That invalid lady on the floor above sits at the window nearly all day, seldom misses a trick.'

'Two names, two identities,' Z reminded him. 'So why not two homes?'

He considered this. 'She hadn't two names. She'd dropped the former one. She'd changed, moved on, jettisoned all the clutter of the past.'

'Maybe. But it's so extreme that I'm tempted to wonder why. What was so wrong with being Annie Lodd? Rather than start on a wild-goose chase through the phone books of the entire south-east of England, I think we should see if the names come up in Criminal Records.'

A wild one, Mott thought; and there was another little job for Z before she went haring off on that. 'See the Boss and collect Annette's description of the clothing worn by Ms Gregory on the Marylebone evening. We need it in the computer.'

He sifted among his notes and found the date of the Gregory deed poll. It was made out over ten years back, when the injured woman was eighteen; when she'd just become legally adult.

It looked as though the change had been no more than a sign of teenage rebellion. Had she also flown the coop at that point? If so, where and how had she spent the missing six years between leaving home and acquiring her luxury apartment in Beaconsfield?

as we've seen. Most thorough, and that's why, in that first talk, I, for one, was worryingly off course. For the boss understood Andrea's dilemma, and the enemy's were as hostile to run the Navy as us. Anyway. We need Fu, the embrace.

He said that, he drew, and found the date of the

SIX

RODNEY FAIRBURN—never Roddy to intimates, because he admitted to no intimates, and those nearest him knew better than to take liberties—read the brief newspaper cutting a second time, then fastidiously retrieved its discarded envelope from the bin.

The address was typed, the smudged postcode could have been Westminster's. No covering letter, no signature, but also no deliberate attempt to disguise where it came from. And he didn't need telling its precise source. A cramped little terrace house off Victoria Street, behind the Army and Navy Store.

Slit-eyed, he stared at the ivory-painted office wall and mentally projected on to it a freeze-frame of the house's narrow elevation. He panned right, widening the vista to take in the street's boomerang curve and then, tracking back towards Greycoats, revealing a perspective of Artillery Row with red buses and black cabs clogging the turn in from Victoria Street. For audio a background mix of city traffic, the *hooh-hah* of a fire engine—receding, not approaching; it doesn't lead on to that sort of action. Titles rolling, names from the past, his own there somewhere down towards the end. But not the name that had sprung at him from the newspaper cutting. Not Miranda Gregory—*Miranda*, for God's sake! The furthest, he supposed, she could get from Annie.

So the old trout wanted him to know. Wanted him to know she knew he knew. (Henry James sort of complications but twentieth-century presentation.)

And the set-up required action. So, action coming up. He

clicked a switch, spoke through to the outer office. 'June, what's in the book for this blustery Monday morning?'

She cooed the three items back to him, total Roedean. (These office types were forever flinging their hair and projecting their prosaic little range of images in the hope of being picked up by Casting.)

'Cancel the first two. But ask Syd Coulter to make it one o'clock instead of twelve thirty. Advise the Savoy accordingly. And order me a car chop chop.'

'Right, Mr Fairburn.' This time a touch of the Southern belle. She wouldn't last: all he needed was a girl to take messages, type, and remember things for him.

He picked up the script he'd been working on when the mail came in, and stayed immersed until the girl buzzed through again.

'Your car's here.'

He grunted, switched off the desk intercom and went to fetch his overcoat from the cupboard. In the full-length mirror inside, he surveyed himself.

Black, wide-shouldered, belted and almost ankle length, the coat made him look seven feet tall. Above it his pale, hollowed face and wispy chestnut hair had a fallen angel beauty. A touch decadent, but he was wearing well, must compare favourably with anyone splatted in a road accident. He wondered if she would be out of coma yet, able to recognize him and appreciate the honour.

No; cut! That sort of humour did nothing for the part: he wasn't playing the villain. Cool, though, and retaining the sort of distance that lends enchantment. He adjusted his mouth and cheek muscles. Yes, nice expression, that. Spot on.

He peered closer, inspected the area under his eyes and opted for the hat. Even more height now, and the crushed wide brim suggested a nice balance of material success with bohemianism. He slid a cordless telephone into the deep right-hand pocket and left the coat nonchalantly open. Now he was ready, big brother all set to visit ailing sister. Now what the hell hospital did the paper say she was in?

SUPERINTENDENT YEADINGS could more easily have rung through for a report or waited until Beaumont sailed in with the latest news on the woman, but he wanted to see her for himself.

'You're like a cat,' Nan had accused him unexpectedly at breakfast that morning.

'Chasing its tail and running up trees when there's a high wind,' she explained as he guiltily withdrew the hand hovering over the children's full-cream milk jug and opted for semi-skimmed on his cereal.

'I'm not running up trees. Nothing further from my mind.'

'You'll be padding off today on your wild lone. I know that expression of yours. A gale like this brings out the panther in you.'

Maybe that was it. Even in the early hours, wakened by a rolling dustbin lid below on the patio, and kept from sleep by a shuddering window, he had become overcharged, wanted to be up and battling out into the gale. Bored to brain-rigor with paperwork, his hamstrings stiffening from lack of legwork, he envied his team actively on the job.

'Just a spot of hospital visiting. That's all I had in mind,' he said mildly.

'Nobody I know, I hope.' Nan was suddenly grave.

'Purely business. An RTA victim, as we thought. But it now seems she was—'

He glanced at his daughter, alerted to her listening, and hesitated.

'Road Traffic Accident,' she translated proudly. Sally was showing too much interest in police matters for his liking. Only yesterday she had said thoughtfully, 'Murder's killing someone, isn't it?' And after a little thought, 'Do you like work like that?'

Nan had quickly intervened. 'Daddy tries to stop it happening,' and the conversation had taken another turn.

Now Sally's blunt little Down's Syndrome face was again solemn. 'Mrs Ford had a road accident.'

'Who's Mrs Ford?' Yeadings asked.

'The old flower-seller at the shopping precinct,' Nan said. 'Sally got to meet her at the garden centre.'

'They're planting her tomorrow. Can I go?'

Planting her? Yeadings almost choked on scalding tea.

'You'll need your heavy raincoat today,' Nan covered for him drily, more familiar with Sally's original conceptions.

Out in the hall with the intervening door firmly closed, she cautioned him. 'You don't always have to shield her from the truth, Mike. Her reality isn't ours. It's—'

'What are you saying? She isn't an idiot.'

'Of course she isn't. She picks up a lot. She knows about people dying, because of the kitten and her plants. She asked me what they'd do with Mrs Ford afterwards. She was quite persistent, so I explained about funerals. That's when she said it. "Oh, they'll *plant* her? That's nice." And she went off quite happy about it.'

'Good God! As if—'

'As if she expects old Mrs Ford to go on growing in the earth, putting up new shoots. Well, why not?'

Yeadings wound his scarf round and tucked in its ends, rammed on his old-fashioned homburg and belatedly tried to kiss Nan from under its brim. All right then, who was to say Sally was so wrong?—apart from Dr Littlejohn and his pathology ghouls. He'd settle for her uninformed faith as easily as all that miraculous business about souls and heavenly rewards. He didn't allow himself to look that far forward. His world was here under his size elevens and his job was to see that the outcome of earthly actions followed as fast as human justice allowed.

But it still rankled, as he went out into the still boisterous

wind, that the child must think of him involving himself
from choice in the seamy side of life. Which, of course,
was what he did. Thriving on others' evil-doing. And most
times enjoying the thrill of the chase.

Halfway down the front path he stopped and turned back.
Nan was still there, smiling, her head tilted expectantly.
'About the funeral. You won't let her go?' he demanded.

'Don't worry, Mike. She's got school. They'll let her
light a candle in the chapel.'

Of course: routine. It let you out of a lot. He grinned,
waved a hand and went on out into the gale.

AS WITH MOST HOSPITALS, morning visitors were not welcome. Now that Ms Gregory was in the offshoot of a public
ward the duty staff were prepared to make him wait. Only
the immediate reaction of the uniformed man who sat at
the entrance and recognized a senior Thames Valley detective warned them of his special status. Within minutes of
his arrival Sister was at his elbow with an assurance that
the registrar with responsibility for the patient was on his
way.

'You understand that Ms Gregory could still be at risk
from whoever was responsible for her being here?' Yeadings asked.

'Yes. Inspector Mott came in to warn us. That was after
the unannounced visitor got in. Since then there's been
someone always keeping the bed in sight. When the constable takes a break one of my first-year nurses takes over.'

'Thank you, Sister. Ideally we should like a private
room, but with the ITU full to capacity and monitoring
needed—'

'I'm glad you understand. Here is Dr Dennis. He'll bring
you up to date.'

Dennis was small, blond, earnest. 'Superintendent,' he
said, 'I hope you've more to report than we have. Is there
anything further on the car that did this to her?'

'Nothing, I'm afraid. It must have happened in the hours of darkness. There were no witnesses and she lay undiscovered for some time. Until some garage notifies us of bloodstains and the kind of damage our bodywork experts are asking about, we can only look for abandoned vehicles. It's not unknown for wrecked cars to be kept under wraps for a year or more before they're sent for repair. As doubtless you know, renewal of licence and insurance doesn't require any check on roadworthiness.'

'No. Well, your lady isn't likely to be roadworthy for a long time herself. Still out cold, though there have been one or two short phases of slightly accelerated brain activity. She's had three transfusions to make up for blood loss, and twice been up to the theatre. The best I can say is that she's holding her own.'

'I'd like to see her.'

'Certainly.'

The small ward held two beds, one of them empty and being made up for the next patient. Ms Gregory's was between two long windows. There were the usual bits of machinery for artificial survival, but he noted that she wasn't at present attached to the ventilator. Her dark hair had been chunkily cut and a small area above one temple shaved where padding was affixed. Her face, strangely haunting, was badly marked and from the strapping at her shoulder level he assumed that her breakages included some ribs and the left humerus.

It wasn't easy to picture how she would look normally but under local swelling the bone structure of the face was delicate. Her long eyelashes lay curving on the bruised flesh. One cheek showed extensive gravel rash, despite her having been found in long grass at the roadside. But she certainly hadn't picked herself up, walked from the point of impact and tidied herself away in the overgrown ditch.

'Dr Littlejohn has drawn your attention to rope marks?' Yeadings asked.

'Yes. On this side there's other damage overlying them. But on the right—' The registrar pulled back the sheet and slid two fingers under the upper arm. 'You see? It's barely visible now. I haven't any experience of bondage, but I can see these marks could be compatible with her being tied up.'

'Wrists too, I believe. No, I don't need to see.' Yeadings was seized by a sudden distaste for the living woman being handled like a corpse. Turning away, he saw through the open doorway a man in outdoor clothes with an armful of hothouse flowers waiting to be admitted.

'Is this Miss Gregory's room? *Miranda* Gregory's?' The voice was light, and Yeadings fancied he caught a satirical note in the second question. As if the man considered the forename ridiculous. He watched while the attendant nurse advanced and took the flowers.

'Are you a relative?'

'Her brother.'

'Right, Mr Gregory. Will you wait until doctor's finished in here? I'm afraid we can't allow the flowers in. Just in case of an allergy. Perhaps you'd like us to put them in the open ward?'

'Ah.'

Dr Dennis nodded at Yeadings. 'Unless I can help you any more—?'

'I appreciate your coming, doctor.' He followed the other out into the corridor, allowing space for the newcomer to go in. From the corridor he watched the man approach the girl's bed and stand unbending to watch her. After a few seconds he turned abruptly to the nurse and asked a question. Yeadings moved in closer to catch her reply. She was assuring him that Ms Gregory's condition was stable.

'But is she going to recover?' There was impatience there. Since the man had brought flowers, had he expected his sister to be in a fit state to enjoy them?

'Mr Gregory, could I have a word with you?'

The man swung round on him. His bony jaw had the arrogant thrust of an unspoken question.

'Superintendent Yeadings, Thames Valley CID.'

'Ah.' It seemed his universal reaction. His dramatically deep-set eyes, slatey grey, met the policeman's. After a moment's challenge he offered, 'Actually my name's not Gregory. I don't belong to that—questionable tribe. I'm Annie's half-brother. We had only a mother in common.'

'Thank you. May I ask how you came to hear that your half-sister was here?'

The man hesitated, then, 'I read it in a newspaper. This morning. Catching up on the last few days' affairs.'

'Do you live locally, sir?'

'London.' His answer was curt. From an inside pocket of the theatrical black overcoat he drew a card case and extracted a piece of pasteboard which he extended droopingly like a forgotten cigarette.

Yeadings advanced his own hand to within a couple of inches and the man flipped the card in. It bore a blue, green and silver logo and the legend Viccentro Broadcasting. Below its SW London address and towards the right-hand corner were the words Rodney Fairburn, Director of Drama, Television.

'Mr Fairburn?'

The man bowed ironically.

Yeadings looked blandly at him. 'I'm afraid this has been a terrible shock for you.'

Cued with an unexpected line, the man quickly adapted himself. 'Quite awful. Even though Annie—perhaps you didn't know that that was her real name?—though Annie and I have rather lost touch over the years. Still, when one hears of one's contemporaries' disasters it sends quite a chill through one.'

'She's rather more than a mere contemporary, surely?'

The mobile mouth pursed. 'Rather less than real family,

Superintendent. We were split up many years ago—after our parents' deaths.'

Yeadings nodded. Light slanting sideways from the window revealed fine lines on the man's hollowed face. He would have been the older of the two, possibly had shown scant interest in his little half-sister.

'How old would she have been at that time?' Yeadings asked. 'I'm hoping you can give us some background about her. She seems to have lived in something of a vacuum.'

'Ah. She'd have been about four. The rest is not so easy. I couldn't even say who'd be best to ask.'

'When did you last see her, Mr Fairburn?'

'Let me see.' He closed his eyes, tilted his head and affected a thoughtful expression. 'I ran into her at a do at the Inn on the Park a couple of weeks back. She was with clients, sleek Middle Eastern gentlemen. I was in a mob of actors. Oil and water, Superintendent. We saluted each other across the room. Before that it would be some months earlier, maybe more. At a private party, God knows whose. Something totally unmemorable.'

'A four-year-old,' Yeadings considered. 'You must have known what happened to her. Was she adopted or sent to a children's home?'

'I rather think someone adopted her. I was only ten at the time myself. Adults didn't go out of their way to explain such things to children in those days. Perhaps they thought we'd miss each other more if they kept mentioning the other. If indeed they thought at all.'

'Were you adopted, sir?'

'For my sins. Firstly by a cousin of my father until he died. Then a more distant connection. Thank God they had the sense to send me away to school when I was thirteen. But I thought it was Annie you wanted to know about.'

'I'm interested in anything that sheds light on her background. Have you had any connection with her at professional level, sir? *Her* profession, that is.'

There was an almost indiscernible tightening of the muscles across the man's cheeks. As if, Yeadings thought, were he a horse, his ears would have twitched back.

'I know of the firm she works for, but I can't remember any occasion when we made use of their services. We have a good in-house PR section at Viccentro and they cover conferences or anything we need of that sort. It's a general tendency since the recession. These expo specialists could be heading for a lean patch.' The prospect seemed to cause him no dismay.

'Thank you. We may need to see you again later, in which case a colleague from the Metropolitan force will be visiting you. Would your home address be more convenient?'

Without a word Fairburn took back the card from the policeman's fingers and wrote on its reverse. He appeared to have completed his sick visit because when he handed it back he nodded peremptorily. 'Good day, Superintendent,' and he made a minor flourish with his wide-brimmed hat before striding off down the corridor.

Yeadings watched his departure from a window near the car park. The man took half a dozen steps into the open and gave a lordly wave, whereupon a limousine began pulling out towards him. A uniformed chauffeur got out to open the rear passenger door at which moment a sudden gust of wind tore off the wide-brimmed hat and sent it cartwheeling across the tarmac.

Fairburn made a desperate grab, shook his fists in the air as the elusive headgear bowled merrily away, turned to glare balefully at the chauffeur who was stifling a guffaw, tossed his head like a prima donna and stepped bareheaded into the car's interior.

There was food for thought in this brief visit, Yeadings told himself. What had it been for? Merely identification, to confirm that the injured woman was who the newspapers said? What else? There hadn't been any affection shown,

nor real regret. The expensive flowers had been a formal
gesture. Fairburn could afford them, just as he could brush
off the loss of a pricey velour hat, one of the dramatic props
of a TV director who chose to dress like an actor; perhaps
was an actor manqué. They were queer cattle, these luvvies
of the small silver screen.

But why should he have given up what must be a working day to visit a half-sister with whom he was at pains to
deny any close link?

Any *recent* close link, Yeadings corrected himself. Anything Annie and Rodney might have been to each other
was by implication in the far past. So, since Miranda/Annie
seemed to lack present context, was that past worth delving
into, and was Fairburn to be seriously considered as a suspect?

Working from previous experience when long-separated
family made a sudden reappearance, Yeadings decided it
could be germane to discover whether the young woman
had made a will, and if not, whether Fairburn was actually
the nearest blood relation.

And still this Gregory case had a possible link with the
man shot dead over a week ago in her London office. No
one had yet identified him, and the injured woman might
even now slip away without being able to give any help.

With so many questions, wasn't it more than time that
the odd answer turned up? He'd have to look upon Fairburn's relationship as the only positive factor at present,
and get the team checking on him. If his emergence was
an answer, it was one that led to still more questions.

SEVEN

ANNETTE BRIERS RETURNED to work on Monday with mixed feelings. A spare office doorkey had been passed to the reinstated PA, so she was to be spared the sickening task of opening up on whatever carnage this weekend might have brought. She was almost convinced that lightning never struck the same spot twice, but nothing had been quite certain of late and she was walking carefully.

Which is why she lingered over combing her hair in the ladies' room until Gwen had preceded her by a good two minutes without any subsequent screams or alarm bells sounding.

Guiltily she admitted to herself that apart from that first awful discovery and the fact of Ms Gregory still in a coma, the past week had had its stimulating moments. It made history to have twice lunched with a man who took some interest in her observations. She hadn't yet decided whether his being a policeman added to or subtracted from the pleasure. At least it was quite outside routine: life was taking on a brisk new tempo. And there had been that visit at home. Even Sergeant Beaumont had been impressed that she was considered sufficiently important to be questioned by a detective-superintendent.

But the strangest event, and by far the most disquieting, had been when on Saturday afternoon she discovered that she was being followed.

It was after leaving the sergeant at the Amersham bus stop. She had reached Wycombe and was walking across the roundabout complex when the fire siren sounded. Amber warning lights flashed and traffic was halted while two emergency machines left the station at speed.

She had been at the edge of the pavement, glancing curiously across, when she saw the tan Toyota. She couldn't make out the driver's features behind the rain-spotted glass but thought he was turned to watch her. Two or three minutes later, as she walked up the hospital approach, a car followed and turned off to park. It was the same one. It struck her then that the driver must be unfamiliar with the complicated roundabout system and had made several circuits to be still coming in behind her. She thought no more of it until she was leaving after her visit.

In the dusk as she waited to pull her rain hood over her head she saw the same car nosing out, and felt the first shot of alarm that Beaumont should have sent someone to check where she went; because there were too many cars of this kind on her heels today, tan Toyotas just like the one which arrived at the Black Lion as they were leaving.

She remembered that during lunch the sergeant had excused himself for a few minutes to use the phone. Had he been ordering a car to have her followed?

But why? Was she seriously a suspect, or did they think she might be in danger?

And then she remembered her momentary disquiet when the man had brushed by them in the pub's doorway. He must have come from the tan car, because rain on its warm bonnet was making it steam under a brief gleam of sunshine. She doubted he would be quite tall enough for a policeman. She recalled the red mark across his forehead, recently made by a tight hatband.

From a *tweed fishing-hat* shrunk by heavy rain?

Now she knew who he was! It was seeing him bareheaded today and without his glasses that had put her off; yet at some level she'd been alerted. This was the man who had followed Ms Gregory and herself out of the buffet, the man the police wanted to interview.

A taxi had just deposited two elderly visitors at the hospital entrance and was close behind her. She waved it down and climbed in. 'Where to, miss?' the man asked.

'Twice round the roundabout while I think,' she said wildly.

He was watching her through the mirror as they stopped at the first red lights. Unfamiliar with the trains from this end of the line, she was scrabbling in her shoulder bag for the timetable.

'One more circuit for good measure?'

She looked out. 'Up that hill.'

From the rear window she saw the Toyota two junctions back. The fishing-hat man would have a clear sight of the cab as it turned off. Little hope of throwing him off her scent since she didn't know the district.

'Something bothering you, miss?' The cabbie sounded amused.

'Some*one*,' she said shortly. 'In a tan Toyota behind. He's been following me all afternoon.'

'Not your dad, is it?' and he clucked.

'No. A nasty bit of work.'

'Is he, then? Well, we'll have to get rid of him, won't we? Mind, this isn't a racing Ferrari.'

'There's a train in nine minutes,' she read off the timetable. 'Could you keep going until nearly then, and drop me in time at the station?'

'You wouldn't rather I stopped off at the cop shop?'

She hesitated, unsure. 'I don't think so. I'd rather just lose him. I want the up-line for London. Can you say how much your fare's likely to be? Would five pounds cover it? If I pay now I can just nip out when we get there. I've got my ticket.'

'You'll not need to cross the railway footbridge. Trains for both directions are leaving from this side. And five's plenty. I'll knock the rest off for the fun of it. Don't get much of this car-chase excitement.'

He had turned right at the top of the hill and was weaving

back through residential streets down towards the town centre again, shot into a car park, made a brilliant U-turn and came out past the Toyota as it entered. Annette caught her pursuer's startled expression as they flashed by.

'How much time we got?' the driver demanded over his shoulder. 'Whoops, nearly bagged that old doll on the crossing.'

'Four minutes.'

'Don't time fly when you're enjoying yourself? What happens if the train's late? Mebbe I'd better hang about in the yard.'

'That's all the spare cash I was carrying. It'd have to be a cheque next.'

The man gave a fierce grin, opened his mouth wide and bawled, '"From a find to a check, from a check to a view!" John Peel, they don't teach kids good tunes like that any more.'

Annette smiled sickly back, recalling 'from a view to a death in the morning'. And now was worse than morning, with the sky overcast, rain gusting again and early autumnal dusk closing in on her.

They gained seconds at two sets of traffic lights and then the taxi careened off up the steep hill she'd walked down oblivious to all dangers only hours before.

As Annette leapt out shouting her thanks she looked back and could see no sign of the pursuing car. She heard the train approaching. Craning from the platform, she saw her cab slewed awkwardly across the station yard, blocking the way of the tan Toyota. The two drivers had their heads out and seemed to be shouting at each other. She fell into a seat and prayed that departure wouldn't be delayed.

A last-minute passenger came flying through the station doors, but it was only a red-faced schoolboy who caught his satchel strap on a trolley and spilled books in every direction.

And still the fishing-hat man hadn't caught up. The train

drew away. She was safe, at least for now. And for one bored cabbie the incident had made his day.

All through Sunday she was restless, trapped indoors by the weather. She had intended visiting Ms Gregory again but her only raincoat hadn't dried out properly and she was still worried about being followed.

She thought of phoning Sergeant Beaumont but she'd already broken into his weekend. If she saw the fishing-hat man again she would report it, but having successfully thrown him off, she'd little for the police to work on. They were looking for him in any case.

Hospital visiting was off, because he might be hanging about to pick up her trail again. Yesterday had scared her enough. His interest could only be through some connection with Ms Gregory, because almost certainly he'd followed her back to the office that night of the murder.

She was thankful when Monday brought brighter skies and the promise that routine demands would keep her busy with other things. Just the same, she took the precaution of covering her gingery frizz with a triangular scarf on her journey up to London and took a magazine to stay immersed in on the train.

GWEN HADN'T WASTED her weekend. There was a list of duties for Annette, and five letters to clients on tape for her to type up. She worked through to twelve twenty-five when a call came through from Reception that a visitor was waiting to see her. No, he wouldn't give his name; said it was to be a surprise.

Lunchtime, so was it Sergeant Beaumont? This was getting to be a habit. Discreet of him not to have said who he was.

'I'll be out in a minute. Ask him to wait, please.'

He had seated himself on the far side of one of the potted palms and rose as she came towards him. Bareheaded, but it was the fishing-hat man just the same.

In panic she seemed to freeze as he came forward, couldn't make out what he was saying. Through a sort of mist she was aware that he had thrust something into her hand. A small piece of pasteboard. His visiting card.

She read it, looked at him, and had to admit now that he didn't look like a criminal. A little intimidating, though. The screwed-up eyes were intelligent, the retroussé nose questing as he took in her utter astonishment.

What a fool he must think her. Yes, she could see he'd grasped the cause of her confusion. 'I'm sorry if I scared you on Saturday. I just needed to talk to you after your hospital visit.'

'The *police* want to talk to *you*.'

'I know. I've already been to see them. Not that I was able to help very much.'

'How much?'

'Suppose we go and find somewhere for a snack. If you feel safe with me, that is.'

She looked down at the card between her fingers. 'I don't know that it's ever safe to talk with the press.'

'Even if that's what I really am, because anyone can get a visiting card printed up for dubious purposes. If you like, look up the paper's number in the phone book, get extension 243, and ask them what I look like. They've split their sides already over the description of me you gave the police. I found it humbling, but totally justified, of course.'

For some reason she believed him. The disquiet she'd been feeling came from the circumstances and not from the man himself. 'I bring sandwiches,' she blurted.

'We'll feed the birds with them, after we've had lunch.'

'All right, but I insist on paying for my own.' Then in horror she remembered she was out of cash.

'Nonsense. Haven't you heard of expenses?'

'But I'm not giving you an interview. I don't know anything you'd want to print.'

'Not now, certainly. But finally, when it's all over, the

public will want to know the whole story. And quite a lot of it is yours. You admired your Ms Gregory, didn't you? At present there's a suspicion she could have killed the man found shot in her office. We might even help prove she didn't. Won't you try to do that for her?'

'You're manipulating me.' But already they were walking out of the building together.

'There, I knew you had your wits about you. I also know a very pleasant little Greek place round the corner where the service is quick and we can be private.' He smiled, his face lively and challenging. Not at all the world-weary misanthropist she'd assumed a representative of the national press would be. All through the meal she searched for a single word to cover him, and there wasn't one. Perhaps sprightly was the nearest.

He reassured her by giving his own story first. He had been in Marylebone station buffet that Friday evening to meet an informant who failed to turn up. He'd given the man forty minutes' grace and then decided the meeting wasn't on. He got up to go at the same moment that the two women left. He'd gone out to the street and seen one of the women enter a taxi. There had been only two waiting. He had to wait for the second while a previous passenger dropped his fare and chased it over the pavement. A tall man who'd followed him out was also keen for a taxi, but he beat him to it. He returned by cab to the office. Yes, his own, at the newspaper, in east London.

'And that is what you told the police?'

'Yes. I never saw which way you went, but I half remembered you both from that occasion. When Ms Gregory's photograph was circulating in the provincial press with the account of the hit-and-run incident it teased me until the scene came back. Eventual mention of the man in a tweed fishing-hat as a possible witness sent me straight to the police with my story.

'I'm London-based, so I rang a CID man I know at the

Met. He passed my name to Thames Valley, who asked me to drop by.

'I'd just come from a meeting with Superintendent Yeadings when I ran into you again. I had no more sinister reason for being at the Black Lion than a fancy for lunch. Incidentally, how's your *moussaká?*'

'It's great. So is the wine. I'll never need another meal for days.'

'I hope you've left room for their *baklavas*. Now tell me about your Ms Gregory. She seems a lady of some mystery. Working together, you must have been as close to her as anyone.'

Annette explained that she worked for her, not with her, wasn't even her PA. Her admiration for the highly competent and attractive woman was evident.

'And that evening you were going off together after work?'

Annette shook her head. 'We were each going home. It was news to me that we lived on the same line, because usually she'd drive in.'

'So where do you live?'

'Wembley.'

'You have your own flat?'

'I live with my mother. She's widowed.'

He hesitated. 'And the friend you were with at the Black Lion—?'

She laughed. 'Pinocchio? He was a plain-clothes policeman. Sergeant Beaumont. Since discovering that awful— that man who was shot, people have taken to questioning me over lunch.'

He considered her gravely. 'Now that you've mentioned that horrid business of a week ago, could you bear to tell me about it?'

'Provided that you don't ask me the stock media question.'

'What's that?'

She upturned a pepper pot and thrust it under his nose like a microphone. 'And how did you feel when you discovered the body?'

'We're an insensitive lot, I admit.'

'It's no good asking me what he looked like. I just had an impression. All I really saw was his face, what had happened to it. Horrible! It won't go away.'

She was gripping the table edge. He saw the trembling go up her arms and he laid his hands over hers. She looked down at them. Small hands for a man, but muscled. Drives a typewriter, just like me, she thought. He's good at his job; he's making me talk. And, surprisingly, it helps.

'Look, I have to get back. I've a new boss now and she's a bit sharp.'

'So at Matherson and Corby life must go on just the same. Heartless, isn't it? Ms Gregory's absence means a colleague's promotion.'

'Her ex-PA who'd taken early retirement was asked to step in temporarily. She's not too bad, I suppose, but Gwen Lodd could never be another Miranda Gregory.'

He was reaching for his credit card in an inner pocket and suddenly froze.

'Who did you say?'

She caught something of his tension and couldn't reply.

'What name was that?'

'Gwen Lodd. The stand-in.'

'But this is weird! Annette, didn't your policeman tell you? That was Miranda Gregory's surname before she changed it by deed poll. She'd been Annie Lodd.'

EIGHT

'I AGREE,' Superintendent Yeadings said calmly. 'It could be pure coincidence. But it intrigues me, two women called Lodd working alongside in a single firm without admitting any connection.'

Angus Mott nodded. 'We know it was over ten years ago that the deed poll was effected. I'll need to look into their dates of entry into Matherson and Corby and their relative ages.'

'According to Max Harris, Annette Briers thought Gwen Lodd was old enough to be the other's mother.'

'And she had been working for the younger one. Food for thought there. What's in it for this Max Harris, sir?'

'A story at the end of it all, maybe, though he's not strictly speaking a scandal-sheeter. Writes a weekly comment column. He struck me as being open to reason, if treated fairly. Naturally he'd like his paper to have the first release on this development.'

'If it is a development. You'd think that any close relative of Ms Gregory's would have been to visit her in hospital. To date the only one to turn up is a half-brother.'

Yeadings nodded. 'A Rodney Fairburn, who claims they shared the same mother.'

'So do I tackle him first on this, or go direct to the Lodd woman?'

'It's your case, Angus. This information is certainly relevant to the Thames Valley inquiry. Let's hope that feeding it to the Met will oblige them to update us with whatever new comes their way.'

'Why didn't Harris pass it to them?'

Yeadings gave a bland smile. 'Because I'd already had

him out here on Saturday. When I knew he'd informed the
Met that he was the fishing-hat character in the buffet, I
asked him to drop by. Frankly he impressed me. He probably had the sense to see that ours is the prime interest in
Ms Gregory and that using his discovery gives us a firmer
footing with the Met for our own needs at that end. Without
close cooperation we could be out on a limb with our hit-
and-run case. I want you fully operative on the London end
yourself, Angus. With Zyczynski. That leaves me Beaumont to cover anything that comes up here.'

Angus looked at his chief and covered a broad grin with
his hand. The Boss had already stuck his nose in twice.
First with the home visit to Annette Briers and again with
calling in the newspaper man. In Angus' absence he could
justify to himself any amount of active sleuthing to skip
routine desk duties.

'Right, sir.'

The answering bright gleam in Yeadings' eyes acknowledged that he'd guessed the way Mott's mind was working
and revelled in his suspicion. 'Then I'll let Meredith know
accordingly. Unless he offers you lodgings, I expect you
both to commute on this one.'

'Yessir.' A deadpan mask concealed Mott's disappoint-
ment that he'd not be staying over. In any case Z's presence
would have made it difficult for him to slope off to his
fiancée Paula's. But working for a few days on the Met's
patch might still afford an opportunity for them to see each
other.

Paula's heavy case-load at the Bailey had prevented her
coming down for a couple of weeks, and their free time
hadn't coincided. Old Wheatman was passing more and
more briefs to her as his junior, resulting not only in increased hours in court but also in more sessions with in-
structing solicitors and mugging up on cases.

Still, she had only herself to blame. If she hadn't been
so stubbornly set on continuing as a defence brief they

might have been married by now, with Paula transferring to the local Crown Prosecution Service.

He was aware that the Boss was sitting owl-like opposite with the sort of knowing stare that always made him feel his brains had gone transparent.

'And if you should run into Paula,' Yeadings said with an innocent-seeming smile, 'give her my regards, will you?'

ROSEMARY ZYCZYNSKI eased herself into the passenger seat of Mott's steel-blue Saab. It was a beauty inside too. She had splashed out two months back on her own modest Vauxhall and envied the inspector's ability to pick up, improve and sell at profit, really stunning cars two or three times a year. He claimed that working as an amateur motor mechanic kept him out of mischief. That and water polo were his main pastimes outside duty, apart from his engagement to the barrister, Paula Musto. Not that she'd been around much of late. And could you really call an engagement a pastime? Especially when you spent less and less time on it.

Mott was frowning quite fiercely as he drove, so she left him to get his thinking done before she asked for updating on the case.

'I want you to tackle Annette Briers first,' he said suddenly. He explained how the fishing-hat character had come forward, was a London-based columnist for the *Courier* and had learned from Annette that Ms Gregory's ex-PA and replacement was a Mrs Lodd.

Her eyes widened. 'That was Gregory's original surname.'

'Exactly. So we'll check the story out with Briers before we tackle the Lodd woman herself. I want to be sure it was the girl who first mentioned the name and not this Max Harris putting it in her mouth. He seems to have a knack of conveniently happening along to hasten on the action.'

'A wily bird?'

'Could be. The Boss seems to trust him. He likes the Briers girl too. But it's increasingly my opinion that nice people can get up to quite nasty things.'

Zyczynski stole a sideways glance at his determined profile. That was a new declared cynicism for the normally sunny DI Mott. So what was eating him?

'And where are we bound for at present?'

'Wembley. Briers will be getting home about now. I'll drop you off and you can find your own way back when you've spoken to her. I'll carry on to the Yard and contact the Meredith murder team. Then we can start together up there tomorrow. I'll pick you up at 7.30 a.m. We'll be going up daily. Any questions?'

'Yes, Guv. When do I get to drive this car?'

ANNETTE BRIERS HADN'T arrived home by the time Z called. Her mother turned out to be a slightly dizzy little lady with salt-and-pepper hair and an arthritic condition. She made tea for them both and sat down for a welcome chance to chat. 'Fancy you being a detective,' she began: a version, Z recognized, of the familiar line, 'What's a nice girl like you doing...?'

'A bit dangerous, I should think. I'm always so glad my Annie's in something safe like secretarial.'

Z looked at her covertly. Hadn't she heard what Annette had walked in on a week ago at work? It seemed not, because Mrs Briers waffled cheerfully on, via some popular scandal in the tabloids, to the topic of her own correspondence.

She brought out a bundle of letters from concealment in a drawer. 'My sister keeps on at me how much I'd like it out there, warm climate and good for my arthritis. But I can't leave Annette to manage on her own.'

Wistfully she laid out a series of colour photographs showing a middle-aged couple with various enticing backgrounds: all outdoor pictures drenched in bright sunlight. A distant view of bubbling mud holes gave a clue to their locality.

Relief came at last with Annette's return. Her apologies were clearly meant to cover more than her own lateness. Z came straight to the point and received an unambiguous answer. Max Harris had not been the first to utter the name Lodd. He'd been quite bowled over when Annette mentioned what the office stand-in was called.

AT THE YARD Mott found they were expecting him, because the Boss had rung through. Chief Inspector Meredith, lanky and lugubrious, seemed content to coopt him into his murder inquiry team. Angus arranged to interview Gwen Lodd next day along with a Met DS called Fox, whose appearance belied the name. He was a laid-back character and his eyes were set far apart to either side of a flattened nose. The two stood each other a beer in a bar off Victoria Street before Mott went off to look up Ms Gregory's half-brother.

Rodney Fairburn shared a flat in Fulham with a sulky-looking starlet who introduced herself as Zara. Rodney, she told him, was in the bath, and sure he could go right through.

Without introduction he did so, and found the TV man, brandy globe in one hand, a script in the other, half submerged in soap bubbles, his feet resting on the gold-finish taps.

'Ah,' he said, glancing up.

Angus pulled the bath stool forward and lowered himself on to it. 'Inspector Mott, Thames Valley CID.' He flipped his warrant card open. 'I understand you have already spoken to Superintendent Yeadings.'

'But now I'm downgraded, it seems. What can I do for you?'

'I'm interested in your half-sister, Miranda Lodd.'

Fairburn dropped the script on the bath mat, downed the brandy and scooped water in a large sponge to squeeze over his cooling chest. 'Annie Gregory,' he corrected.

'Annie Lodd,' Mott compromised. 'Also known as Miranda Gregory, having changed her name by deed poll.'

'*Born* Annie Gregory,' Fairburn insisted, 'whatever she changed it to later. Lodd was the name of the family who adopted her, now I come to remember.'

'So she changed it twice? The second time going back to her original surname?'

'Look; since ancient history is what turns you on, it went like this. My father's name was Fairburn and he was married to my mother. That made her a Fairburn, and myself—their only and legitimate child—a Fairburn too. After my father died, my mother was crazy enough to marry again, this time a hoodlum called Gregory. The result of their miserable union was a weedy female infant called Annie. That's all I know, or care to.'

'Except that you now remember the name of the family who fostered, and—presumably—later adopted her. Can you tell me anything else about them? Forenames? Address?'

Fairburn half closed the deep-set slatey eyes. 'Nothing. It wasn't important.' Abruptly he sat up and began sponging one leg after the other with long, leisurely strokes, pausing to ask over his shoulder, 'Ever thought of modelling? I could probably fix you up with a thermal underwear commercial.'

Mott rose to his full height and suppressed the desire to push the other's head under. 'Thank you for your help, Mr Fairburn. Good evening.'

Out in the Saab again, he reflected that Paula's flat was only three streets away. At least she would appreciate hearing of the new career prospect insolently on offer to him.

SUPERINTENDENT YEADINGS switched off the desk-lamp and reached into the cupboard for his overcoat. Rapid foot-

steps in the corridor outside halted his movements. Someone rapped on the glass panel of his door. 'Come in, Beaumont.'

His detective-sergeant slid into the room. 'Sir, we've
traced the car that hit her.'

Yeadings switched on the light again and nodded to the
upright chair facing his own.

'It would have come to light earlier, but it was hired for
a week, Saturday to Saturday.' Beaumont pulled out his
notebook and rattled off the licence number.

'Red Ford Sierra hatchback from Vortex Car Hire,
Slough. They followed up its non-return, couldn't contact
the hirer and phoned in its registration as a missing vehicle.
A patrol man notified us that it's been for several days in
the station car park at Gerrards Cross running itself up quite
a bill. Smashed windscreen and buckled offside wing. Of
course it's rained plenty in the meantime, but SOCO's had
it bagged in hope of finding some traces.'

'You're keeping the best to the end. Spit it out, man.'

'Sorry, sir. Anticlimax: it was loaned to a Ms Miranda
Gregory, driving licence particulars correct according to
records.'

'Are you asking me to believe, Sergeant, that Ms Gregory was run down by a car she was driving herself?'

'Sir, it was hired for a week, Saturday to Saturday. And
her own car was due back the Friday night before. It was
only a lighting fault and they promised to fix it in a day.
So what would she need a second car for?'

'You think it was someone other than Gregory who ordered it.'

'I know it, sir. The description was all wrong. This one
had fairish hair, height about five two to five five, plumpish,
aged between eighteen and twenty-five.'

'But she had Gregory's driving licence on her? They
actually looked at it?'

'Took down the details from it, sir.' Beaumont gave him a moment to get accustomed to the leaping suspicion.

Yeadings sucked in his cheeks reflectively. 'Well, we both know someone who fits the description and might have had access to the licence without much difficulty, don't we?'

'Except that she's more ginger than fair, sir.'

'It depends on the light and whether the observer is good on colours. And then there are such things as wigs.'

'Yessir.' He sympathized with the Boss's momentary deflation. The girl had had him fooled too.

Yeadings stood up again and for a second time reached for his coat. 'So Zyczynski will have something else to follow up tomorrow when she's at Matherson and Corby. Progress, Sergeant. We've taken a small step forward.'

ANGUS MOTT, himself in need of tender ministrations, found himself cast instead as provider. Paula was weary and stiff-limbed after a long day in court. She sat slumped on the floor between his knees while he kneaded her shoulders and neck.

'Just there, yes. Excruciating, but um, great.'

'What you need is—'

'What I need is a long, long vacation and never, ever, to hear the word libel again. The trouble is there's so much money in it. People get greedy.'

'You should have it out with old Wheatman. He's driving you into the ground. What does he need all that money for at his age?'

'It's because he *is* at that age. I think he has an idea of retiring. There's that widow down Salisbury way. Maybe he's working towards a target. Once he's hit it, then it'll be wedding bells and a future of gentleman-farming. He's keen on pigs, would you believe? Not much difference from the clients we've been defending of late. God, I am

so tired of all this shit-digging. I got wound up and told
him so yesterday. Know what he said?'

'Tell me.'

She pulled a long face and mimicked the silk's over-
precise diction. '"My dear, it's the ideal brief for you.
What jury will doubt the client of someone like driven
snow? I see a long and highly profitable career ahead of
you." I could have knifed him—well, ledgered him anyway.'

'Maybe that's where the word "legerdemain" comes
from.'

'That's an old one, Angus, but you could try it on Beaumont. Oh Lord, let's take a lovely long, hot bath.'

'I've just come from one. Not such good company,
though.'

She turned and eyed him suspiciously. 'Who?'

He told her, and the circumstances.

'Rodney Fairburn? Well, well.'

'You know him?'

'Know of him. A possible future client, at least his company is. They put out a TV series about advertising scams
and one of the victims is back-biting. It wasn't Fairburn's
script, but he did direct the documentary. The plaintiff's
gone wild and is suing everyone, nearly down to the studio
cat.'

'Will he succeed?'

'Not if I can help it. But let's not talk shop. Can't you
think of some alternative?'

He bent over and gently bit her shoulder. 'Maybe I could.
If I tried really hard.'

NINE

TUESDAY MORNING'S CALL to the hospital assured the superintendent that there had been no change in Ms Gregory's condition. At least she was stable, and the registrar had insisted that low-level brain activity was present, but Yeadings wondered whether the longer she was unconscious meant the less she would remember if and when she did recover.

Inquiries at legal firms in Beaconsfield, Amersham, Wycombe and Aylesbury had failed to turn up any solicitor who had had dealings with the injured woman, apart from over the purchase of her flat. In the absence of any will being found among her few personal papers, it had been assumed that her half-brother was her nearest living relation.

Yeadings had briefly hoped to prove kinship with the Lodd woman at her workplace, but now Mott had discovered from Fairburn that a couple of that name had merely fostered the orphan Annie.

Orphan Annie! Lord, had she been old enough to come across that character in the American comics? If so, small wonder that she'd chosen to be called something different; even before she was of an age to insist on reverting to her original surname. It had been insensitive of the adoptive parents to foist their own on her, even from possibly well-intentioned motives. The child had been four years old. At that age she would remember being part of an earlier family. From her later actions it looked as though she had resented such a wholesale takeover.

Sifting through families of that name locally was continuing without success. It rested now with Angus Mott to look into the seeming coincidence of the Lodd onetime PA, retired for health reasons and then recalled temporarily following Ms Gregory's injury.

Beaumont too was in London, chasing up certificates of birth and death at the Public Records Office. Z was tasked to tackle the Briers girl. Which left the superintendent overseeing current cases at base: two of arson, an aggravated burglary, a missing Swedish au pair, and a double sexual assault.

He read conscientiously through the stack of reports, debriefed the arson team, liaised by phone with the Fire Chief and took a turn round the outside of the building for the good of his lungs. When he resumed his chair he still had the same image at the back of his mind: Annette Briers getting herself from Wembley to Slough—how? since she claimed not to have a car nor be a driver—and booking a red Sierra hatchback from Vortex Car Hire in her boss's name. Booking it for a week when said boss would have full use of her own car.

If Z was up to form she should get the story quite soon. In the meantime, couldn't he work it out for himself?

Annette Briers might have been following Ms Gregory's orders—or orders she supposed had come from Ms Gregory. There could have been a note left for her, or a phone message sent through a third person. In which case she was an innocent party. Ah, but there had been the driving licence.

How often did a woman make sure that her licence was actually on her—in her handbag or whatever? It wasn't a thing he checked on regularly himself. He patted his pockets until his own came to light.

Women carried a lot of unsorted junk around with them. He'd heard Nan complain that the linings of handbags were always black (to hide dirt), so nothing in there showed up. She'd said there was a fortune to be made by anyone who patented a handbag with a light that automatically switched on, like a fridge's.

Yes, it was reasonable to suppose that Ms Gregory's driving licence could have gone missing some time back without her realizing the fact. Only a spot check by police would have required her to dig it out.

It wasn't necessarily Annette Briers who took it. Anyone Gregory came into contact with over a period could have searched the bag and found it. And there were plenty of young, plump girls of five two to five five with fairish hair.

He sighed. As ever, there were too many options. Speculation took one further into quagmire. He must curb his restlessness and wait for Z to report back. But whoever made the car booking had a nasty sense of irony, using the name of the victim the car was later to run down. Premeditation. In his eyes it smacked at worst of attempted murder, at best of deliberate GBH.

Why should Miranda Gregory be targeted for violence? What was there in her unknown past that merited it? If only he'd access to more of her material possessions, they'd give him a lead. He spared a passing thought for his own recent perambulations through the junk of his loft; all those clues to his own and Nan's personal histories. They'd be easy meat for scavenging archivists. But Ms Gregory seemed to have existed in a vacuum, yielding only a succession of names.

Which surely must have some importance for her. She had opted to be known as Miranda, and as soon as she was legally of age she had chosen to drop the surname foisted on her. Teenage rebellion; why not? The first, hurtful move of independence as the chick flies the nest. So was the intention to identify herself again with her dead parents, or merely to flaunt her new freedom from chafing authority?

And why in the first place had these adoptive parents seen fit to cut her off from the little past the child had? Could it have been for more than personal reasons?

That question hung on him more heavily than the preceding ones and led on finally to suspicion. Yeadings pushed himself from his desk and made his way along the corridor. There was little point in following up this suspicion until Beaumont returned with something definite from the Public Record Office, but he felt a gambler's itch on this one.

He found DC Silver alone in the detectives' office and wrote the names Gregory, Lodd, Fairburn on a memo pad which he laid on the desk. 'Try Criminal Records for these,' he said. 'You'll probably need to go back quite a way.' He felt remiss because Z had meant to follow this through and been diverted to another angle.

As Annie Gregory had changed family at age four, they would need access to records nearly a quarter of a century back. Yeadings mentioned the year in airy fashion and watched Silver's jaw quiver in a controlled drop.

'Just an offchance in the penny dip,' he murmured blandly, 'but it might come up with something.'

Having, as he saw it, served his desk sentence for the day, Yeadings looked out at the sky's sunlit blue raked with the tail end of wispy clouds and decided to risk going hatless. He shrugged on his overcoat, treated his loaded desktop to a contemptuous survey and left the building.

AT THE HOSPITAL he found slightly more optimism over Ms Gregory's condition. Her heart was apparently emitting more encouraging beeps through the monitor, and one unit of the array of plastic tubing had been removed, together with the drainage bag with its residue of blood. From this he was relieved to assume—ever finding clinical details distasteful—that fear of further internal haemorrhaging had ceased.

'We're hopeful,' Sister told him. 'The next twenty-four hours might see her coming round. Would you like to sit and talk to her a while?'

Surely she hadn't taken him for family? Or was just any-one expected to take a hand when help was thin on the ground?

He brought a chair across, dropped his coat on the waxed floor and unburdened to the unconscious woman a rambling account of his views and doubts so far. 'So if you could manage to come round soon, it could save us all a lot of extra delving. Too much, perhaps, to expect you to remem-ber exactly what happened, the driver's face and so on, but if you'd just shed light on why anyone should have it in for you—well, that would be a beginning.'

There was no reaction, as he'd expected. Perhaps he should try a more personal line, though what could be more so than a possible attempt to murder her?

'You're a popular lady, Ms Gregory. Miss Briers is in to see you nearly every day. And your brother—whatsisname. Fairburn.' Roderick, was it? No, Rodney.

'Rodney,' he said loudly, proud of the name's recovery. 'Or as a little girl perhaps you called the boy Rod. *Rod,* was that it?' He leaned forward to watch the white face.

A vertical crease had appeared between her brows and the eyelids momentarily flickered. He called for a nurse, but by the time she reached him the face had returned to how it was before. The comatose woman's lips made a soft *pp* sound and she seemed to settle into deeper breathing.

'She's got a long way to come back,' the nurse said. 'She could half surface several times before she finally comes out of it.'

Yeadings made for his car, to ring Matherson and Corby in London, asking for Inspector Mott.

'Angus,' he ordered, when they were connected, 'I want you to inform Z that Ms Gregory could be starting to come round. And be there when she tells Annette Briers. Report back on the girl's reaction; it could be crucial. Has anything interesting come up from your end?'

'I've been talking to Gwen Lodd. She is the adoptive

mother we were looking for. She and her husband, since
divorced, first fostered the child as an orphan, then two
years later adopted her. This was the third fostering they'd
taken on, having failed to produce any children of their
own. Miranda, as she was by that point, left their home at
seventeen, changed her surname—as we know—at eighteen, and seems to have been an ungrateful little baggage,
though the woman's surprisingly uncritical of her behaviour. She's a very restrained lady all round. Despite Miranda's cutting herself off, Mrs Lodd was willing four years
ago to sponsor her when she was looking for work. It was
through her that Ms Gregory came to be at Matherson and
Corby, and so got her chance to climb over the older
woman's head. It says something for the long-suffering
Lodd that she was reconciled to acting as the younger one's
assistant until, recently, failing health obliged her to take
early retirement.'

'Did she say anything about Gregory's half-brother, the
TV director?'

'Merely that he was adopted by a different family. She
didn't feel at the time she took Annie Gregory that she
could cope with both children. Had they been twins or true
siblings their separation would have been frowned on officially, but they weren't.'

'M'm. I had a call from Aldermaston this morning about
the hit-and-run car.'

'That's quick, sir.'

'Only a preliminary report. To say that the interior had
no dabs apart from anonymous smudges that could have
survived cleaning by the hire firm after previous use.'

'Which confirms that the driver who ran Gregory down
had reason to avoid identification.'

'Not necessarily. It's been damn cold of late. I've made
a point of driving in gloves myself. We're not all hot-
blooded young athletes like you. Talking of which, how is
Paula?'

'Fine, fine.' Mott cut the automatic, robust line and had second thoughts. 'No; actually she's a bit brown at the edges. Disenchanted with presenting libel defence on behalf of media toughies.'

'Could this be a good thing in the long run?'

'I ask myself that as well.'

'Too much running with the jackals might make her ready for an alternative. Well, nobody would be more pleased than I to see her make the change and settle in down here, if only to instil some courage into our Crown Prosecution Service. Give me a ring at home tonight, Angus. Let me know how you and Z get on with the Briers girl.'

ANNETTE HAD WALKED IN on the waiting detectives when she arrived at work. Their presence seemed to offer a way out from the quandary she found herself in.

Already curious to find out what connection if any there was between Ms Gregory/Lodd and her ex-PA replacement at Matherson and Corby, she had been wondering how to raise the question tactfully herself. It couldn't be done without divulging that she had again been in touch with the press and learned of Ms Gregory's earlier surname from Max. Now, it seemed, the question was to be raised officially.

Apart from both women being tall and lean, she could recognize no family likeness. Certainly, Gwen indicated none of the classy background she had imagined for the younger woman. Nor were they alike in personality, Miranda being assertive, imaginative and assured of her own magnetism. Gwen was none of this. Efficient to a fault, and demanding as high standards from those working for her, she could be sourly discouraging and would never command the admiration that Ms Gregory did.

Detective-Sergeant Fox had been working here the previous day. He now introduced the other two from Thames

Valley. 'This is Inspector Mott and Detective-Constable—er—Bailey. They have a few more questions to ask.'

Annette recognized the policewoman she had earlier met as Beaumont's partner. The big detective with the crisp blond hair and his Met shadow shepherded Gwen off to interview her in their temporary office. She seemed, if anything, to be even more offhand about the inquiry than before, vexed that the questioning should disturb office routine. Thoughtfully Annette turned back to her desk and found Z seated ready to question her in her turn.

'I've told Superintendent Yeadings everything I know,' she said, judging that name-dropping was permissible in the cause of a more rapid return to work.

'Unfortunately he doesn't see fit to brief me in detail. I have to make my own report, so bear with me.'

She had a sweet face, Annette thought. It could be hard for her holding her own alongside the men. And such a macho-seeming superior as Inspector Mott. 'Your name isn't really Bailey, is it?' she asked.

The woman detective smiled. 'It's Zyczynski,' and she spelled it out. 'It's not surprising that you don't remember it. Sergeant Fox clearly found it too much. Actually "Mott and Bailey" sounds an inspired double act.'

'Would you like some coffee?'

'If it's no trouble, I'd love some.'

Annette went through to the outer office and switched on the filter machine. She was beginning to enjoy the atmosphere of girls-together. She went back, leaving the intervening door ajar so that she would hear the coffee burbling.

Rosemary Zyczynski was standing by the window. 'So this is the office where it happened.'

'The shooting, yes. They've changed the chair, of course. The bullet went in at the back, and out—'

'At the front, yes. The thick padding muffled the sound, which is why no one heard it. Look, I don't need you to go over all the details. It must have been horrible for you.'

'It was, at the time. Since then so much has happened that it hardly seems possible. Or it's as if it was someone else coming in and finding it, not me.'

'Still nasty.'

'You must see some terrible things yourself at times.'

Zyczynski didn't answer, busy with her shorthand pencil in the office's electric sharpener. 'Have you been in this firm long?'

Annette explained how she had been picked from the pool by Ms Gregory, worked for her under Gwen until her retirement, then directly for Ms Gregory. Now—temporarily, as she hoped—Gwen was back in charge while Ms Gregory was on sick leave.

'You don't get on so well with Mrs Lodd?'

Annette was almost tempted to ask which one, to get the subject launched. 'She's all right. Ms Gregory was more—inspiring.'

'So you find the work interesting?'

'Yes, much more so than insurance, which I was in before. Here you can help shape a project, and although I've not yet followed one the whole way through, I've seen some finished results and they're really impressive.'

'So you take an active part in the expo end?'

'Just at secretarial level for Ms Gregory. And twice on loan to conference delegates who didn't bring their own staff.'

'How fascinating. What expos were these?'

Annette pulled illustrated folders out of the filing cabinets and spread them over the desk. Zyczynski pored over them.

'Did you ever get the impression'—she paused as if uncertain how to put the rest of the question—'that by her actions, or her manner, Ms Gregory got up the nose of any of her clients?'

'They didn't always jump at her ideas straight off, but

she could be very persuasive. Her presentation was good
and she'd a lot of experience.'

'And then she knew how to charm her clients.'

'She certainly did.'

'I was wondering if—putting together contracts like
these, where there's money involved—is there anything
similar to the casting-couch element? I mean, would personal feelings be likely to influence the outcome of a business discussion?'

Annette stared back with round eyes.

'As a woman yourself you must sometimes have wondered about your boss. So attractive, and with contracts
depending on her salesmanship—'

'She had relationships, yes. But I don't think it was all
that mercenary. Some of the men clients she was dealing
with were quite—well, personable. She hadn't any ties that
I know of. I mean, she was free to please herself, and nowadays—'

Zyczynski nodded. 'Standards. I know; they vary as
much as skirt lengths. But in changing partners she could
have made enemies. Sad but true. So many of the violent
crimes at present are committed by lovers who feel rejected.
I'd like you to go through the last three or four months'
contracts and think whether any of the clients were likely
to have been on intimate terms with Ms Gregory. Can you
do that by this evening and let me know?'

Annette heard the passage door open and someone come
in. 'Marvellous smell of coffee,' the big blond detective
said.

'There's some left if you'd like it. Help yourself.'

While he made noises with crockery Annette turned back
to Zyczynski. 'I suppose I could try. If it would help her.
But I wasn't really close enough to notice much. She wasn't
all that obvious, you see.'

Mott came through with a steaming mug. 'How have you
two been getting along?'

'All right.' Z stood to relinquish her seat.

'No, carry on.' He went to stand against the wall behind her. Annette was aware that the atmosphere had changed with his entry. She felt herself withdraw, on the defensive.

'You do know, don't you,' Z said, 'that we aren't treating the hit-and-run as purely an accident?'

'That's rather obvious; there are so many of you on the case. Then these last questions: you're looking for someone who could want to harm her.'

'We have...' Z seemed to be considering how much to tell. 'We have the car that was involved. It seems that it was hired by someone in Ms Gregory's name, and using her driving licence.'

'The car that actually hit her?' Annette appeared puzzled.

'Yes. It's still the subject of forensic examination. Fortunately we have a good description of the person who hired it.'

Annette sat forward eagerly. 'So it could be easy to trace him. But the driving licence—Ms Gregory would surely have kept it on her?'

'In her handbag, I'd have thought. Did you ever get to see it?'

Annette shook her head. 'She'd no call to show it to me. And I certainly never looked through her bag for anything. In the office she always locked it away in the bottom drawer of her desk. She was careful about things like that.'

'So whoever took it would have had to distract her attention to something outside the office and use duplicate keys.'

'I don't know about her desk keys. You could ask at Reception, but I can't imagine Ms Gregory letting them be held by anyone but herself.'

'You haven't asked about the person who hired the car,' Mott pointed out. 'Aren't you interested?'

'I didn't suppose you'd tell me. Who was it?'

'A woman of five feet two to five feet five with fairish

hair, plump and aged between eighteen and twenty-five. Does that suggest anyone?'

Annette stared back with slowly dawning outrage. 'But that's ridiculous. I mean, if you think *I*—' Words failed her.

'Anyway,' Z said, gathering up her pencil and notebook preparatory to leaving, 'we may soon know all we need to know. Mr Yeadings has been in touch with the hospital, and it seems that Ms Gregory is starting to come round.'

TEN

DESPITE THIS LAST GOOD news, with the detectives' withdrawal Annette felt her last defences crumble. She gathered her shoulder bag and a handful of tissues and fled to the ladies' room. There she found Gwen Lodd leaning against the tiled wall by the basins, dabbing at her mouth with a handkerchief. She looked terrible.

'Oh,' the woman managed to get out, 'how sensible of you.' She commandeered the tissues and bent again over the basins.

Lodd, Annette thought: so there *was* a connection. They've got her to admit she's Ms Gregory's mother. Now that it's come out she can be open with her grief.

Worrying about herself being accused—no; it was just a *suggestion* as yet that she had ordered the hit-and-run car—Annette had forgotten the more obvious line the detectives would be pursuing: the mystery of why the two women's relationship had been concealed. While Annette had been granted the softer option of DC Zyczynski, the two men had been working on Gwen. *Working over*, wasn't that more the expression? The poor woman was shattered.

'Is there something I can do?'

Gwen Lodd shook her head, blinked back the moisture in her eyes, wiped her mouth again and then set about rinsing the basin thoroughly.

'I think,' she said, straightening and facing herself severely in the mirror, 'we'd better go back and try to catch up with our work.'

'I don't know that I can. I feel—so—angry.' If Gwen wasn't going to open up, at least she should be made to listen to Annette's complaints. 'Do you know what they think I did?'

Gwen looked at her as if for the first time really seeing her. 'No. What?'

'That I ordered the hire car that knocked Ms Gregory down. I know nothing about cars. I don't believe I've ever been in Slough. I'm not actually sure where Slough is. I told them so.' Her voice took on a desperate howl. 'They probably think I drove it too and was responsible...'

Tears burst out at last, too long held in check. But they were tears of anger.

'Did they believe you?' There had been a silence before she asked, and Annette looked up to meet a cold stare of appraisal.

'How would I know? They came here believing it was me. Their minds were already made up. I don't know how I can prove otherwise.'

'You can find someone who'll say that you were elsewhere at the time.'

'What time? They never said when. They just sprang it on me, no details. They said I'd be questioned later at home, because the hit-and-run isn't a London case. What will my mother think? She's never been told about any of this. Only that my boss was in a traffic accident and I've been visiting her in hospital.'

'When did you see her?' The voice was sharp.

Annette ceased wailing and looked up. She felt ashamed. Gwen must be feeling so much worse, because it was her daughter who was suffering. She'd been carrying on stoically and then suddenly this invasion of police with their insinuating questions. Gwen could even assume Annette was guilty, just as the inquisitors did.

'When did you last see her?' Gwen insisted.

'Last night. Did they tell you? She's starting to come out of coma.'

Gwen didn't answer. She was looking at her with something very like distaste. There was another marked silence, then, 'In that case perhaps she'll be able to tell us herself—who was driving the car that ran her down.'

'Oh, I hope so. And from that they'll find out I wasn't the one who hired it.'

For a moment Gwen Lodd appeared to have difficulty following Annette's logic. 'But if the police really suspect you they could arrange an identity parade. The car hire people would have to pick out—whoever they thought it was.'

'Yes. Yes, of course. Gwen, I wouldn't for the world do anything to harm her. You must believe me.'

They had passed out into the corridor, Annette trailing behind. When they had regained their shared office the girl closed the door and stood with her back to the panels. 'Gwen, why didn't you say? You're her mother, aren't you?'

The woman's head snapped up. 'Who told you that?'

'No one. It was the name. Someone mentioned that she'd been Lodd before Gregory. It seemed too much of a coincidence. You are her mother, aren't you?'

'I tried to be. God knows, I tried hard enough.' She collapsed on to her chair, elbows on desk, and covered her face with her hands. They were blunt-fingered with unpolished nails. UnGregory.

'I'll make some more coffee, shall I?'

'If you think it can help.' She sounded exhausted. 'But first let me explain, and then we'll never have to refer to it again. Sit down, Annette.'

She sketched out how Annie Gregory had come to her for fostering and they'd later adopted her, she and her then husband. The child had become increasingly wilful as she grew older.

'She seemed almost to resent us,' Gwen said. 'I believe that's often the case with adopted children when they're determined to find their natural parents. But hers were dead.

She had no home but ours. Yet she couldn't leave it soon
enough. Once she was eighteen she had her name changed
by deed poll, back to Gregory. We let her go. It seemed
best not to thwart her, but it was very hurtful. We lost touch
for years.'

'And you met up again here.'

'That wasn't by chance.' Gwen blew her nose softly and
blinked behind the big spectacles. 'She had had two or three
jobs before this, the last one in advertising. She found I
had a position here and asked me to back her application
for a vacancy.'

There followed quite a long silence. 'Perhaps I shouldn't
have done it. I was one of the two who interviewed her and
I gave a favourable report. I didn't mention the relationship.
I never have done since. Certainly *she* wouldn't have
claimed any connection.'

She stared down at her hands clutching the damp handkerchief. 'I thought it was going to come all right at last:
she needed me, she'd softened. But I was wrong. Once she
was here she treated me as a stranger. We worked in parallel, and as time went by she began to make her mark.
She won us several important new clients, was promoted
twice. Until I found myself working as her assistant. And
there had never been so much personal distance between
us.'

Annette didn't know what she could say for comfort. 'I
think she was a very private person,' she suggested, 'despite seeming so outgoing.'

'A swan I'd cared for and protected when she'd been
quite an ugly duckling,' Gwen said wistfully. 'She's come
a long way, has made a real success of her career. Even at
her harshest, people have to acknowledge her talents.'

Annette fetched coffee and slid the mug along the desk
to the other woman. She was shocked for the second time
that morning. Her own handling at the detectives' hands
seemed less upsetting now against what this wretched Mrs

Lodd had suffered. And it wasn't only today's questioning, bringing out all those carefully concealed troubles from the past, but also the long hurtful history of disappointed hopes, and wasted affection poured out over the years.

'Perhaps it will be different now,' Annette said hopefully, 'once she recovers.'

'I thought that before, and I was wrong. Well, here we are. Let's put it behind us and deal with whatever's the next thing. So—back to your own desk, Annette. You've been very patient. I trust you'll prove equally discreet.'

Of course she would. Poor woman, how awful if she had to endure office tittle-tattle on top of the assault the police had made on her privacy.

At 12.30 p.m. there was a lunch appointment in the diary. Annette reminded her and asked if she should cancel. On no account, she was told: everything must continue as normal. At 12.10 Gwen tidied her desk, picked up her handbag and went off.

Annette gave her another ten minutes, then rang the number Max Harris had given her. He was the only person she could confide her own troubles to. He listened without comment—she could see him in her mind, head cocked, the screwed-up eyes merely slits, one forefinger pushing back the centre of his glasses as they slid down the bridge of his nose.

'I'd come now but I've a meeting in half an hour. What time are the police to visit you at home this evening?'

'They didn't say, left it open.'

'So—suppose I come by when you finish work, run you home and cadge a meal while we wait for them to materialize? I'll bring a camera and we'll give them a good likeness of you to show to the car hire people. That should save you having to meet them in the flesh.'

'Max, that would be wonderful. I don't want to see the police on my own again, and my mother would be hopeless.'

'Right, then. Be with you after five.'

As she laid down the phone she wondered what on earth Mum would make of him, would make of her bringing any man home.

Then she recalled that Max was expecting a meal. She couldn't deliver him up to one of Mum's rehashes. She must dash out now for something appetizing. No time even to bolt her sandwiches. But it didn't matter; she was in far too great a turmoil to eat.

DC SILVER HAD EXPECTED little of his search through Criminal Records. The name Lodd had already brought up a couple of complete irrelevances, one a teenage burglar, the other a fraudster selling non-existent properties in Ibiza. Fairburn looked like another non-starter. There were two Fairbairns and he looked them up in the hope that the entries might have been misspelt, but one was a woman sentenced on a child abuse charge and the other was a twenty-year-old serving a stretch in Parkhurst for a series of violent muggings.

It was with the third name that Silver pulled a big one. He printed out the information and went in high glee to knock on Superintendent Yeadings' door.

Inside he found DS Beaumont and the Boss poring over some papers together. 'Shall we let him tell us?' Yeadings asked his sergeant.

'Better not spoil his fun.'

'You *know* about the Gregory criminal record?' Silver demanded.

Yeadings passed across a duplicate death certificate for one Ellen Rita Gregory. The date indicated that the child Annie would then have been seven, three years into her acceptance by the Lodd couple. The place of registration for the death was Her Majesty's Women's Prison of Holloway.

'And Mrs Gregory's husband had died three years ear-

lier, at their home, of multiple stab wounds,' Beaumont
stated.

'I'll get a transcript of the case,' Yeadings said heavily.
'Just to be sure of the background, but it needn't trouble
you two any further. It suffices that the Lodds took the child
in full knowledge of the circumstances, which may have
coloured their treatment of her, either over-protective or
suspicious of genetic inheritance. We have to consider how
this would have affected the child Annie when eventually
she learned the full details—that she was the child of both
killer and victim.'

'It was brought in as manslaughter,' Silver said in miti-
gation. 'Which means there was likely provocation and the
woman acted in self-defence. Nowadays she might even
have got off with a suspended sentence.'

'What did she die of?'

'A heart attack. Left ventricular collapse. She could have
been pretty unfit all along.'

Yeadings grunted. 'It's just possible the children were
witnesses, if not of the killing at least of any earlier violence. How much would a four-year-old remember or understand? In the boy's case, six years older, I guess he had
quite a good idea of the score.'

'Does this actually have a bearing on our hit-and-run?'
Beaumont asked. They were all silent, turning it in their
minds.

'Probably not,' Yeadings granted at last, 'except as essential background. It all went into the character-building
of everyone we're considering so far in the wider frame. It
could explain something about the rather aloof nature of
the injured woman, the distance between her and her only
sibling, the strain in relations with her adoptive mother. It
accounts too for the fact that she's kept nothing to remind
her of the past. Yes, it's useful information in that it helps
us to get in there with them.

'What I'd like to know as well is what Annie/Miranda's

motives were in discarding the new Lodd identity and returning to her original family name. Was it meant to bat
off the intrusions of the Lodd couple, or somehow to embrace a parent she'd lost? If the latter, which parent did she
want to claim her link with—the killer or the killed?'

'Or did she do it in a mood of damn-your-eyes-I'll-go-
my-own-way?' Beaumont put in, sore at sporadic rebellion
by his adolescent son.

Maybe, Yeadings thought, but did not say, she saw both
parents as victims, and herself as yet another. Eighteen's a
precarious age of often misdirected compassion. But whatever she decided then, she'd stayed with it, she was still
Gregory. Not that the name would invite censure such a
long time after the forgotten scandal.

'So let's come up to date,' he said abruptly, rising from
his chair and walking to the window. There he looked down
for a moment on cars manoeuvring in the yard, then turned
to face them, leaning his big frame against the warm ribs
of the radiator.

'Mott and Z are on their way up. We might at last be
getting something concrete to work on. Fill the machine for
a brew-up, Silver.' He strode across to fold back the doors
that partitioned off the next office and stood aside as Beaumont brought through more chairs.

Mott came in briskly with Z at his heels. 'The Met have
had some movement since I rang through about Mrs Lodd,'
he said. 'The bullet extracted from the office wall was
a .38, and they think they've an ID on the dead man. He
could be a private investigator called Collins, from Nottingham. DS Fox has gone up there with a woman constable
to see the wife.'

'Nottingham,' echoed Beaumont, as the superintendent
remarked, 'It took her long enough to notice he'd gone
missing.'

'According to the girl who runs the man's office there,
he'd intended to be away for a week. That week wasn't up

until Wednesday, and she expected him to phone if the case was taking longer. When another weekend went by and he didn't get in touch, she started to worry, discussed it with the wife, and then rang the lodgings he usually went to in London. All his stuff was still in his room there, but the landlady assumed he'd slipped back home and would return in his good time. He'd paid her in advance.

'When she realized there was some anxiety at the other end she decided to cover herself by reporting him missing to the Met. They contacted his office who faxed through a photograph of him. Well, you know the body had a messed-up face, but they were pretty certain of the ID and have asked for a dental check. I've given Fox my home number and he'll fill in the details when he's tapped Nottingham sources.'

'And the job this Collins was on down here?'

'His office won't give any information until the ID's conclusive.'

'Which means a stalemate for us on that. Are there any further ends we need to follow up in the meantime?'

They looked inquiringly at each other. 'There's still another Lodd to be looked at,' Beaumont offered. 'I know we've got the adoptive mother, but she did have a husband. Divorced, but it seems he's still alive.'

He consulted a page in his notebook. 'Peter Martin Lodd. It might be helpful if he could verify her story—until we can talk to Annie/Miranda herself.'

'I'll leave that with you, then.' Yeadings turned to Rosemary Zyczynski. 'Can I ask you to be mother? I'm not really coming the male chauvinist, but I'm a bit scared of that fine glassware. Things seem to crack so easily in my hands.'

She smiled, rose and went across to the new filter machine. 'Can I give my report at the same time?'

'Do. How did you fare with Miss Briers?'

'She was—er, gobsmacked,' Z said. 'There's no other

description. But so angry at the implication, that I couldn't tell whether it came as complete news to her, or merely a shock that we'd caught up with her. Denied all knowledge of the car. Inspector Mott and I were going to see her again at home tonight when she'd have had a chance to worry a bit—'

'But since I'll be hanging on for a call from Nottingham,' Angus put in, 'Z will now be going on her own.'

'That all right by you, Z?'

'Yes, Boss.'

'Get it over by 8.00 p.m. if possible and ring me at home straight after.'

Fusspot, Rosemary told herself. As if I can't take care of myself. She transferred the tray of steaming mugs to a corner of Yeadings' desk and let them reach for their own.

'Biscuits,' Yeadings reminded himself, and delved into the desk's bottom drawer. 'It's a packet Nan turned down,' he excused them, 'but they do fill the odd corner.'

THE FINAL LODD on Silver's list drawn from the Greater London phone directories had the required initials P.M. and a home address at Wandsworth. There had been no reply to three phone calls earlier in the day, but if the man had been at work then, he might be found at home after six. DS Beaumont decided to drive over and see for himself.

He found that it was the upper flat in a pair of semis, and approached by an outer concrete stairway. Through grubby net curtains he could just make out a small sitting-room visible in the dim light cast from the open door of a room beyond. He rang the bell hopefully and waited.

There was no answer. He put his head close to the glass panel and could hear no sound of voices or radio. With a hand torch held close to the glass he tried to make out more of the interior. It seemed empty, the light possibly left on to deter burglars. Not that a break-in would be likely where so little of value seemed to be on offer, but he had known of less promising places laid waste.

Pressure on the door produced a loose rattle, seeming to promise that a good shove might overcome the lock's resistance. Only a week before Beaumont had been looking over a flat where the owner hadn't been seen for a matter of days. He'd had a Leading Fireman with him who'd mock innocently said, 'I do believe I smell gas. You can smell gas too, can't you, Sergeant?' and without waiting for an answer hatcheted the glass and they were in.

Beaumont now sniffed the air exaggeratedly, stepped back and then came forward with his right foot raised. It met the door squarely at lock level and the thing gave way first time.

'Mr Lodd?' he called. 'Anybody at home?'

The living-room was modestly furnished, shabby, but with signs that efforts had once been made to add comfort. The grey cloth-covered settee had several multicoloured cushions. From a wide bowl filled with dried-out soil a dark vine-leafed plant straggled up the wall, embraced a sepia print of Polperro with drunken mateyness and then drooped floorwards, its edges brown and crinkled.

'I know how you feel,' said Beaumont.

There came a creaking sound from the direction of the light. He went through the door into a short passage. To the right the beam of his torch showed the tiny kitchen, travelled past the gas cooker and lit directly on the bleary-eyed gaze of a large basset hound curled in a basket. There was an overpowering smell of old dog. It acknowledged his presence with a sound of complaint, somewhere between a moan and a mew.

'You're supposed to bark,' he told it.

It took no notice, just sighed, dropping its floppy jowls back on the basket's much-chewed edge.

Back in the passage Beaumont opened the left-hand door

and entered a room which held an untidy double bed with
a table lamp alight on the low cabinet beside it.

The reason for the untidiness became clear as he approached. The bedclothes were humped about the body of
a man lying on his back, arms and legs outflung, mouth
open.

But he wasn't drunk, didn't snore. Beaumont put two
fingers on the cold neck, then lifted an arm by the wrist
and let it fall back.

Rigor had come and gone. He could tell as much from
the too-familiar sweet-decay smell of the room. How long
the man had lain there was for the pathology experts to
decide. Too long for them to get accuracy from body and
room temperatures. Possibly they'd do it from the amount
of potassium in the eyes, which would increase after death.

There were sounds again from the kitchen. Beaumont
went back to the survivor. The basset hound ceased chun-
tering, rolled bloodshot eyes at him and crawled out of the
basket, trailing a piece of greyish blanket caught in an un-
trimmed claw. Beaumont detached it and reached for the
identity disc the animal wore. It lumbered to the outer door
and leaned there while he turned the handle to let it out.

Maybe he'd never see it again if the garden wasn't
dog-proofed, but this did appear part of a set routine. Beaumont stood at the open door to watch, taking deep breaths
of clean night air.

Hudson—as faintly engraved on the metal tag hanging
from his collar—made heavy weather of the concrete stairs
but managed quite a brisk trit-trot across the back patio, his
heavy undercarriage swinging rhythmically just short of the
stone flags. He attempted as brisk a leg throw against a
washing post and toppled over. Then, undaunted, he squat-
ted and did a girly job. From there he disappeared into a
dark cumulus clump of shrubs before lumbering back.

'Showing off, weren't you?' Beaumont greeted his return. Gutsy though, he admitted. In any sense you wanted.

In the sitting-room he located the phone, lifted the receiver in his handkerchief and rang through to the Met. Caught on their patch after a questionable entry, he didn't want to step any further in the clag.

When he'd filled the dog's water bowl he sat down to await his colleagues' arrival.

Two flat-cap constables were the first to arrive, parking their patrol car two houses down. He took them through to the body then joined them in checking on the other rooms.

'Empty pill bottle on the bedside cabinet,' said the one called Rogers. 'Nothing else springs to the eye. Looks like an OD suicide.' He radioed through for CID and was rewarded with an address in the High Street which required an immediate visit.

'There'll be a full search by the experts,' he told Beaumont. 'OK if we leave you with the body?'

That, Beaumont told himself on their departure, and the problem of Hudson's disposal. He supposed he'd have to pass him to the RSPCA, who would probably class him as an undesirable and put him down. Which seemed a pity when the poor old thing was so harmless, even tried to put on a mild swagger. There were a lot of candidates he'd give greater priority to for the disposal job.

Alternative, however, there was none. He had no intention of acquiring a crumpled raincoat and playing an imitation Columbo. He picked up the grubby blanket and, trailing it, made chirruping noises for the dog to follow him. Hudson swayed on splayed feet, gazed back suspiciously and belched emptily.

'Food,' Beaumont told himself as an inspiration, and started looking through the cupboards for a tin of dog meat.

It was then that he found the bloodstained tea towel wrapped round a meat cleaver.

ELEVEN

MAX HARRIS ARRIVED WITH two bottles of rosé, in ignorance of what it might have to accompany. Annette, an unpractised cook, had opted for loin of pork divided into six chops, to be fried with onion then gently baked in a cream sauce. Mum was deflected from possible gaffes into salad-washing duties, while Max put the first bottle in the fridge, poured them each a glass from the second and buried it up to its neck in ice in a convenient china plant pot. He seemed not to feel one whit out of place in the kitchen.

When the doorbell rang, Annette was liquidizing a dollop of mango chutney to jazz up the anaemic-looking sauce, so it was Mum who dried off her hands and went to open up.

'Oh, it's you, love,' they heard her greet the newcomer. She returned to the scene of action with Rosemary Zyczynski in tow. 'It's the lady who came before,' she announced. 'Well, this is nice, all Annette's friends together. I'll just go and lay another place.'

'I'm sorry,' Z began, but Annette shrugged.

'She gets the wrong end of the stick sometimes. We were just going to sit down for a meal. You really are welcome to join us. I've made plenty.'

Z hesitated.

'Have you eaten?' Max demanded.

'Actually, no.'

'Oh sorry,' Annette interrupted, 'this is Max Harris, the "man in the tweed fishing-hat". He's a columnist with the *Courier*. Max, this is—er—'

Zyczynski told him, adding, 'but you can call me Z.' Perhaps it was hunger, she thought, that made her rashly accept their invitation, slipping into the casually domestic

scene. By the time she had accepted a glass of wine she
had a heady sense of flouting social conventions and police
rules of procedure.

'To PACE,' Max said wickedly, raising his glass.

Z flushed, Annette demanded what's Pace? and Mrs Briers beamed on them all.

'The Police and Criminal Evidence Act,' Max explained,
'and a right headache to the force.'

'I think,' Z said uncertainly, 'I'd better go out and come
in again. This is all terribly irregular.'

'You heard what Mrs Briers said: all Annette's friends
together. And she'll need them if you're going to take seriously that business about hiring the car.'

'What car?' asked Mrs Briers, but she wasn't bothered
at being ignored.

'If it helps,' Max offered, 'I intend taking some Insta-
matic shots of Annette which you can show to the car firm
at Slough to eliminate her. But let's eat first and do business
later.'

I must be crazy, Z told herself; but there had never been
much likelihood of Annette's involvement. No woman
would have described the girl's hair as 'fairish', and it was
too obstinate a mop to be crammed convincingly under any
wig.

The surface of the pork dish had baked to a golden
brown, to Annette's surprised gratification. She put on oven
gloves to draw it out. 'Let's go through, then.'

Z picked up her glass and followed, marvelling how differently it would have gone if she had come with Inspector
Mott as at first arranged.

ANGUS MOTT LAY SPRAWLED on the settee of his bachelor
pad sourly savouring his frustration. If Paula's ageing boss
hadn't invited her to stay on after her pupillage it wouldn't
have been a bachelor pad any more. He would have traded
in this one-bedroom apartment for a ground floor two-

bedroom affair with a patio and a bit of garden thrown in. A suitable place had come on the market just before the date they were to have married. Every time he passed it now he witnessed its new owners branching out with enterprising additions. He begrudged them their brick barbecue site, the striped sun awning, the new brass door-furniture.

He acknowledged that Paula had a job which meant a lot to her. By now he almost accepted it as having an equal importance with his own. But when push came to shove it was the man who provided, and the woman who needed support while she went through the female thing, had babies, set the toddlers on their feet. And Paula had wanted children as much as he did. But she was determined to make her way professionally first. Otherwise, she said, some day she'd wake up to feel tied down and have never been anywhere, never achieved anything.

Right; so he could take that, in small doses. But it was hell waiting when he wanted his woman with him. When he expected her to feel the same about him.

He swung his feet down and padded to the phone, dialled her number. Her flatmate answered. 'She'll bless you,' Lottie warned him. 'She's shut herself in her bedroom, literally with a wet towel round her head and about twenty-seven law books all over the floor. I wouldn't, Angus. I really wouldn't.'

He sighed. 'Right. I ought to keep this line free anyway. Expecting a crucial call. Tell her I rang when she next emerges, will you?'

He shuffled a few compact discs, tossed up between Shirley Bassey belting out something fortissimo and a quiet classical, settled for Max Bruch's violin concerto and agonized along with half the first movement before the expected call came from the Met.

Fox was back from liaising with Nottingham's city force. At the private investigator's office he'd drawn a blank as

far as the London case was concerned. The teenage girl
assistant had proved no more than a telephone minder, too
dim to be trusted with client information. Collins, a lone
operator insistent on discretion, had taken the current papers south with him. Since none had been found at his
London lodgings it must be assumed that he had held them
to pass to his client there, whose name—as entered in the
office diary—was M. Gregory.

A cheque for an advance fee and estimated expenses
made out with that signature had been paid into his bank.
Because his first meeting with the client had taken place in
London, his shorthand notes weren't available in the office.
He had prided himself on carrying the broad inquiry outlines in his head. Anything he discovered in following the
trail would have been entered in his personal notebook.

But his pockets had been empty when the body was
found. There had been no briefcase.

Big fat zero, Mott informed himself. That was all they
had until such time as M. Gregory pulled out of her coma.
There was not even any witness to say that it was the
woman herself who had called in the investigator. If a car
could be hired in her name by a stand-in, why not a detective? Experts would have to be used to verify the cheque's
signature.

Fox had reported that Gregory's bank was the Beaconsfield branch of Lloyds. The manager there would feel
obliged to cooperate in a case of murder, even although it
wasn't Ms Gregory who'd been killed.

There were two possibilities about the shooting. Either
Miranda Gregory had returned to her office, shot the man
and taken away the evidence she required him to find, or
someone else had done the killing and removed it because
it implicated himself. Himself/herself: sex equality being
insisted on in all things.

Gregory's current cheque book would most likely have
been kept in her handbag, which was still missing. But if

the cheque was made out some time back, then the coun-
terfoil could be found along with her bank statements at
the flat. Mott wished Fox had given details of the cheque's
number and date. Now everything must wait on his return
from Nottingham.

Stalemate all round. He wondered what the chances were
of Gregory coming out of coma.

THE WARD SISTER HAD phoned through for the houseman
who now stood by the bed, biting at his lower lip. He
checked the electronic display, then concentrated on the
patient's face, the mere flickers of muscle movement.

Several times she had been on the brink of waking and
then sunk back, as though at some deep level she wouldn't
allow herself to return. There should have been family here,
someone who related to her. The brother had eventually
agreed to be entered as next of kin, but two attempts to
phone him had proved fruitless.

Dr Dennis knew she went under two names and he had
no way of telling which might have the greater power to
stir memories.

He leaned over her. 'Annie?' Sometimes the earliest experiences were the most profoundly felt. Annie was her
childhood name; Miranda, an artificial adoption, would be
connected with a later more complicated period. If the police were right in thinking she was the victim of a deliberate
attempt on her life, then it could be a zone of some risk.
Which left him to pin his hopes on 'Annie'.

'Annie,' he insisted. 'Come on, Annie. You can make it.
It's all right. Out you come.'

He picked up her hand and squeezed it gently. 'That's
it. Get those eyes open.'

THE WALLS OF THE WORLD are black as hell.

She didn't know where the words came from. Nor quite

what they meant. But they were there in her head and all around.

She understood walls, could feel their crushing resistance as she began pressing forward to penetrate them. She seemed to move slowly and they parted a little, started to close again behind. 'Push,' she told herself. 'Push!'

She burst softly through with a liquid sound of tearing, to emerge in terrifying space. The walls slipped back a little. Not total dark any more. The limitless medium she found herself in had a faint luminosity more dreadful than familiar night. Blurred shapes slowly moved against each other, merged with a strange transparency so that outlines were indistinguishable.

It was a sort of beginning, vertiginous, like birth. She was utterly alone.

Crying silently inside, she swam about, turned, reaching for the familiar dark, and the walls opened narrowly to receive her back.

'Damn,' said the registrar. 'I thought we'd got her, but she's gone again. Well, maybe next time.'

IT WAS PAST ELEVEN when Beaumont got free of the Met's Scenes of Crime team in Wandsworth. Chief Inspector Meredith had turned up in person on learning that the apparent suicide's name was Lodd, and greeted the Thames Valley sergeant sourly. Beaumont put on his most wooden puppet-face as he delivered the account of his break-in.

'Thought you smelled gas?' Meredith echoed, total cynic. 'That excuse has whiskers.'

'You have to admit there is a pong, sir, even now. I just got the wrong analysis. Just as well I did take a look, though, seeing what was waiting inside.'

No one could deny that. The dead man had obviously lain there several days and the dog was dehydrated, lapping up bowl after bowl of water before promptly bringing back the canned meat he had wolfed too greedily.

Beaumont was included in the ban when Hudson was driven outside. They sat together at the foot of the concrete stairway in companionable gloom.

A young woman doctor had spent no more than three minutes with the body to confirm death, and as soon as the close-up shots were taken the hands and head were separately wrapped, then the whole zipped into a body bag. Examination at the morgue would certainly include chemical tests to see whether Lodd had fired a handgun shortly before taking his own life.

If it was indeed a DIY job.

The idea of his committing suicide after killing the man Collins struck Beaumont as being too easy a way to tidy up the shooting at Matherson and Corby. That simple solution overlooked the hit-and-run incident. Lodd had surely been alive at that time, so could he be considered a suspect?

There had to be a strong motive for him carrying out the shooting. If he was indeed the gunman, had he emptied the man's pockets to obtain some report which could incriminate him, and to remove any identification that might lead back to himself through a connection with Ms Gregory?

Had he managed to forestall her by stealing evidence of his own questionable conduct? But in that case there should have been no need to wipe out the woman.

Or were the two in collusion, with Lodd pulling the trigger and Gregory helping herself to the papers which she had commissioned Collins to obtain?

That option was unlikely, since she'd every right to them without resorting to violence. But perhaps they incriminated her too, and Collins himself had intended to use them against her.

But whatever the favoured option, someone on the team would now have to inquire of Gwen Lodd what relations had existed between her ex-husband and their sometime adopted daughter.

And then, after all, perhaps Peter Martin Lodd had no

link whatsoever with the two crimes under investigation, but the poor sod simply got tired of living, as anyone might.

Yet another patrol car was drawing up behind the two with flashing blue lights, and beside Meredith's silver Volvo. A constable stepped out, fitted on his helmet and adjusted his raincape. He came across with heavy tread to where Beaumont sat, looked over the sorry pair and demanded officiously, 'Is this your dog, sir?'

Beaumont looked at it. Why not? Though more properly he supposed he'd been taken on as its man. 'Temporarily,' he admitted.

'I must ask you to move on, sir. There's been a crime committed. And fit a leash on the dog.'

So this was the Plod put on guard duty, the Paganini of the plastic tape. 'I'm a witness,' Beaumont said wearily. 'And a bloody jack.' He pulled out his warrant card.

They were finishing upstairs. Meredith was the first to leave, walking past Beaumont (who obligingly rose from the steps) as though he were invisible; then came the photographers. Finally a ferret-faced man sealed off the door, abandoning the flat for a more thorough daylight search.

There was a little knot of neighbours by now in the street, some hastily dressed, others huddled in their night-gear. All fell silent at the Yard officer's approach. A bald elderly man in a puce dressing-gown ventured to address him but he went tight-lipped past.

All three cars had barely drawn away, the tail lights following each other round the bend, when with a screech of tyres another tore up from the opposite direction.

Beaumont glimpsed the white PRESS card on the windscreen, turned up his collar, tweaked his handkerchief, by now attached to Hudson's collar, and slunk off with bowed head.

Wasn't it a marvel? Whatever happened—scandal, scam, misery or mayhem—there was always some excited onlooker with a phone who thought the greater British public had the right to be informed.

Informed of what, though? Surmise and conjecture. Fiction, if there wasn't any fact. For himself he was prepared to wait for the morrow and certainty of a carpeting by Superintendent Yeadings, followed by a formal summons to the Yard.

He scowled at his watch-face. Despite the hour, he'd have to put in a call to the Guv to warn him what was on the cards.

MOTT BARELY HEARD the phone's summons through the drumming of the shower. He cut the flow, shook himself, pulled a towel round his shoulders and padded into the next room to locate the instrument.

'Guv,' he heard Beaumont begin, 'did I wake you?'

'I wasn't in bed. What's up?'

'Lodd. The onetime adoptive father of Ms Gregory. I went to check on him. He's dead, apparent OD. I found the body coupla hours back.'

'Jeez! The ground's getting covered with them. Where?'

'At his flat. Wandsworth. Couldn't raise him by phone, so I went round. Light on inside but nobody came to the door. So I leaned on it a bit.'

'Broke in.'

'Sort of. Whiff of gas excuse. Plenty of whiff in fact. He'd been dead a few days.'

'How many? Prior to the shooting or the car business?'

'Can't say for sure yet. The post-mortem's tomorrow.' Beaumont hesitated on the brink of really bad news. 'Meredith came down himself. He's not best pleased.'

He heard Mott quietly swearing. It sounded as if he was muttering through a thickness of cloth.

'Anything else I ought to be warned about?'

'Only minor details.' After all, who would want to know about the dog?

'One thing, Guv. They took away a bloodstained cloth wrapped round a meat cleaver. But no sign of what it had chopped up.'

'Well, it certainly wasn't used in the Collins shooting. And Littlejohn would have picked up a hatchet job among Gregory's injuries.' Hell, Mott thought, it was sticking one's neck out ever to ask the pathologist to run a second check. That would have to be tackled at Yeadings' level.

'OK, Guv?'

'Far from. Where are you now?'

'On my way home.'

'Try to keep your nose clean till you get there and then go straight to bed!' He rang off on a snarl.

'We're in the shit, Hudson,' Beaumont told the slumbering dog. 'And don't expect anything better at journey's end.'

It was almost 1.00 a.m. as he pulled up at home. Someone had parked a white van opposite the driveway, and no one had thought to open the garage door. As the rain was deluging again he abandoned the car behind the van, standing on the handkerchief lead while he locked its doors by hand. Hudson whiffled sadly, nose to ground, and paddled after him. There was a light in the downstairs front room and a sound of amplified, factory-beat music. Indignant, he didn't bother with his key, rang and waited to be let in.

The sound cut out and a head was silhouetted against reflected light in the hallway. Beaumont pressed his face against the leaded glass panel. 'It's me.'

Stuart opened up. 'Hi, Dad. You're late. Been having a wild time?'

Beaumont controlled his language. 'Where's your mother?'

His son gave him a swift, quirky look which clearly said, 'You mean you care?' Since Cathy had returned home after her brief tussle as a reborn single there had been an icy gulf between his parents.

'I mean why isn't she reading the riot act over the infernal row you were making?'

'She's in the kitchen—er, entertaining. What you heard was an audio smokescreen. Like I'm being discreet, man.' The boy's jaw suddenly dropped as a dejected Hudson emerged from behind Beaumont's ankles. 'It's a dawg!'

'They've demoted me to the dog pound. Or they will tomorrow.' Beaumont took on a chirpy air. At least the house was warm, and despite the hour he detected a scent of fresh baking. Cathy must have someone special in the kitchen with her. Inviting a friend home? This was worth investigating.

He loosed the dog, who shuddered and shook himself, then all three continued through to the kitchen.

On the far side of the table, which was piled with all manner of edible goodies, stood a rosy-cheeked woman almost as broad as she was tall. Cathy turned from her station at the draining-board where she had been busy with a clipboard and pen.

'Hallo,' she greeted Beaumont with unaccustomed warmth, 'you can tell us what you think of the beef and onion pasties.'

The fat woman circled a finger over the assortment on offer and plunged it towards a caterer's tray. There must have been four or five dozen of the things to choose from. Beaumont boggled.

'Oh.' Cathy recovered her manners. 'This is my husband, Margie.' She looked defiantly at him. 'Margie owns the China Platter down by Market Place, and she's starting up a party-catering operation. I've just been showing her what I can do.'

'So I'm taking her on,' grinned the rosy woman. 'Aren't I the lucky one? This'—she waved at the display of confectionery—'is a real *tour de force*.'

Beaumont nodded. 'Like *La Tour Eiffel*, compulsive: once seen, you have to go up it.'

Margie flipped a fat arm in his direction. 'Not like that at all. I meant it metaphorically.'

'Ah, speaking all educated.' Beaumont sounded impressed.

The fat woman chuckled. 'Bit of a joker, your husband. I like that. We shall get on famously.'

She waddled past him, pulling on an enormous purple sweater from the back of a chair. 'Well, I'll be off then, if you'll all lend a hand loading the stuff in m'van.'

They did: it seemed less bother than protesting, and in the coming and going Hudson's shadowing presence was observed but not remarked on. As Cathy finally closed the front door Stuart had a kitchen knife and was cutting down one side of a large grocery carton to form a bed-box for the dog. 'He'll need a cushion or something,' he said over his shoulder.

'There's an old quilt I was going to send to Oxfam,' Cathy told him. 'I'll fetch it.'

'He can have my brown pullover,' Beaumont offered. 'It's got a tear at the front.' Implying she should have noticed and mended it.

Cathy retorted with spirit. 'Keep it. Wear it inside out.'

He stared after her, astounded that she had made a joke.

Stuart stood watching. 'She does sometimes, when she's on the up. You don't notice, always batting her down.'

'I don't do anything of the sort!'

'No? Have it your way,' and Stuart gave a flick of his forelock. At the window he lifted the edge of the curtain. 'Raining again like there's no tomorrow,' he said.

His father shrugged. 'Could be the Last Chance Monsoon.'

Stuart groaned.

Cathy had come in again with the quilt folded in her arms. She looked at her husband coolly. He felt briefly ashamed of trying to sound clever when his son clearly thought him a turd.

Yawning hugely, Stuart opted to leave them to it. 'See you at breakfast,' he offered. ''Night, dawg,' and slouched off.

TWELVE

AT THE YARD NEXT MORNING, Mott encountered less rancour over Beaumont's actual break-in at the Wandsworth flat than over the suspicion that Thames Valley force had been sitting on information and expecting Peter Lodd to top himself. He needed to strike a delicate balance. Too much insistence on the sheer chance discovery of the body could leave the DS more open to reprimand for unauthorized entry. In fact he'd had no reason to suppose anything untoward in the flat. Therefore the claim of suspected escaping gas had to be pushed hard, however well worn an excuse.

Mott was able to parry serious criticism, and the final outcome was no more than a telephoned scorching for Beaumont's ears and an extra coolness between the two working teams.

It hadn't pleased Mott to learn from Z last night that she too had stepped out of line, but the news she carried back—of Annette Briers' alliance with Max Harris—was intriguing. As a result he was inclined to accept the WDC's taking a meal with involved persons as an act of infiltration, and let her off with a warning. Today she had been dispatched to Slough with Max's photographs of Annette and instructions to show them to the car hire firm.

The national press would tomorrow carry a photograph of Miranda Gregory in the hope that someone would report a sighting of her between leaving Marylebone on Friday and being found injured on Sunday morning. The hospital report still claimed she was stable but unconscious. They were cautiously hoping she might come round within a matter of hours.

Meanwhile, a video was today being made in and around Beaconsfield featuring a policewoman of the same build, wearing a wig and the identical black raincoat and mustard yellow dress, as an attempt to jog the public's memory.

An initial report from Aldermaston, where the suspect car was under examination, mentioned minute quantities of partially wiped blood of Ms Gregory's general group on the offside wing, shattered windscreen and headlamp rim, but there were no fingerprints to indicate that she had ever driven the car. No helpful dabs at all, for that matter. So many negatives, Mott thought; and now with Lodd dead they could have lost a source of information. Not that the two were known to have stayed in touch. Yet there had to be some reason why he'd chosen this particular time to kill himself, and it could well have a link with Gregory's injury or the subsequent police inquiry.

Mott joined Fox in a further visit to the offices of Matherson and Corby to interview Gwen Lodd, only to find that she had phoned to say she was unwell and would not be coming in.

He consoled himself with a few searching questions to Annette about her relationship with Max Harris, and accepted provisionally her assurance that they had only met as a result of a common interest in the Gregory case. He warned her of the dangers of too close an association with members of the press, who were liable to distort one's least considered remarks and blow them into sizeable fictions.

He left her blinking back tears, because what he had said reinforced her own doubts after last night's talk with Mum, who, in a cosy glow after the departure of their two guests, had remarked what nice friends, then cast a gloom by wondering if Max hadn't been more than a bit smitten by Miss Z. Such a pretty girl, and she couldn't want to stay forever in the police force, could she?

Which had struck at Annette's faint hope that Max was showing some interest in herself. On waking this morning she already saw the two bottles of rosé as his signing-off fee to herself as informant. Her confidence plunged further at Mott's warning that the newspaperman could be using her for his journalistic ends.

She'd been a fool to let him take away her copy of the annual staff photograph in which she was shown standing behind the seated woman who was soon to become her boss. There was no guarantee of its return when he'd blocked out the rest and made an enlargement of Ms Gregory.

Faced by again being left in charge of the office, she attempted to force her personal feelings into the background. But there was no cheer to be had at work either. It seemed that Gwen Lodd couldn't take the strain. One of the senior executives would surely be moved in from another department, and there was a chance she could be sent back to the typing pool herself. Nothing today, it seemed, was set to go right.

AFTER THE FRUSTRATION of Peter Lodd's apparent suicide, and failure to find his ex-wife at her office, Mott felt trapped in a negative phase and, on their way to Gwen Lodd's address, voiced gloomy fears that they might find yet another corpse there.

To his relief, after a short pause Fox's ring at the door was answered. Mrs Lodd opened up, dressed in a housecoat and slippers, looking unmistakably ill.

Mott let Fox offer their apologies for troubling her.

'I don't want to pass the bug on,' the woman said shortly. 'It's a sort of gastric flu. Quite fierce. I was up all the night. You'd do well to keep your distance.'

They followed her in and Mott signalled to the sergeant that he would take over. 'I'm afraid we have news that may further distress you, Mrs Lodd. Your husband—your ex-husband—was found dead at his home last night. We think he may have taken an overdose of barbiturate.'

She blinked once or twice in quick succession, her thin fingers working at the top button of her quilted housecoat. 'How awful. He—but I suppose I shouldn't really be surprised.'

Mott was alerted. 'Why is that, Mrs Lodd?'

'I know one shouldn't speak ill of the dead, but he was so—ineffectual, easily depressed.'

'Was that the reason you parted company?'

'To some extent, I suppose it must have been.'

'Was there something else? Something specific?'

She stood up, winding her fingers together. 'Inspector, I really don't see that this is any concern of the police. In any case, it was a long time ago. It isn't always easy to remember what the reasons were for our disagreements, and since then I've consciously tried to clear it all from my mind. One shouldn't harbour resentment or cherish past injuries. We were incompatible, simply that. For a long time we tried to make something of our marriage, especially when we had a child to be responsible for, but in the end the strain told. After Annie—Miranda—left home there were just the two of us. I went out to work again, something he was opposed to.

'At that point nothing either of us did seemed to please the other. The situation became impossible, and eventually we decided to go our separate ways.'

'There was a divorce?'

'Yes. It was my decision. Not that I had any intention of remarrying, but it left him free to find someone to look after him. Men aren't so good at living alone.'

'And did he? Find someone else?'

The question seemed to throw her. 'I—I really don't know, Inspector. After we sold up, I moved here into London. He got a flat in Wandsworth somewhere. As far as I heard, he never married again.'

'So you didn't keep in touch? We were hoping you could

ell us something about how he lived, who he associated
with.'

'I'm afraid not.'

'Perhaps we shall have more luck with your adopted
daughter. She could have recent news of him.'

'Oh no, I should think that's quite unlikely. They—he
wasn't a very fatherly person at all.'

Mott eyed her speculatively. 'You haven't asked us about
Ms Gregory's progress.'

She drew herself up tightly. 'I am in daily contact with
the hospital, by phone. It would hardly be acceptable for
me to visit any patient with my present infection.' She
faced him with chill haughtiness.

But she'd had no infection last week, Mott thought.

'It's been an anxious time for you,' he conceded. 'I'm
sorry we had to bring you this latest bad news. We'll leave
you now to get some rest. I hope you'll be better soon.'

'WELL?' HE ASKED FOX when they were again in the car
and joining Horseferry Road's traffic flow towards the
river.

'That's a cold-blooded one, if you like. Must have been
like marriage to a frozen fish.'

'I think Lodd's death was news to her. But not too upsetting. She certainly doesn't wear her heart on her sleeve.'

If she has one at all, Mott added to himself. He couldn't
imagine her adequately mothering the child of a woman
driven by cruelty to kill her husband. But give her the ben-
efit of the doubt.

'We know from her workplace that she's the efficient
type, probably makes a virtue of controlling her emotions.'

'Our new stiff,' Fox gave as his opinion, 'was well off
when he got out on his own. Not that he stayed that way.
I had a call just before you turned up. They've found quite

a bit of women's clothing and stuff at the dead man's flat so if they do find suspicious circumstances we may even end up *cherching la femme*.'

ANNETTE DROPPED HER sandwiches into the waste bin. Without Gwen Lodd to dictate the pace and then interrupt the flow, she found she had got through her work more quickly, even boldly took the initiative when two possible clients phoned, offering to send them brochures with the promise of detailed costings. After so much dizzy dealing she deserved more, she felt, than tinned tuna between wholemeal bread.

The outside air was bright, fresh, blowy, more like April than October. You could even imagine a scent of grass from the parks mixed in with the car exhaust. It made her restless, ambitious enough to go somewhere special to eat.

So it was the 'little Greek place' again, this time on her own. There was a newsstand near the entrance and on impulse she bought a copy of the *Courier*. When she had ordered, she turned to the inner pages where Max had said his midweek column would be found.

He wrote well, jauntily but not jokily, and the article had a serious theme. Nothing to do with murder or politics or scandal, but about bringing up children. Was he a father then? Simple soul that she was, she had imagined him a free spirit, just because he seemed able to come and go without ringing home with excuses.

She started to turn the pages back to their original order and was arrested by a photograph. It was of a man in his late fifties, the face long and lugubrious. She knew immediately how his voice would sound. It would be reedy, calling out to her as he raised a bony hand. 'Excuse me, miss—'

It had been in the hospital corridor when she came from visiting Ms Gregory. So how did he come to feature on the Home News page?

The headline below read 'SOLITARY'S DEATH AT WANDS-

WORTH', and underneath—'Was it Suicide? Police are investigating the death of a man found last night at his flat in Wandsworth. Neighbours, who had not seen him for several days, described Mr Peter Martin Lodd'—*Lodd! Oh God, no!*—'Mr Peter Martin Lodd as a shy man who avoided social contact, preferring the company of wild birds which he fed twice daily on the Common.

'Mrs Phyllis Daniels, who lived opposite said, "He was a nice old boy. We all felt a bit sorry for him, but nobody got to know him properly. He didn't have anything delivered, not even milk, so how were we to know there was anything wrong?"'

Dismayed, Annette crushed the paper between her hands. Lodd wasn't a common name. There must be a connection. Why would anyone living at Wandsworth go to *Wycombe* Hospital if he was ill? It was right out of his way.

No, he'd gone to visit an in-patient. And who else but Miranda Gregory, once Lodd, and—given his apparent age—possibly his adopted daughter?

If only I'd turned back when he called me, she thought. He'd be dead today just the same, but at least we'd have spoken.

She could recall him quite clearly now. He'd been trying to get free of a little knot of visitors outside the Intensive Therapy Unit, surely wanting to know where Ms Gregory's ward was. Poor man, distressed about the woman he'd cared for as a little girl. And he was Gwen Lodd's husband. *Former* husband, because hadn't Gwen once said she was divorced, making it sound like a distinction?

And then it struck her: *another death.* First the shooting; next the hit-and-run, which had been meant to kill; now this, and he'd taken his own life. Epidemic death.

When the newspaper mentioned suicide they'd put a query after the word. And why should the police be interested, unless they suspected something more?

Since it was in the *Courier*, surely Max would have seen

the photograph and the name. Or did he only check on his own column? She must ring him for more details. Before she saw Gwen again—Gwen, supposedly off sick—she must make sure whether this dead Peter Lodd was really who she thought him.

MAX WAS IN A BAR off Victoria Street when the call came through from the *Courier*. Some woman called Briers wanted to contact him about a photograph.

'Right,' said Max. 'It's not forgotten. I'm up to the gills, chasing an interview at present. If Annette rings again, be nice; tell her I'll post off the enlargements tomorrow at latest.'

'We're at cross-purposes, Max. This was a mug shot in our today's edition she was on about. Suicide called Lodd. She wanted you to know she'd met him. He's the body found at Wandsworth, page five.'

Max hesitated. 'I must have missed it. Lodd, you say? Can you give me the outline?' He listened. 'And she says she's met him? When, for Gossake?'

But that was all the *Courier* knew. 'Is there anything worth following up?' checked the newshound.

'No.' Max sounded firm. 'It's just coincidental to something I'm working on at present. Comment, not news. Thanks, Dick. I'll see to it.'

He had hung up his coat with today's copy in its pocket. He went now and dug it out. The page-five second-column story had only three short paras, undeveloped. But it mentioned a police interest, and the surname was certainly Lodd. So he had to assume it was—just possibly—an offshoot of the Gregory hit-and-run story.

And Annette Briers claimed to recognize the man from the photo, which was smudgy enough.

Could she be right? He knew how easily some people deceived themselves, over-willing to share in press notoriety.

Yet if she was working alongside the man's ex-wife, there was a chance that she'd somewhere caught sight of them together. Yes, he liked the idea. Annette was observant enough and, although inexperienced, nobody's fool. As soon as he was through in Westminster he would slip across to Matherson and Corby to get it from her direct.

He glanced up to see the man he was to contact standing by the entrance, glancing searchingly around. He raised a hand and stood up, spinning an empty chair to face him.

Lance Grünig was a parliamentary correspondent, himself the son of a onetime Liberal MP. Little of note or of political speculation occurred west of the Tower or east of Oxford that he hadn't access to. With a phenomenal memory for faces and sufficient discretion to hold on to facts until their exposure became necessary, he was trusted by many to whom the press were anathema.

This was the man who had phoned for a meeting because he had seen Ms Gregory's photo faxed through to the *Telegraph* when he happened to be in the newsroom. Since Max was mentioned as a witness to her last known sighting, it was to him that Grünig now turned for further information.

'What'll you have?' Max greeted him.

He joined him with the Macallan. It seemed disrespectful to drink anything less in that excellent malt's company.

'The lady in question,' Max prompted him.

'Yes, what's the whole story?'

'You first. Declare your interest.'

Grünig rolled the whisky appreciatively round his tongue and closed his eyes. 'She might have been extending her little puddy claws into a rather vulnerable person.'

'That sounds too cautious to be useful.'

'I happened to catch sight of her three times in this person's company, and wondered. That's all. But I'm very curious. I'd like to know more.'

'More than what?'

Lance rolled his eyes this time, comically. 'Her background, her job, her salary, her home address. What can you add to that?'

'Her parentage, next of kin. Let's trade. I'll fill you in, and you tell me where and with whom you saw her.'

Grünig didn't quite care for that.

Max sought to reassure him. 'You know me, Lance. I'm not a newshound. I don't tittle-tattle. The scandal, if one breaks, will be all yours.'

'So what's your interest, if not the thing that killed the cat?'

Max considered his next words carefully. 'I have an acquaintance in common with Ms Gregory. Someone I'd not want damaged.'

'So.' He looked round at the crowd of afternoon drinkers. 'Let's take a walk, shall we? The park's looking rather pleasant after the rain and I've a standing assignation with some ducks.'

They made a circuit of St James' lake, and leaning over the bridge, facing the distant prospect of Whitehall's roof-tops, Grünig spoke of seeing Miranda the first time at an international trade fair at the Queen Elizabeth II Conference Centre.

'Did she appear to be part of the organization?'

'No. I took her for a hanger-on. Watched her on the quiet, assumed she was an expensive horizontal touting for custom.'

'You said she was *with* someone.'

'Yes. Three days later they were dining together, discreetly and intimately, at Browns.'

'And the third time?'

'I was leaving the House of Commons when Feaist-Rivers' limo slid alongside to pick him up. It has darkened windows, but she was leaning forward as the rear door opened for him to get in. She gave him a special, welcoming smile.'

'Feaist-Rivers? Lord, he's old enough to be her—'

'Let's not be trite, Max. Old enough for her to be his mistress. You see now why I have an interest in the lady. But there are no whispers abroad—as yet.'

No open scandal, maybe. Members of Parliament had all sorts of little arrangements on the side but, as Grünig had said, Feaist-Rivers was vulnerable, not yet of cabinet rank but a trusted junior minister, and rising.

So far the police had discovered no valid motive for a deliberate attempt to run the woman down. But if she was having a secret affair with a member of the government—well, any number of people might find the fact an embarrassment. There had been too many competent men in the party tripped up by their animal instincts of late. And accidents had been known to happen before, to save a promising career.

A lot depended on the sort of woman she was. Certainly one of expensive tastes. He knew that from the glimpse he'd had of her, from the neighbourhood he knew she lived in, and the car Annette had said she drove. He doubted that Matherson and Corby valued her services enough to supply all that. If this attractive woman's second source of income was from politically powerful men it meant she was a force to be reckoned with, maybe an influence exerted with mercenary intention.

So—an exciting luxury while cherished; but if later scorned, a potential threat?

So how far had this relationship with Feaist-Rivers gone? Had he tired of her already, and met with her refusal to be quietly set aside? Had he felt forced to think of a tidy way to remove the embarrassment of her interest?

Or could his political friends, watchful for trouble, have taken matters into their own hands?

THIRTEEN

SUPERINTENDENT YEADINGS tossed his newspaper on to the kitchen counter and took his place at the breakfast table. As he tapped the shell of his boiled egg he observed that Nan wore make-up and her second-best suit.

'Going shopping?' he inquired. 'Can I give you a lift?'

'That would have been nice, but I won't hold you back. The children have a ten o'clock dental appointment. No school for Sally because it's one of those special saints' days. That's one advantage of a convent education.'

He looked up as Sally presented herself at breakfast in a new T-shirt which screamed, in red on white, DO IT IN THE ROAD.

Seeing Mike's mouth open for some crashing protest, Nan rushed in quickly. 'Oh, new T-shirt, Sally. Rather smart.'

'M'm. I got it at school.'

'Someone *gave* it to you?' her father asked, suspicious that Sally's simplicity could be a butt for more sophisticated humorists. His eyebrows made a thunderous black line, and she hesitated.

'I—bought it. Judy had four. She wanted my lunchbox.'

'So you swapped? I see.' Nan sounded ice-lolly cool, one restraining hand on her husband's arm.

Nevertheless he had to ask, 'What exactly is it we're supposed to do in the road?'

Sally beamed. 'The Green Cross Code.' She frowned in concentration: 'Look right, look left, look right again, and if...'

'Of course,' Nan said. Then, doubtfully, squinting at the

shirt again, 'I'm not altogether sure about the dye. Sometimes print smudges when it's washed.'

Yeadings turned away before he should encounter her too-innocent gaze. Wicked woman. Red dye run? She'd damn well make sure it did!

The phone rang before he had finished eating, and he swung round to reach the receiver off the wall. 'Yeadings.'

'Sorry to bother you,' said Mott, 'but Max Harris has been on the blower. He has something he won't share with me. I've asked him to drop by after nine. Is that all right?'

'Doesn't he know it's your case? I assume it is about the Gregory hit-and-run?'

'It is, and he does know. He says he's happened on something sensitive. He wants you.'

Yeadings hesitated. He resented the implied slight on his inspector, but it was just possible that Harris had access to something on the verge of Special Branch interest. 'How did he strike you?'

'Concerned and a bit apologetic.'

'Between nine and half past, then. It won't harm him to cool his heels a few minutes.'

He turned to Nan. 'I've time to run you in, save you the trouble of parking. It's always a bit tight down there mid-morning. You can get a cab back.'

'Thanks, love. That's one small problem settled. After the dentist we might start looking for Christmas presents and stay out for a bite of lunch, if Luke behaves himself.'

Yeadings regarded his small son proudly. Luke had reached the stage of taking food seriously, and seldom spoke at table. 'I'm sure he will.'

'So long as he doesn't fall asleep over his meal: That's the trouble with children who stuff themselves.'

The toddler eyed her solemnly while manoeuvring the last triangle of fried bread into his bulging cheeks.

'Joke,' his mother said fondly. 'I really love my little trencher-man.'

MAX HARRIS ARRIVED to find that Beaumont had been appointed to entertain him until the superintendent was free. The detective was leaning against the counter in Reception, casually flicking through a sheaf of typewritten pages. On the wall behind him a poster depicting a beaming patrol policeman showed the double row of square teeth blacked out alternately to match his chequered cap band.

'All quiet on the constabulary front?' Max assumed.

The duty sergeant looked sharply across from behind his glass screen. 'Crime is thriving, Mr Harris. Though you wouldn't think so to judge from some people. A very relaxed character, our Sergeant Beaumont.'

The CID man nodded serenely. 'I'm the proverbial three-toed sleuth.'

The uniformed officer noted that there was a breeziness about him this morning which had been missing of late.

'Mr Yeadings is held up at the moment,' Beaumont confided. 'So how does the idea of a coffee grab you?'

'By the parched throat.' It wasn't hard to drop into the idiom, but Max was aware that under the detective's light manner lay a questing intelligence. Three stripes didn't come easily in a force like Thames Valley, and Beaumont's were of the subtler, plain-clothes kind.

They settled in the canteen, Max exhibiting his publicized tweed fishing-hat on the Formica tabletop as if to advertise his part in the action. When Beaumont brought their coffees across, he explained, 'I'm not an investigative reporter. This case is right outside my zone of interest until after it's closed. I just pontificate on life in general.'

'I know your column,' Beaumont assured him. 'I liked the one about men in the kitchen. Passed it to my son as a heavy hint. I take it you're a family man, with a crowd of kids.'

Max shook his head. 'Bachelor in bedsit.'

The detective collapsed dramatically against the chair back, throwing in his own stage directions. 'Steps back in amazement; wipes amazement off shoe.' His voice returned to normal. 'So where do you get your ideas from?'

'Sufferers among my many acquaintances. That and imagination. Well, that's my job; how about yours?'

The Pinocchio features reassembled sombrely. 'There's a choice of answers to that.' He hesitated before admitting, 'Nothing else would fit me so well, given the crowd I fell among.'

'So the job wouldn't be the same in other places, other circumstances?'

'I'll say. I've got a good guv'nor. And the Boss is the best, with the right kind of back-up, for all that half of it's female.'

He made a lemon-sucking grimace. 'And if you ever quote that last bit, I'll deny it to my dying day, because officially—rank apart—all guys are equal in the job, whatever their sexual trimmings.'

'I've met the delectable Z.'

Beaumont eyed him evenly. 'She's short on granting the delectables, so you can forget the sugar coating. What's inside is formidable. But she's all right. In a few years she'll be a good jack—jackess, jackass, whatever.'

'And I've also met young Annette Briers.' Max sounded contemplative.

Beaumont's mouth twisted. 'It's no good trying to tap me on that one; I've been around too long. Nice try, though.'

'Not even a hint whether she's a serious suspect?'

As Beaumont's mouth opened, Max knew what he was going to say. They pronounced it in duet: 'Everyone's a suspect in a murder case!'

Conversation at the other tables had ceased at their raised voices. Faces were swung round to regard them curiously.

'Time we were elsewhere,' Beaumont said, rising. 'Come up to our office.'

WHEN Superintendent Yeadings arrived he was informed where his visitor was. He threw off his overcoat, riffled through the papers on his desk and then had him brought along. 'I'll ring if I need you,' he told Beaumont and the sergeant withdrew.

'I'm told that you have information of a confidential nature for me,' Yeadings began.

'For your ears only. At least for the moment.'

'This conversation is not being recorded, though I may take notes at the end for my own use if I feel it necessary.'

'I leave that to your discretion, Superintendent.'

'Good. So what have you to tell me, Mr Harris?'

'It concerns the hit-and-run victim, Miranda Gregory.'

'Go on.'

'It isn't common knowledge yet, but a particularly keen pair of eyes has picked up her close friendship with a member of the government.'

'Namely?'

'Julian Feaist-Rivers.'

Yeadings sucked in his cheeks, rotating a slim ballpoint pen between his fingers. 'Ah. How close a friendship?'

'I trust the source. He believes she's his mistress.'

Yeadings sat slumped, considering this. 'You haven't passed this on anywhere?'

'No.'

'I shall have to ask you for the source.'

'In confidence?'

'I can't guarantee that. You know I can't. Are there photographs to back this up?'

'Nothing but this witness speaking to me of what he's seen: three occasions of their meeting discreetly together.'

'I need a name for your informant, Mr Harris. It will be passed by me to only one other.'

'And from then on to how many more?'

Yeadings didn't answer. He heaved himself from his chair and went to peer between the slats of cream blind that covered one window. Max wasn't deceived by his apparent casualness. He let him take his time. When Yeadings turned back and resumed his seat his face was inscrutable.

'I appreciate your misgivings, Mr Harris, while regretting them. For the moment let's leave it there. At rumour level. Unfortunately the lady herself is in no position at present to provide either confirmation or further action.

'I can pass on a general query regarding the other party. He does enjoy special security provisions, so he's not exactly invisible. One of the officers involved will know if he's been slipping his leash of late.'

Harris nodded. 'There's another small matter. Yesterday I had a phone call passed through from Miss Briers. She recognized the press release photograph of Peter Lodd, found dead in Wandsworth. There was no mention of his connection with any case under investigation, but she obviously thinks there must be one.'

'How did she come to know him?'

'I haven't discovered that yet. We're meeting for lunch.'

'Then perhaps you'll ask her to get in touch with me. Thank you for coming forward, Mr Harris. I can trust to your discretion about the first matter?'

'If it breaks, it certainly won't be my doing, but since one pair of eyes has remarked on it, then others may as well. Ms Gregory's photograph in all today's national newspapers could jog memories.'

Yeadings grunted, rising. 'Thanks to my officers' determination to find out where she was up to the moment she was run down. Now it seems we may discover more than some public figures will like.'

He hesitated, one hand on the door. 'You appreciate I can't make any move on investigating the Feaist-Rivers rumour myself.' He rasped a hand over his chin. 'You, on the other hand, are not equally hog-tied. Not, of course, that I would ever approve of a member of the public interfering in what may become a Special Branch interest.'

Max Harris nodded. 'Fortunately you don't choose my research topics. I might tackle articles on home backgrounds of the justly famous: tycoons' toddlers, the grass widows of overworked MPs, the charivari of entertaining royals; that sort of thing.'

Yeadings pursed his lips. 'I imagine your research extends well beyond what you actually publish?'

'You would be amazed how much is binned as unusable.'

'Shredded and burnt might be better in some cases.'

'I'll certainly bear that in mind, Superintendent. Thank you for giving me your time.'

BEAUMONT WAS GRANTED the dubious pleasure of attending the post-mortem later that morning. The pathologist, a London professor whom he hadn't previously met, was already at work on an earlier corpse.

'Thames Valley CID,' Beaumont announced himself, joining the half-dozen present to watch the examination.

'This isn't your body.'

Professor Oliver glanced dreamily over his half glasses, scalpel raised. 'Interesting one, though, with a quite horrendous liver. Positively friable.'

The possibility of an intended pun alerted Beaumont's own penchant. 'An alcoholic? Spirited away, then.'

'Er, quite. I assume from that that you must be Sergeant Beaumont. Your—er, fame has preceded you.'

Whipping off his plastic apron and surgical gloves, Professor Oliver binned them, noisily ran water in the adjoining room and came back ready to be kitted out for the next job.

'I understand you found the body?'

'Quite by chance. I'd gone to interview him about another matter.'

'Now, now; don't drop me any clues. I need to be totally unprejudiced. He's male, he's dead. We start from there.'

Oliver beamed round at the other officers present, waving his mortuary assistant in to perform the preliminaries while he stood by, humming reedily and tapping one shoe on the tiled floor.

'And—in—we—go!'

As he carved, sawed and drew off fluid, he delivered his findings on the body to a girl taking shorthand notes at a table behind him, and these he interspersed with a Hibernian-type mouth-music with as vague a tune and rhythm as the burble and gurgle of water flushing the table's gutters.

Beaumont kept his eyes off the slicing of yellowy rubberized flesh, concentrating on abstract patterns of blood stringily forming and parting, reluctantly dispersed by the flow. This red stuff was quite dead, dead as unmourned Lodd himself.

Peter Lodd. Peter Piper picked a peck of pickled peppers. Peppers...pimentos...pizza-topping...topped. Was Lodd topped by another, or was it a DIY job?

It wouldn't take the Prof long to confirm what drug had been used, but it wasn't his job to discover whose hand had administered the stuff. Only the police experts combing the dead man's flat could come up with that, and even then they'd need an element of luck. Overdoses were the very devil to be one hundred per cent sure about. For the final verdict some coroner's jury could be reduced to spinning a coin.

MAX WAS A MINUTE or two late for the meeting arranged by telephone, dropping off from a taxi at the restaurant door and entering with apologies. 'Peace offering,' he claimed and slid a large envelope along the table towards Annette.

Inside, with the original photograph, was the enlargement of the seated Ms Gregory. The rest of the Matherson and Corby staff had been blocked out, with an out-of-focus effect of bushes as background.

'That's clever,' she said, delighted.

'And then there's this.' He offered her a second envelope.

She drew out another photograph taken from the same original. This time Ms Gregory too had been removed. The remaining head and shoulders were her own.

'Like it?'

She had never had such a flattering portrait, but modesty forbade she should admit so much. 'Oh, thank you. I wasn't expecting this.'

'It's good of you.'

They left serious discussion until they had been served, then Annette said, 'Peter Lodd—the man who was found dead—was it really suicide?'

'They can't tell yet, but it looked that way. Did you meet him through his ex-wife?'

'So he *was* Gwen's husband? No, it was at the hospital. I only caught a passing glimpse of him. He must have gone to visit Ms Gregory, but they'd moved her from Intensive Therapy to a ward and I guess he'd got lost. I was just coming away, so I never knew whether he found her.'

'He did. One of the ward nurses saw him there but he hurried off before she could talk to him. The police thought at first he might be the person who'd run her down, come to check how she was.'

'And he was simply her adoptive father.'

'But could still be the one who'd hurt her.'

'Only if he'd used someone who looked like me to hire the car,' she reminded him.

'I don't think the police seriously suspect you of anything to do with it.'

'They may reconsider if they know Peter Lodd and I were at the hospital at the same time.'

'You must take that risk, Annette, because you'll have to tell them. Give Mr Yeadings a buzz from the office. He'll understand. They're not going to make a case against you for as little as that.'

'Even although there's no other suspect?'

'You don't know that. I had to admit today that I'd come across Peter Lodd myself. It was only briefly. He brushed past me to try and take the second taxi, as your boss left Marylebone station. And I'd seen him earlier, sitting on one of those circular red benches. Wouldn't have noticed him then but he was reading a *Courier*, my page.'

'So do you think he followed Ms Gregory to the office?'

'It's something the police will have to ask themselves. There's no one else to ask, since he's dead now.'

'Max, what's happening? Haven't they a single clue? There are two dead already, and Ms Gregory was meant to die as well. Who's doing all this? What's it about?'

He pushed his glasses up his tip-tilted nose. For all that his eyes were small and screwed up, there was a deal of kindliness in them.

'Maybe Ms Gregory will come round soon, then she can tell us herself.'

IN THE NARROW HOSPITAL bed the woman moaned, barely above a sigh. She thought a sound had reached her, again the boy's high, thin scream from the attic. She couldn't bear it. Part of her was up there, with him and the man, flinching at each brutal stroke. The pain flamed in her.

She loved the boy. She always had done. But it wasn't until another lifetime that she'd known. It was cruel how they had been separated. So suddenly.

She'd been snatched away, without warning, barely wakened from her sleep. She remembered being lifted from bed, covered in a blanket—even her head, so that she could hardly breathe. And some unknown man had carried her downstairs, right through the house and out into the cold night air where there were cars and people waiting. Someone else—a woman—had pulled the blanket away from her face, said, 'Poor little scrap,' in a soft northern voice.

She had looked up and seen the dark sky pinpricked with

tiny bright stars. There was a smell of frost and of the
cigaretty, rough woollen cloth of the man's dark uniform
that he held her crushed against.

And then she was in a car being driven away; sleeping
some more; waking in a strange place with unknown people, alien children kept at a distance, who stared and silently pulled faces at her.

They had promised she should see her mother, but when
they took her it wasn't to her home. Another place, bare-
looking and smelling like the one she had already fetched
up at. And Mother had been different, her face gone puffed
and mottled, her pretty hair dragged back. She looked ill,
and she cried. They cried together in each other's arms,
though she didn't know why, and then she was taken away
again.

She didn't remember any more for a while. It hadn't
mattered. Places changed. The weeks and months trailed on
and on. People told her what to do and where to go, and
she did it, but all the time she had been waiting for something real to break through. Waiting and waiting; she didn't
know how long, except that she was older when she saw
him again.

He had changed, was taller, less delicate. She'd had hold
of her new mama's hand, was being towed along through
the crowd outside Victoria station, and he'd been standing
there with his luggage beside him. Just a schoolboy, but
she knew at once it was him.

His fine chestnut hair had the same way of flopping over
dark-shadowed eye-sockets. The look in his eyes—a wild
thing burning inside the tightly fleshed face and staring out
through slitted mask-holes. His lips were still curly. There
was that same cleft in the centre of his chin. And, older,
he had a new force, a physical magnetism. When he was
fully grown he would dominate the others round him, like
Nureyev did.

He had stared right through her without recognition.

Which hadn't surprised her because she was someone else now, a taken-over girl called Annie Lodd. At times she felt invisible. Nothing was left of how she'd been before.

Except needing him. As, without open admission, she always had done. All her life long she would be waiting for him to reappear: the boy. It even struck her then that she'd rather be back in the past hearing him scream than not have him at all. The agony of the thrashings he'd endured was slight against her pain at him not being there.

She groaned more loudly and a face came close, out of nothing. 'Pain,' she breathed. 'Pain.'

'She's coming round,' said the ward sister. 'Have Dr Dennis bleeped.'

FOURTEEN

ANGUS MOTT HAD NO EXCUSE to prolong his interest in the London deaths. Both the West End shooting and the apparent suicide of Peter Lodd were being energetically tackled by the Met, if without notable progress to date. His immediate duties being back in Thames Valley, he reluctantly surrendered any hope of staying near Paula to work on her present disenchantment with libel defence and so hasten a career change.

The prospect of marriage seemed as distant as ever. He was beginning to question whether enforced celibacy was really his style. There was no lack of female talent locally, even within the force. Working alongside Z, for instance, constantly reminded him that she was more than a decent chap with a deal of horse-sense. There were embarrassing moments when he could have done with her being less of a woman.

He had come from a debriefing with Yeadings and was considering a visit to Miranda Gregory's bedside to check on her reported recovery, when a call came in from Sergeant Fox.

'Thought you'd like to hear about the blood test on the tea towel and meat cleaver from Lodd's flat.'

His voice was dry. A negative, then, Mott assumed. 'Oh, yes?'

'*Not* human traces. Same for both.'

'Right, then.' But there was something about the other man's silence. Not the end of the message.

'Like to make a guess what it was?'

'Lodd had a dog, hadn't he? Rabbit, perhaps, to feed it?' Fox gave a little grunt. 'Not a bad guess, but not spot on. Lodd also liked to feed wild birds, so his neighbours said. Maybe that's why he chopped up one of their cats.'

Mott grimaced. 'A bit vicious, but you're not suggesting he afterwards did himself in out of remorse?'

'No. It's just another curiosity. He'll go down as a suicide at the inquest. Depressed loner, thrown over by his woman friend. Off-balance. Nothing for any of us in this.'

Nothing except a vague coincidence, Mott thought: Lodd having been adoptive father to the young Annie Gregory. And, suicide or not, he was still a disturbing element, because there was something pretty unwholesome about the cat-killing. Fervent gardeners often threatened felicide, but seldom went further than a bloodcurdling shout or a tossed flowerpot.

What would move a seemingly peaceable middle-aged man to stalk the creature with a meat cleaver and do it in? An unlikely act, even if it was a bird-snatcher or yowled under his window every night.

'Whose cat was it?' Mott demanded.

'Well, anybody's. I mean, the things aren't registered. No need to report if you run one over. We've received no complaint of a missing moggy.'

Which was understandable if the neighbours were shaken by the man's death and conscious of falling short in socializing with him. Maybe Beaumont should be sent back to have a word with some of them, keep an ear open for any rumour of Lodd acting viciously before. Loners could more easily go round the bend. Premeditation of this sort wasn't so very far off hiring a car to run down a human victim. Both acts symptomatic of mental deterioration in someone hitherto apparently normal. So how much later had his death followed the attempt on Ms Gregory?

'Did the Prof's report give a date for Lodd's OD?' Mott pursued.

'He had the sleeping pills prescribed on the Tuesday after Gregory was found Sunday. He collected them from Boots the same day. Just when he took the overdose is uncertain, dependent on too many unknown factors. Time of actual decease was probably mid-morning on the Sunday before your man found him on the Tuesday evening. No wonder the dog seemed hungry. Says something for the beast that he didn't take a nibble.'

The dog, yes. Mott would have to ask Beaumont what had happened to it. As for the time of the supposed suicide, it neither implicated nor ruled out Lodd as the driver who ran Gregory down. Certainly he had got to know of her being injured because, according to Yeadings, Annette Briers had seen him at the hospital.

'Right, thanks,' he told Fox, and rang off.

So where did that leave him? With Lodd as a possible suspect merely because he'd still been alive at the time of the attempt on Miranda's life? And later killed himself, either from remorse or because he'd not quite succeeded and she might live to accuse him?

A bit far-fetched, Mott decided. But it was all they had as yet. He questioned whether it would be worth while checking with Gwen Lodd about the man's attitude to Ms Gregory. A recognizable motive would make the possibility a great deal stronger.

Something the ex-wife had said earlier came back to his mind: 'He wasn't a very fatherly person at all.' In which case it was unlikely the two kept in touch once Miranda had left home.

Yet he'd visited her in hospital. It could be just bad luck that that late flash of sympathy made him feature as a possible suspect for her attempted murder. Could her pathetic condition have exasperated his depression so much that it tipped the scales to suicide?

Causing him to abandon his old dog to a slow death from starvation? Wouldn't the sort of man who fed wild birds have been merciful enough to share his overdose with Hudson? Or had he expected someone to call and find the dog in time?

But then if he'd flipped his lid over a cat...

There were too many possibilities, and the people in the case hadn't firmed enough in Mott's mind. He wished the Boss had leaned towards some theory when they discussed the case that morning, but Yeadings seemed willing to wait on the woman's recovery. Meanwhile Mott was to take over questioning on the recent series of aggravated break-ins at Holtspur and Wycombe Marsh, leaving his sergeant and Z to keep an eye on any developments in the Gregory case.

Z came in, heavily wrapped against the outside weather. She had a dead beech leaf caught in her brown curls. 'It's blowing half a gale,' she said cheerfully. Her eyes sparkled and the colour was high in her cheeks.

'What have you got?' he asked, wryly telling himself that he knew well enough and it was already disturbing him.

'I wasn't happy about the Slough hired car that ran Gregory down, so I had another go at the clerk who booked it. She sticks to her description of the plump young woman who came in, and the driving licence details check out, so she's straight on that. She's doubtful about the photographs of Annette Briers; says the hair's wrong and maybe the nose.'

'But...'

'She needed a little coaxing, then she remembered a folded piece of paper the girl took out of her pocket. It was typewritten, and it looked like a set of instructions. They covered where the car was to be left parked on the Saturday morning and that its keys should be taped under the offside front wheel arch, which we already knew.'

'Thereby doing away with any need for the collecting driver to appear at the office to claim it in person.'

'Yes, and this unknown young woman signed the hire papers with Gregory's name. It's acceptable in some firms for staff to add each other's signatures on trivial matters when pushed. She paid the deposit in cash. Finally she checked with the note, sort of "Blah-blah-blah", then folded it up as if satisfied and put it away again.'

'As if acting on orders. I see. So, if not Annette Briers, you think there's a second plump young woman in the firm we should question again?'

'Possibly an innocent agent who found the instructions in an envelope on her desk, together with the money and licence, and thought she was being asked to do a favour for Ms Gregory.'

'So why hasn't she come forward now that everyone knows what happened? Isn't it more likely that she stole the licence herself and has good reason to stay schtoom? She could have written out her own intended moves to make sure she followed them to the letter. She sounds dodgy to me. Remember too, they haven't yet pulled anyone in for the shooting. It had to be someone in the firm who stayed behind after the others left, and then hid from the cleaners. All visitors that day were signed in and out at Reception. Which simply leaves the staff. Could be the same girl.'

'Guv, I'd like to go up to Matherson and Corby and nose around again,' she pleaded.

He didn't like it, mainly because he'd been withdrawn from the London end himself, and he felt his needs were paramount. OK, so it was sour grapes. His second thought was that the Met wouldn't want Z interfering further in their case. Even if he cleared it with Yeadings, it would need Meredith's approval.

'Get yourself a coffee,' he said dourly, 'while I think about it.'

On his way to Yeadings' office he passed Beaumont in the corridor and picked up the report sheets he saluted him with. 'What happened to the dog?' he inquired.

'He's perking up,' Beaumont told him, suiting his puppet

face to the words. 'Takes on a helluva lot of food, has a heavy paunch and a hearty belch. He's a natural for uniformed branch.'

'So what's his future?'

'Until there's a legal claimant I'm game to keep him, failing other offers. He's sort of settled in at home.'

With the somewhat neurotic Cathy and the quirky son? Mott had his doubts, but Beaumont appeared almost cocky about it.

'Clear it with Lodd's solicitors, whoever they are. We don't want a complaint of dognapping.'

'Right, Guv. The Gregory woman—'

'Yes?'

'Came to last night, but they're not too pleased with her. Got to operate again. An aneurism. There could be permanent brain damage.'

'Just what we need! The Boss is depending on her. I'd better drop him the bad news. Keep checking back with the man at her bedside, but also take a look at the Wycombe break-in reports on my desk. See if any bulbs light up in your brain.'

He found Yeadings' door open, a recognized invitation to disturb his immersion in paperwork. 'Angus, come in. It's at least ten minutes since we talked.'

His grin vanished as Mott passed on the news about Miranda Gregory. 'H'm. So what progress elsewhere?'

'Z wants to follow up the stealing of Gregory's driving licence—at Matherson and Corby.'

'Haven't the Met come up with anything definite on that?'

'They've enough problems with their shooting case and they're thin on the ground with these recent bomb alerts. This little problem seems to belong in our court.'

'We and the Met could both lose out if we're not careful. Liaison's vital. I'm convinced the two cases are linked, Angus; maybe the Lodd suicide too.'

Yeadings pushed himself away from his desk and rose stiffly. 'Z isn't known up there, is she?'

'Personally only to Annette Briers. She just whisked through otherwise, no introductions. She could change her appearance enough to get by.'

'They must be getting short-staffed at Matherson and Corby, with Gregory in hospital and Gwen Lodd off sick. I'll suggest to Meredith we lend him Z to put in undercover as a temp. Her secretarial skills are well up to it.'

'And Annette Briers? She's a risk if she lets on who Z is.'

Yeadings grunted. 'When I've spoken to DCI Meredith I'll give her a call at work. I think she might respond to a word from me.'

ANNETTE RANG THE superintendent back on an outside line as he suggested, eager for an update on Ms Gregory's progress, and was dashed to hear of the new development. The idea of Z joining Matherson and Corby's staff, even as a temporary measure, restored her spirits a little and she gave her word not to do anything that would spring the fact that Rosemary was an undercover DC.

Two hours later, as she was dealing with the second postal delivery, Sally from Personnel ushered in a tall newcomer in high heels, a side-slit black skirt and a Cleopatra hairstyle. For a moment the wig deceived her, then she picked up Z's closed eye signal.

'This is Jill Wilson, Annette. Make her feel at home. She'll be temping in this office for a few days until Mr Franklin rejigs the department. Nothing's decided yet, but you do understand, don't you, that there will have to be some changes. So we don't know yet quite where you will be fitting in. All right?' The woman smiled, switched off and departed.

'Already? How on earth did he manage it?' Annette demanded.

'The Boss?' Z smiled. 'He doesn't let grass grow under his feet. The Met were quite pleased to have a spare body on offer. They had a word with your MD who "personally recommended" me. I just hope my work's up to scratch, that's all.'

The upper echelons — no, I set at its approval...
by now. The MD were quite pleased to have a man down
on spot. They had ... the MD with personally
loyal clued-up... Franklin ... was sure to assist
that a ...

FIFTEEN

Z HAD COME TO POLICE work after several years in an advertising agency. With no shortage of reports to draft for the Thames Valley force, her shorthand and keyboard speeds had not been allowed to fall off. Towards the end of her first afternoon at Matherson and Corby she was summoned to the MD's office ostensibly to stand in for his secretary dispatched on an invented task outside.

He had been strongly opposed to allowing a police spy within the firm, as he saw it. But DCI Meredith had thrown his full weight behind the requirement. Mr Franklin could accept that or suffer suspension of all operations while the place was taken apart and the whole staff's backgrounds rigorously examined. There had really been no choice.

Already mollified on sight of Z's qualifications, he was more reconciled when she presented herself. He waved her towards the vacated desk. 'I think you'll find all you asked for there. You understand, I must insist on your total discretion about any information not relevant to your present inquiry.'

The files released for Z's examination covered details of staff employment, lists of clients, and office diaries for the past year. When she had been making notes on these for some twenty minutes, he asked, 'Is there anything I can do to help?'

'Would you mind dictating some letters on tape? I'll need to type them up and leave some file copies, to justify my being here.'

'Do you think that's necessary?'

'I'm afraid so. The first thing your secretary will do on Monday is check on whether my work was up to standard.'

He threw up his hands. 'And eat her heart out thinking you'll be asked to replace her! If only you would. I must admit I could see some advantages in that.'

'I'm a policewoman first and foremost, Mr Franklin,' Z assured him humorously, tucking her legs and the slit skirt decorously behind the desk front.

'Well, I suppose I might as well make use of your secretarial skills. I trust my voice won't disturb your concentration?'

'I can block out distractions at will,' she came back, and he took the smiling slap-down good-humouredly.

He went home soon after completing the recording, leaving her to work under light from the desk-lamp. A few minutes later, Annette looked in wearing her outdoor clothes. 'I'd offer to help out,' she said, 'but I don't suppose you'd allow it.'

'Off home?'

'Yes. I'd hoped to go and see Ms Gregory first. I rang the hospital this afternoon. They were operating again. It was a nurse I hadn't met; she wouldn't tell me anything because I'm not family. Do you think it sounds ominous? I do hope she'll be all right.'

When the girl had left, Z worked on, isolated in the pool of light, conscious of the gathering darkness outside the windows, the emptying city.

She was unusually aware of her own isolation, not just physically in this building, but in her life. Outside in the streets other women were hurrying home, to families, husbands, lovers. She'd none of those, had deliberately cut herself off.

It didn't worry her that she quite liked being alone—for most of the time—but she knew it was unnatural; knew too well what the barrier was; acknowledged sometimes that sooner or later she must tackle it, this aftermath of a young life made miserable by abuse. In the job she had met too many victims who carried permanent scars with them, who

cherished them as reasons for not living fully, for never
daring to take the risk of entering real relationships. Unless
she broke out she could become embittered and a permanent prey to fear. But for a long time there had been no
one she thought she could trust her life with.

She rose and went across to drop the latch on the door.
With the action she also cut off the unwelcome interruption
inside her own mind, went back and resumed work on the
files. When eventually she came on something significant
she picked up the phone to ring Angus Mott, then had second thoughts. Although she'd been given an outside line,
there might be an automatic recording system.

She typed the letters Mr Franklin had put on tape, and
addressed the envelopes, leaving them for his signature.
Then she collected her things and went down by the lift to
the entrance foyer and into the street.

Standing there in the biting wind which flicked little sliv-
ers of ice against her cheeks, she was reminded that it was
Friday and the office block behind her emptied of day staff.
This was just how Annette and Miranda Gregory had left
exactly a fortnight ago. And to travel home she must take
a train from Marylebone, as they'd meant to do.

She had a disturbing sense of—not déjà vu, because she
hadn't been here then. It was more as though she was standing in for a crime reconstruction, the policewoman who
wore the victim's clothes, followed the same route, prompt-
ing people to remember what they had witnessed.

Although there were no alerted spectators to put on the
act for, she felt compelled to follow the same pattern as far
as she knew it: take a cab to Marylebone station, miss the
Chiltern Line train as it pulled out, drink a coffee in the
buffet, sit at the identical table.

She followed it through, feeling apart as she observed
the other people around her in the buffet, ordinary commuters; an elderly man breathing wheezily, with a younger

one anxiously in attendance; a woman sharing crisps between two noisy children under school age.

Any repetition was solely in her own actions. There was no tweed-hatted Max Harris in the corner by the door, as he'd been on the real occasion; and the girl serving behind the counter was different, Pakistani instead of Caribbean.

Because the scene wasn't identical, it ruled out a valid experiment; but she continued, even riffling through her shoulder bag and leaving in a hurry, as if sight of something in it (or missing from it?) had alarmed her.

Outside, there were several taxis waiting at the kerb. She took the first, asking for the Matherson and Corby building. Following the movements the Met had learned from Miranda Gregory's cabbie, she left it near Harrods, and found it made good sense to go the rest of the way on foot, saving time on the traffic snarl-up.

She was conscious now of a need for haste. Hadn't she a rendezvous with the Midlands detective back at her office? He was bringing her the results of his inquiries, vital proof which she had paid him to find. And yes, she was sure by this point that he'd been somewhere in the building earlier—perhaps infiltrating after a visit to the floor above—and managed to slip a note in her handbag.

There was little difficulty in getting into the building unseen. The porter on duty had his back turned in the foyer, busy behind his counter. Z removed her high heels, stole across the tiles and went up by the stairs.

There she found that security had been improved since the shooting. This time the outer door to Matherson and Corby's suite of offices was locked, although lights and the subdued hum of vacuum cleaners reached her through the glass panels.

She used the labelled key-ring Mr Franklin had left for her, let herself in, went quietly past open doors where the cleaning team were working and made for the office she

had shared early that afternoon with Annette Briers. She
opened the door and slid in.

A fine line of light showed under the closed door to the
inner office.

She felt a surge of rare excitement that her intuition
could be proved right. Angus Mott had listed hard work,
luck, and native instinct as his recipe for success. Superintendent Yeadings believed in much the same, referring to
his celebrated hunches as 'a touch of my old Welsh
granny'. Z couldn't boast descent from any Wise Woman,
but she knew how she'd felt out in the street as she left the
office, recognizing the parallel, identifying with Miranda
Gregory; like her, walking in now on unknown danger.

Because Miranda *had* come back here. There was no
proof of it, but she knew, she felt in every nerve of her
body, that the woman now in coma had stood here trans-
fixed by an identical sense of unease. She had gone on in,
to confront something terrifying in the next room: a killer,
or the dead man just wasted. Or even, perhaps, someone
she must herself kill because of what he had unearthed for
her in his searches.

She listened, one hand on the knob of the door, and
fancied she heard slight sounds of movement like a drawer
shutting in the steel filing cabinet. She waited, holding her
breath, regretting she hadn't phoned Mott after all, so that,
if anything went wrong, at least he'd know how far she'd
got.

Everything was quiet now. If the intruder was examining
documents this was the moment to try opening the door,
just a crack, enough to look in.

She used both hands to slow the movement, watching a
vertical bar of light appear and gently widen. With her
cheek flat against the jamb she peered round.

The overhead neon bar wasn't on. With only the desk-
lamp, the outer edges of the room were in semi-darkness.
There seemed to be no one there, but the replacement green

leather chair was pivoted to face the window. Z stared at its back and remembered the single bullet that had gone through the earlier one, muffling the shot so that the cleaners, busy vacuuming, had heard nothing.

Someone was sitting there now, hidden by its tall back, and she had no way of knowing who. Sitting doing what? Reading perhaps, but—just as possibly—waiting. For whom? Was someone else due to appear? Someone who could walk in now behind, and catch Z spying?

She drew the door back against her thumb, with the palm of her hand flat on the jamb to control any sound in closing. In the dark outer office she began to retreat towards the corridor, brushed against something trailing from the desk, became entangled, and the phone went crashing to the floor.

As she groped about the carpet, behind her the inner door was flung open, throwing in enough light to catch her struggling to free her ankles from the flex. She hopped round. In silhouette a tall woman stood staring down at her.

'Oh shit,' said Z in a casually exasperated voice, 'just look what I've done. And I'll bet I've gone and bust it.'

'Who are you?' the woman demanded harshly. 'And what on earth do you think you're doing in here?'

Z straightened, adopting a truculent expression. 'I could ask you the same.'

'I happen to work here. But you don't. Who are you?'

'My name's Jill, *if* it's any concern of yours. And as of today I *do* work here. This is my office. Or half of it is. With Annette. She's showing me the ropes.'

'A temp?' After a pause to draw breath, the woman's voice had changed. The panic turned to wariness. She was still suspicious.

'That doesn't explain what you're doing creeping around in the dark at this hour. How did you get back in?'

Z bridled, deliberately ignoring the note of authority in the other's voice. She scowled blackly. 'I walked, didn't I? Listen, I don't have to take this hassle!'

It was a relief to discharge the build-up of fear as seeming anger. Muttering, Z bent and slapped her shoes back on, retrieved her shoulder bag from the floor and straightened belligerently. 'I'm off home, now I've got my railcard back. And a ruddy goodnight to you, whoever you are!'

The woman stood rigid, her eyes smouldering. 'Don't trouble to come in on Monday,' she said with controlled anger. 'You're fired. We need no relief typist now that I'm back. Not even a properly trained girl. Personnel will send on whatever is due to you.'

At the door Z halted, seeming momentarily deflated. Under the circumstances of her being here, she couldn't be dismissed out of hand by this woman. But there was no doubt that Mrs Lodd thought she had the power to get rid of her. Mr Franklin would be in a spot having to override her ban.

So he needn't. Already there was information in her handbag which Z was sure could give the investigation a new lead. So, accepting that she'd burnt her bridges, she turned defiantly, fist on hip. 'You know where you can stuff your rotten job,' she said waspishly. 'I can find better than this crummy joint any day.' And she stalked off.

Maybe the tarty effect was a bit overdone. She'd known a lot of temps, and they were an amenable lot on the whole. So—silent apologies, girls; but she'd had to behave totally different in character from the detective of her earlier visit.

Then, Gwen Lodd had given her only a passing glance before being ushered to a separate office for questioning, while the WDC interviewed Annette. Even so, it was lucky that tonight's encounter had been in the half-dark.

And why hadn't the woman reached for the main light switch? Wasn't that the natural thing to do, encountering an intruder on her own ground? Perhaps it meant that, while demonstrating her authority, Mrs Lodd too preferred not to be identified.

FEAIST-RIVERS LEFT the House feeling definitely uncomfortable. There had been that intuitive flash as he'd entered the Committee Room, triggered by a sharp break in the conversation. Keen glances had darted his way and then interest was abruptly transferred to briefcases, rapidly shuffled papers. There were over-casual greetings. Only Piggy Everton's blue stare retained the hard gleam of speculation.

So they'd just been talking about him. There was gossip of some kind. He'd need to step warily.

They had settled to discussion and all had gone normally, with the usual haverers and hair-splitters lengthening the process to the point of tedium. But his unease remained. He'd been glad to get away at the end, declining the customary socializing offers.

Piggy had hovered, so that Feaist-Rivers could scarcely avoid leaving with him. And, at the outer door, while they waited for their cars, the man had been unable to resist uttering a caution. Bluffly offhand, turning up the collar of his British warm over his Guards tie: 'Pretty brisk wind blowing up. Do well to cover y'flanks, eh?'

So Feaist-Rivers knew they were after him; knew that somebody—in time, *everybody*—had scented a reputation at risk.

He was soon to find out just what rumour was abroad. It was in the fastness of the Reform Club atrium that the approach was made. Quietly, as he relaxed in his discreet corner; but it was official. No one he'd met before, but the type was familiar: correct, smooth, bespectacled, urbane, almost deferentially authoritative. Wanting to know—no; knowing, but wanting him to admit—what his relations were with a woman known as Miranda Gregory.

He had already rehearsed the answer several times, but even as he opened his mouth to speak, he hadn't decided which version to give.

'Gregory?' His modulated voice and fine arched brows questioned recall of the name. His smile promised willingness to be of help, but alas... 'A constituency worker, perhaps?'

The man was no amateur. He didn't overstep any predetermined mark, and his very correctness, his carefulness, made the junior minister suddenly certain that he wasn't yet working from proof, but bare speculation. If there had been something concrete to hold against him—photographs, or some complaint from the woman herself—they would have sent a different kind of person, and to his home. This one was gently probing, not leaning on him. It meant that as yet they had nothing, nothing at all, to take to the cabinet committee.

A murmured word came out at him. '*Browns?* Yes, I do lunch there on occasion. Rather a favourite place of mine when I'm encouraging an informant. I trust you aren't about to tell me that I've ventured into questionable company?'

'Miranda Gregory,' the man reminded him, and Feaist-Rivers permitted himself a frown as he tried to conjure up a face to match the name.

'Miranda. Now that's a name I should surely remember. But I am afraid it rings no bell at all, Commander. Gregory—wait a moment, wasn't that the—? Remind me, Commander, what the connection would be. Oh wait, I have it now—thought she was Miss *Graham!* Representing Matherson and Corby, the conference and expo organizers.' His smile expanded with delight at his own recapture of detail.

'A charming young woman, quite efficient; but her scheme was on altogether too grand a scale for the purpose I had in mind. A modest local function, just a couple of hundred party supporters. I fear she would have taken the bit between her teeth and turned it into a G7 Summit. Sometimes these ambitious young people lack a sense of proportion.'

'A very experienced member of the firm, as I understand.'

'No doubt; and I'll admit I was quite impressed. But, for my present purpose, altogether too—er, exploitative.'

'So you haven't been in further touch, then, sir?'

'Quite so.'

'And the date of that intended function would be—?'

'I should have to consult my desk diary, Commander. A few weeks back, however. Really, I must confess to a certain curiosity about the reason for these questions. Has Miss Graham—er, Miss Gregory—disappeared, or been accused of some shady dealings?'

'She was involved in a serious accident, sir. I thought you might have seen some reference to it in the press.'

'My dear Commander, I try to read all the national newspapers. Which means that I inevitably skim over a great deal of the matter that is not germane to my current interests. Had she been the victim of a judicial sentence which was open to question, or concerned in major company fraud—' He waved a hand generously, permitting his inquisitor to complete the sentence.

A club servant hovering nearby picked up the signal and came across to take a repeat order. Declining Feaist-Rivers' offer, the commander stood and tilted his head in leave-taking. 'I won't take more of your valuable time. Thank you for your help, Mr Feaist-Rivers. Perhaps your secretary will supply that date for me if I telephone you tomorrow.'

It was not a question, but a Service requirement.

And that was all? The junior minister could hardly believe it, as the other moved away among the club chairs. The commander had asked so few questions, and given a minimum of information in return. But then Feaist-Rivers had asked him for none. Maybe he should have demanded what kind of accident; and what injuries the girl had suffered; shown some concern? Had he been too reticent, unnaturally detached?

But no; he was a junior minister, a man of some standing. Why should anyone imagine it of interest to him if a woman he had brushed against in a professional context was later run down by some car?

And yet someone somewhere had seen fit to have him questioned. These days there was no such thing as a private life, he reflected bitterly. They had been discreet about their meetings, or at least he had, and he'd assumed the same of her. Normally the association might have passed as acceptable. God knows, he wasn't the only one in his position acknowledging a need for something beyond the barren existence of a wasted marriage.

But Miranda was dead. Must be, to necessitate this inquiry. Which should have ended his liability for scandal. Special Branch need have no fear of leaked documents or of outside pressure exerted on his political conduct. It was over, done with.

So it was the death itself they were interested in. It wasn't accepted as accidental. Behind the commander and the mandarin activities of Special Branch there had to be plain men doing an unpleasant job. Traffic police, a pathologist, forensic scientists; none of them open to soft persuasion. They could be the sort of men to take satisfaction in querying his immunity from such sordid probings.

The commander had so far only inquired about their association. And gone away. But the matter didn't rest there. Like the mills of God, the arm of the law was ponderously slow, but had almost infinite patience. It was only a matter of time before some other more earthy officer asked him to check with his diary for the night Miranda was killed.

And by then they would have found out other things he could not afford to have made public. If only it were a simple matter of a little harmless dalliance. Adultery was common to all walks of life, even the highest families in the land. But the other, no. He couldn't face the scrutiny, would be destroyed by the findings.

SIXTEEN

THE HOUSE MAX WAS seeking lay midway between Eton and Datchet, close to the river. At the end of a short, curving drive the white portico, rather too grand for the size of the thirties building, would be attractive when the wistaria was in bloom trailing over red brick and painted wood balconies. There was a double garage, and shrubberies neatly trimmed for winter. Evidence of money, he thought, but not excessive ostentation. He had expected something more impressive as the home of a rising light in the government.

Of course, Feaist-Rivers didn't spend much time here. He had a flat in Albany. The family home had been in Surrey, but after the fire Constance moved back to this area, where she'd lived as a child. Daughter of a housemaster at Eton. Rather a solitary, from all accounts.

The previous house had been virtually destroyed. It would have cost the earth to rebuild. Probably underinsured, or else Feaist-Rivers felt the extensive property had served its purpose by that point. They had already been starting to drift apart.

Not divorced, because Constance Feaist-Rivers did turn up on necessary occasions, to show the flag. Not really a town sort of person, though she used to make more effort in the early days of their marriage.

As Max mused, bachelor that he was, on the incomprehensible nature of some permanent relationships, launched on sex and ending at best in protracted boredom, the front door was opened to him by a quiet-voiced middle-aged woman who introduced herself as Mrs Dean. 'Mrs Feaist-Rivers is expecting you in the winter garden,' she told him.

A new concept to him, it turned out to be a glorified

conservatory complete with a trickling cascade and ferny
pool. The lady of the house sat on an extended rattan
lounger with a plaid rug over her legs. She made no effort
to rise but extended a languorous hand towards him. Re-
serving herself.

Not that she was old, nor necessarily frail. She would
probably be about fifty-five or -six, and was heavily built
with an unlikely baby face surrounded by pale, flat curls.

'You managed to find me, then?' she asked in a gaspy
voice. 'My first-time visitors usually end up in Old Windsor
or Eton Wick.'

'I know the roads round Eton pretty well,' Max told her.
'I was in New House for three years, until the family's
money ran out.'

Mrs Feaist-Rivers' eyes went round. 'My dear man, how
dreadful for you. And they didn't offer to keep you on?'

'I imagine my grades hadn't impressed them enough,' he
said lightly. 'Anyway, my parents decided to go abroad and
take me with them. It helped my languages. I came back
in time for Oxford.'

'And from there to fame as a newspaper man.' She
waved him to a chair beside her.

Max beamed. 'To the *Courier* by roundabout routes. But
I came to talk about you, Mrs Feaist-Rivers. Not for a
glossy *Homes and Gardens* number; something a little
more cerebral perhaps.'

If she were a cat she would have purred. As it was, 'Do
call me Constance,' she invited. 'What sort of thing had
you in mind?'

'The Eton of your childhood compared with its present
image. From schoolhouse to the House of Commons. The
supportive role of the government wife. Your views on
Women's Lib, modern education, the present moral climate. How you see your future role. Anything you like,
really. You have enjoyed very varied experience. Your

opinions will be of interest to thousands of readers who
envy such contacts with people and events of importance.'

Inside himself he would have blushed for his duplicity,
but that he had a serious quest in view. On the surface he
remained sincere and socially concerned.

Mrs Feaist-Rivers was eager to comply. Max couldn't
help thinking that time's passing had created pleasurable
reminiscences from what had once been less welcome political duties. In retrospect the lady was drawing on a
slightly fictional image of herself, as if to expunge her present non-involvement.

Their conversation was broken as Mrs Dean came in
pushing a trolley with refreshments. There followed a fussy
little ceremony with tiny plates and napkins, then cream
pâtisserie presented in silver tongs. For drinks they were
offered coffee, tea and a choice from a crowd of intrigu-
ingly shaped bottles. When Max and his hostess were
served, Mrs Dean seated herself alongside, poured herself
coffee and selected a heart-shaped pastry dredged in icing
sugar. So not the housekeeper, but a companion.

Mrs F-R was in spate by now on the subject of her brief
early period as lady-in-waiting to Princess Alice. Her plate
of pastry lay untouched on a side table as she lay back
alternately waving languidly and trailing one hand, for all
the world like a twenties picture of a flapper in a punt on
the Cam.

She went on to her part in the two most recent general
elections. Max saw no reason to take notes; there was nothing profound or quotable in what she said. It was just as
well that he'd had no serious intention of sounding out her
opinions, because she presented herself as central to the
scheme of things; all the big events were peripheral and in
the past. The woman was pathetic, not in any way material
for a column of topical comment, unless to be scathing
about.

As she spoke, she became more voluble, her colour

higher. She had refused the tea and coffee, preferring re-peated recourse to one of the bottles. More and more Max felt embarrassment on her behalf, and distaste at himself for leading the woman on.

He made some mention now of the fire at the family home, and was alerted by Mrs Dean suddenly leaning for-ward, seeming apprehensive how her employer would react.

'That was a long time back,' Mrs Feaist-Rivers said, waving a hand loosely as if plagued by a swarm of midges. 'We don't talk about it.'

And for a short while she seemed intent on demonstrat-ing this, falling silent, glass in hand, her eyes distantly brooding.

Mrs Dean rose and presented the cake dish again. 'Me-ringue, Constance?' she prompted, and the other let her deposit one on her plate beside the ignored éclair.

With a visible effort Mrs Feaist-Rivers recovered her vi-tality. 'Would you like to see over the house? I must show you my little collection of memor-mor-or—'

She took a deeper breath, carefully lowered her feet to the floor and stood with one hand on the high back of the lounger. 'Mem-or-a-bil-i-a,' she said distinctly and with some pride. 'I'm sure you'll be interested, Mr—er—Harris. Come along, then.'

Mrs Dean fell in behind as Constance Feaist-Rivers pro-cessed on Max's arm, overtopping him by half a head. If she collapses, he thought, she'll crush me. It would be far-cical if it weren't rather sad.

'My little den,' the lady announced proudly as they ar-rived in a square room with its blinds drawn against non-existent sunshine. Mrs Dean busied herself switching on pink-shaded lights and the details became clearer.

Three walls were almost totally covered with photo-graphs, in most of which Mrs Feaist-Rivers featured. There was no chronological order, so that a sepia posed study of a debutante in white and ostrich plumes—surely Constance's late mother—appeared between a fat baby in monochrome and a more modern group at Ascot. There were Indian backgrounds, house party backgrounds, various European backgrounds, bathing scenes, tennis groups, hammock poses, cruise-ship poses, even hard-hatted entrance-to-coalpit poses, and groups of political wives both informal and in terminal Romanoff array. The dates, partly discernible from dress and hairstyle, showed the fat baby's progress to thickset teenager, to tall and imposing (almost anorexic) young woman-about-town, to imposing wife figure and ultimately to harassed mother caught stormy-eyed in confrontation with an angelic youth with yellow hair wearing cricketing flannels. His switched-on smile showed him more quickly aware than she of the camera's approach.

'Your son?' Max queried.

Mrs Feaist-Rivers leaned close, uncertain. Her reading spectacles were back in the winter garden.

'That's Robin, yes,' Mrs Dean answered for her. 'Just before he left for Sydney.'

Sidney whom, or Sydney Australia? Max wondered.

Mrs Feaist-Rivers drew their attention to a ring of keys suspended from a hook among her gallery of treasures.

'My last car's. My darling old Daimler. We went everywhere together. They don't let me drive any more. My health, you know.' She touched the keys tenderly, the romantic heroine fondling her last token from a dead love.

They passed on to examine an aerial photograph of an imposing stone-built house, its eighteenth-century symmetry broken by later additions, the whole set in landscaped lawns and shrubberies. Max lingered a moment studying it before passing on. This was the house which was later burnt down. Weren't there any happy endings in this woman's life? What had happened to the golden-haired son?

As he moved to take his leave, his hostess was fidgeting with her hair at a mirror down the hall. He dared quietly to put that question to Mrs Dean.

'Oh, he did rather well, I believe,' she said vaguely. 'Sheep-farming, I think.'

In which case it had been the Australian Sydney. 'Doesn't he keep in touch?'

The woman gave him a long, interrogative stare. 'From time to time, I imagine.'

Surely she knew what post Constance received? Especially as she appeared to be more of a minder than an ordinary companion.

Being steered to the front door, Max worked at full throttle on his thanks. In the car, leaving the driveway, he looked swiftly back. The door had closed on the two women. The whole house had a noncommittal air, giving nothing away. Perhaps there was nothing to be gained there. And yet...

He'd been digging for a connection; following up the rumour about her distanced husband. The visit had been invasive, could have offended. Yet he believed the woman had been left with the feeling that she had entertained him well.

And Mrs Dean? Would she be reporting back to Feaist-Rivers that the press had started poking about, on the lookout for scandals in the past?

The only unusual incident had been the fire, and that was fifteen or sixteen years ago. Which was about when Mrs Feaist-Rivers retired from public life. She would still have been quite young then. And she seemed to have no interests. A pity she'd not had a big family to keep her busy and abreast of new ideas.

So—back to the golden-haired son. His name was Robin. There'd been just the one photograph.

For a dangerous instant Max forgot he was on the motorway. He should have remembered before! There was nothing about the issue in Feaist-Rivers' biographical entry. So what had become of the boy? Even if he'd died, the fact would have been recorded. How old would this Robin be now?

In the photograph perhaps about seventeen. The background was the terrace of the Surrey house, so it was taken before the fire. By now he should be in his middle thirties.

But he didn't have to be Feaist-Rivers' own. Constance could have had a son before she married him, and for some reason they now kept the fact dark. And then the boy went to Australia, sheep-farming, according to Mrs Dean. It didn't sound as if he'd stayed in touch with his mother.

The only son of a lonely lady who'd given up on herself, preferring to live in the past? And she wasn't bothered about how he was? Did that seem likely?

I think, Max decided, I'd like to know more about Master Robin and his mysterious disappearance; like what the date was, and what else happened at about that time. It smacks too much of oldtime melodrama, the son of the grand house dismissed abroad to avoid a public scandal, and paid to stay there. A remittance man.

He made a late attempt to check his runaway suspicions.

This has nothing whatever to do with what I was looking for. If Feaist-Rivers kept a dozen mistresses there'd be no evidence of it at the house in Datchet. Right, so I've missed out on that one, but there's an interest here, something that doesn't fit. Admittedly, I'm not an investigative journalist, but I never could resist a puzzle. And somehow I'm suddenly a bloodhound on the scent.

He smiled wryly, thinking of Yeadings the professional bloodhound. They had agreed to keep the original rumour under wraps, waiting for the lengthy process of investigation by Special Branch to report back on the Gregory connection.

If there is a link between Feaist-Rivers' affair with Gregory and any indiscretions in his earlier life, he acknowledged, then it's tenuous in the extreme. But for what it's worth, I should pass it on.

But bother Superintendent Yeadings with such tittle-tattle? Admit to prying into the *wife's* private life? Hardly on. All he'd found was confirmation that the Feaist-Rivers marriage was a non-event these days. Which might make any public man feel himself entitled to seek alternative company.

Negative information, but he could pass on that much. If not to Yeadings, someone less elevated. There was Z, of course. He took a firmer grip on the steering wheel and asked himself sombrely if, behind all the probing, that wasn't what he'd been getting round to all along. An excuse to see the personable Rosemary Zyczynski again.

SEVENTEEN

THE LIGHT WAS PAINFUL, brutally white. It flashed suddenly on her and was as suddenly withdrawn. She could hear voices, coming like the waves of the sea, breaking and swirling about her, drawing the shingle away underneath as she tried to find her feet.

A man's face swam out of the mist that had replaced the glare. A mass of dimmer white, out of focus. One voice was insistent now, calling her Annie. But he was nobody she knew. She tried to turn her head away.

Then the words reached her. 'Your brother is here,' he said.

She opened her eyes fully. There was a second figure there. It wasn't the boy. Instead, a sallow beanpole of a man, with cavernous eyes, lean-cheeked: a sort of ballet-dancer's face.

'No,' she said inside, refusing him. She drew herself in, away from the threatening light and the deceivers.

Over the screen of her eyelids a viscous pattern flowed, colours running, a swirl of shapes constantly changing. I can mix what I want, she thought. And she wanted the boy: the boy as he was that time when his new mother invited her for his birthday.

HIS HAIR WAS BRIGHT yellow.

'Oh, they will get up to such tricks,' the woman said, fondly forgiving. 'He came home from school like that.'

'I got gated for messing about in the chemi lab.' He threw it out casually, smiling. 'It'll look weirder as it grows out.'

'I've rather come to like it,' the woman admitted.

Annie agreed. It made him look special. No; *showed* he was special. She admired his daring. Nobody stepped out of line at her junior school. The rule was—hair clear of your collar or tied back in a bunch. And heaven help you if you wore a ring or had your ears pierced.

She didn't know how to talk to him, but that didn't matter. There were other people there to do that, mostly boys and of about his age. He was fourteen years old today.

She trailed behind in their activity games, a head shorter than the others, unable to catch a ball well, never having tried to bowl. But she could swim, although she hadn't thought to bring a swimsuit. The families she knew had no pool in the garden.

His mother found spare trunks to lend her, so she imagined she could pass as a boy too, until they laughed because she had a flatness at the top of her legs instead of a bulge like them. But *he* didn't laugh, just stared, and she was grateful that he said nothing.

Cars came in the evening and their parents took the others away, but it was arranged she should stay over that night. Next day the boy's mother would drive her home, because the Lodds hadn't any transport.

There was supper on offer, but the boy whispered not to eat anything. They'd have a midnight feast on their own when everyone else was asleep. It seemed wonderful fun.

She awoke in total darkness to find him there, leaning over her bed and pressing on one bare arm until she opened her eyes.

'Here, take the candles,' he said, thrusting a package on her. He was wearing pyjamas and carried a canvas sling-bag over one shoulder, a torch in the other hand.

'Quiet!' he ordered as they stole past closed doors where the grown-ups slept. Tugged by one hand, and with her package in the other, she kept stumbling over the hem of her long nightdress. He stopped on the third stair up, put down his bag and fixed the skirt for her, twisting it like a rope so that she was left with a sort of blouse, then tucking the spare tightly up inside at the waist, so that it stayed there. It felt chilly but she didn't like to say so.

They went on up. She began not to like it. 'Where are we going?' she dared to ask.

'The attics. There's nobody up there. You can look out and see all the lights of Guildford. Just like stars.'

But she was afraid and hung back until he pulled her impatiently after him. 'Come on, *girl!*'

She knew what it reminded her of. Attics, and someone being pulled up there, unwilling. By the time they were there she was snivelling, but hoping he'd not notice.

But it wasn't cold any more. The day's stored heat hung under the roof, seeming to press down on them. A half-dead bluebottle buzzed intermittently in a dusty corner of the single sealed window. And when the boy spread the paper cloth and put out the cakes and trifles, the four candles which he lit and set at the corners of their feast added to the oppressiveness.

'I am the High Priest of the Sacrifice,' he intoned, smiling fiercely, and she laughed as he poured a red drink for her in a waxed carton. 'Drink to the Celebration of the Act.'

She drank and ate. She was thirsty and there were such lovely things to taste. On bare boards they sat cross-legged opposite each other, and, despite his yellow hair and the quite new way he noticed her, she felt she had never lost him, never gone away to be made into someone else. Next time she woke up she would be at their real home again, in her own bed, with her real mother coming in to open the curtains.

He was staring again.

She followed his eyes and felt shamed by what he stared at. She hardly dared ask, 'Does it matter I'm not a boy?'

He didn't answer, but he leaned over and touched her. It didn't seem that he minded. He moved across and began to stroke her hair, her shoulders, her arms. His fingers on her legs were hard, bruising the soft parts. 'Lie back,' he told her. He climbed over her. 'I shan't hurt you.'

But he did. It hurt and hurt and hurt. Muzzily she seemed to be the boy herself, beaten: thud, thud, thud. They were in the attic at the old house. This time it was happening to her. But she couldn't see properly. Everything was muzzy and strange. She clung with desperate fingers to the boy and tried not to cry out.

When she was little his screams had gone through her. Her own moans now were stifled in his chest, distanced by his body. She felt defenceless when he pulled away. And messed and sticky.

Just when she needed him to hold her he got to his feet and went to stand at the attic window; looking down, she supposed, at the lights of Guildford, which he'd said were like stars. And he held his boy's bit in his hand.

She floundered, trying to rise, but her head was swimmy. Falling forward she dislodged a candle, and it lay spluttering until suddenly a whoosh of flame swept over the wrappings, the cartons, the paper plates.

The boy swung round, shouted and came stamping barefooted on the debris of their feast. 'Little fool!' he hissed. He was angry with her, and she knew she had let him down, spoiled everything.

There was a horrible smell of charring, and she found that the hem of her nightdress, untucked now, was glowing, bubbling into a sort of black jelly. She beat at it with her hands and the little flame disappeared; the cloth fell away in charred pieces. She knew she would be scolded when she got back to Mama's. Tears kept welling in her eyes and she turned her face away to hide her guilt at it.

'You'd better tear that bit off,' he said shortly, already shovelling the mess from the tablecloth into his sling-bag with both hands. But there were still scorch marks on the floorboards.

'Here,' and he came at her with a knife, sawing jaggedly at the cloth until all the black had disappeared. 'You can say you tore it.'

She watched, awed, as he returned the knife to a little leather sheath strapped on his calf. He seemed able to cope with everything that happened.

'Listen,' he said, surveying the room before they left, 'someone's bound to come up in the morning to see what the pong is. It's best you say you know nothing at all. Pack that nightdress in your case. Say you slept right through, see? Then you won't get into trouble.'

She didn't want trouble. He seemed to understand that. If any came, he was willing for it to fall on him. Because he wanted to guard her.

Still shaky, and with her head quite muzzy, she could have done with a helping hand on the stairs, but he had his torch and his bag and went on ahead, alert for sounds of anyone moving on the lower floors of the house. She gathered her nightdress in one hand and clung with the other to the handrail, limping down, one foot and then the other beside it, on each stair.

He was waiting at the door to her room and went in with her, snapping on the bedside light. 'I've got a better idea.'

He gave her a funny little secret smile. 'I'll take your nightdress. Then you can just say you lost it. Your mother won't dare write to ask what happened to it.'

'But it's new.' She had gone with Mama to British Home Stores to buy it specially for coming here. It was a good one, bought extra large so that she'd grow into it, could keep it for years. Mama knew she wouldn't let it get lost.

'*Was* new. It isn't any more. Come on, I can't stand here all day.'

She looked hopelessly at him, then reluctantly pulled it over her head. He tugged it off roughly. She watched him roll the pretty stuff up and cram it into his bag along with the remains of their feast.

'Don't forget: if anyone asks you, you've been in your bed all night. Slept right through. Didn't hear a thing,' he reminded her sternly, before opening the door to leave.

Shivering again, but with her head reeling and burning, she climbed back into bed to the cold embrace of stiff sheets.

She never saw the boy to talk to before she was driven home. But at breakfast, when his mother demanded to know what she'd thought she was doing, wandering about with a naked candle in the night, he was out in the hall, looking through the doorway with a finger to his lips, reminding her. So she denied it. Which meant a lie, but they'd agreed to it.

Then his mother was twice as cold and nasty, calling her a wicked little liar. And irresponsible: she could have burnt the house down with them all inside it.

There was more trouble when she reached Mama's. Annie was sent into the tiny back garden while the two women spoke together, only being allowed in to say goodbye, and thank you, and how sorry she was.

All of which she did, not understanding. And not understanding the final sidelong glance the boy's new mother gave her, muttering something about 'bad blood'.

Mama was furious: she'd disgraced them. She'd been given this wonderful opportunity to make useful friends, and she'd thrown it away. She needn't think they would ever want to see her again.

Confused, and tied up inside her own lie, she could only go on saying what she'd said before. If she told the truth, maybe the boy would be blamed too, for taking her up there. The candles had been his, but his mother said there hadn't been any in the house; which meant that Annie had brought one with her, and hidden it away after the accident, for fear of being found out.

Everyone was quite sure she was to blame, creeping

round the house, being nosey. And she *had* knocked the candle over, so it really *was* her fault.

Sent to her room for the rest of that day, she lay on her bed, aching with misery, an outcast to everyone—except to the boy. He at least knew the truth, and by now he wouldn't be angry any more.

She remembered, as if it was a dream, what he had done to her because she was a girl. Much later, someone at school told her people did that to show that they loved each other.

She still felt it was like what the man had done to the boy when he was little. Because it hurt. But then it didn't seem so *bad*, because now she'd been hurt, like him. It was something they shared, and secret.

ON HIS WAY HOME, Beaumont looked in at the hospital. 'How does she seem?' he asked the officer on duty at Ms Gregory's bedside.

The man grimaced. 'She did come round briefly, but she seemed awfully groggy; couldn't recognize her brother when he came in. Since then she's gone under heavily again. The docs say it's quite normal to be confused for a while after what she's been through. But it's my guess they privately think there's a fifty-fifty chance of some permanent brain damage.'

'Right. Let us know at once if she does show signs of rallying again. We badly need her help to get that driver who ran her down.'

IT WAS TOO LATE now to catch Mott at work. Z came out of the station and waited her turn at the phone box, hunting in her diary for the inspector's home number while the stream of travellers thinned.

He answered on the third ring. 'Paula?' he queried, as she hesitated.

'Sorry, sir. It's Zyczynski.'

'Oh, Z. Yes.' His tone of voice had changed.

'I think I've found what I was after. Shall I give it to you now?'

'Over the phone? Better not. Where are you?'

She told him.

'Well, hang on, and I'll pick you up. Give me twenty minutes. I'm wet from the shower.'

'My car's only five minutes away, Guv. Shall I save time by coming to you?'

He hesitated, then, 'Do that, Z. I'll leave the door on the latch.'

Walking to the car park, head lowered against the sleet, Z queried her own motives. Hadn't those few sentences between them been a paraphrase of the proverbial 'Your place or mine?'

The suspicion wouldn't have occurred to her a week or two before, but just recently— Just recently, what? There was something rather different between the two of them, a tension unconnected with any aspect of their work: a new awareness of each other as breathing the same air, sharing experience. Needing the same things?

She had never been inside Mott's flat. This evening would make history. There was no call to hurry. Then, if she caught him still in his bathrobe it would be because he wanted it that way.

He was barefoot, but had changed into a tracksuit. He left off towelling his hair to open a bottle of wine. 'Drink, Z?'

'Lovely. I nearly dropped off on the way back for a stiffener.'

He turned to look at her. 'Why? What happened?'

She took the glass he held out. 'It went off fine at the beginning. No one questioned me, Annette and the MD were discreet. After he left I turned up something promising. There's a young member of the typing pool called Myra Shanks, at present on leave, due back on Monday.

According to her photograph she could be the one. She lives at home with her parents. The address is Slough.'

'Good. Any connection with Gregory?'

'Myra had recently been working in the adjoining office. Went on two weeks' holiday to an uncle in Canada. Flew out the day before Gregory was found injured.'

'Was in Slough at the time the car hire was arranged?'

'Probably. I can check that with her family before she gets back.'

'No. Maybe I'll go and see them tomorrow. What else?'

Z turned her glass, staring into the rich claret glow. 'I tried a little experiment.'

He was beginning to look stern. 'Did it pay off?'

'I'm not sure. Perhaps it did. Gave myself a scare, though. For a moment.' And she told him of her reconstruction of Miranda Gregory's Friday night return to the office.

'You were out of order, Z. God knows what you might have walked into. Never, ever, do anything like that again without back-up.'

'There was no reason—no logical reason—to suppose the office would be any more dangerous then than when I left it three-quarters of an hour before. Just a feeling that I ought to run through the actions, see if anything new came up.'

'And it was Gwen Lodd. Who hadn't been in all day, then decided to do so once everyone had gone home. How did she get in?'

'Probably the same way I did. Behind the downstairs porter's back, and then using a key to the Matherson and Corby floor.'

'So why did she come in?'

'To read through some files. Which could have been from a genuine desire to catch up with any projects she'd missed out on during her day's absence.'

'But you think she was up to something irregular?'

'We shan't know until I find out which files she was

interested in. I can get Annette to check for me. It was the second drawer down. She'd left a plastic divider sticking up as she closed it. It had either an E or an F label on the top.

'Whatever brought her there, it was something worth covering up. She was more than just startled at the thought of an intruder. Guilty, I felt. She seemed relieved to find I was someone unknown to her, and even then she was a damn sight too keen to get me out of the firm. I know I set her back up, but dismissing me on the spot was high-handed. She didn't even ask at what level I'd been recruited.'

'She could have come back after work in the same way the fortnight before,' Mott said thoughtfully.

'She wasn't working there then. She'd retired some weeks before.'

Mott jabbed a finger in the air. 'Or that's euphemistic for getting made redundant. And with Gregory wiped out she could be reinstated. Hardly a motive for attempted murder, though. Or has unemployment got to us so badly that we're killing to keep our jobs now?'

It seemed unlikely. 'Gwen Lodd was Gregory's adoptive mother,' Z pointed out doubtfully. 'And murder is most often a family thing.'

'Dammit, what was it the dead investigator had found out? It's plain crazy that the only record he seems to have had was the copy he intended handing to Ms Gregory.'

'Which he might actually have done, and then she disposed of it elsewhere.'

Mott gave a choking little laugh. 'Wouldn't it be just too rich if one of them had filed it there in the office? Under E or F. And you walked in on Gwen Lodd helping herself to the information?'

They stared at each other.

'Fanciful,' Z said, 'but life *can* be ironic. Maybe I should go back and take a proper look.'

'There's always Monday. Oh, cuss it,' Mott said carelessly, upturning the bottle. 'We seem to have finished that one. I'll get another. It's the end of a working week when we've been getting nowhere fast. Let's relax.'

Z stayed silent while he fetched more St Emilion and refilled their glasses.

'Your car should be quite safe outside,' Angus said. He was looking at her quizzically. 'We can ring for a cab to take you home. Whenever, or if ever.'

EIGHTEEN

Z WAS FAMILIAR WITH the Boss's facial expressions. Normally on encountering her he would slightly relax any hint
of grimness, then assume a paternally instructional air, or
else, keeping his head down over some procedural problem,
he'd finally glance round with a humorously exasperated
grimace, all eyebrows. He also had a gale-force glower, so
far used on her behalf but seldom at her directly.

This time she hadn't seen him coming—Saturday morning, and none of them needed to come in—so she missed
his initial expression. By the time their eyes met, his face
was a blank, and such inscrutability meant only one thing.
Whatever his reaction—and there certainly had been a positive one—he had swiftly wiped it off.

Disapproval, Z guessed. Because he was astute enough
to pick up a difference in the way Angus and she stood
together. She could feel it herself, was fired with it. It had
to show.

And beyond the judgemental, he'd be simply worried,
because he'd hand-picked his team and he wouldn't want
anything to happen that might split it up. Which must happen if...

If what? Now she was obliged to look at it squarely,
admit that so far what she was doing was no more than
experimental brinkmanship, but fraught with dangerous
consequences. Mott couldn't afford to get involved with
anyone in the job. They already had a firm relationship,
and it wasn't a sexual one. And there was Paula to take
account of too.

Wasn't it just her luck that the only time she'd been
really tempted of late was with someone totally out of

bounds? She couldn't afford to look for personal therapy, when keeping the team intact was of such importance.

'Sir,' she said to Yeadings, mentally coming to attention.

'It doesn't matter. Monday will do. I take it you're off now? Both of you?'

Mott hesitated. 'Officially we're not here. Z's just written up her report on her visit to Matherson and Corby. I wanted to check that no immediate action was needed on it.'

'And there's nothing vital?'

'Sir, I've rather blown it,' Z put in. 'In fact I got summarily sacked. By Gwen Lodd.' And she outlined her attempted reconstruction of Miranda Gregory's Friday evening return to the firm, and what had resulted from it.

'When she caught me I acted up, gave her good cause to think I was up to no good. I'm sure Mrs Lodd had no idea who I really was,' she ended.

Yeadings had already experienced some of Z's thespian repertoire and now permitted himself a wan smile. 'I'm equally sure. But, in any case, if Gwen Lodd has returned to work, it's better you don't continue there.'

'I'd found most of what I wanted. Personnel department keeps photographs of all employees, together with their CVs and annual assessments. There's a Myra Shanks, at present on leave, who answers to the description of the plump, blonde young woman the Slough clerk remembers applying for the hire car. And her home address is also Slough, only a few streets away.'

'She sounds a likely one.'

'Not that she'll necessarily know who sent her to make the arrangements. As discussed, sir, it would have been easy to leave the request in a memo on her desk, together with the stolen driving licence.'

'Which she would have returned to Ms Gregory's desk afterwards.'

'Or wherever her instructions said.'

But the superintendent wasn't listening. His startled gaze

had swept down the corridor past her. 'What on earth is that?'

She turned. It was Beaumont. Or part of it was. The rest was a low-slung dog affecting what looked like an affable grin.

'Hudson,' Beaumont introduced the beast. 'Wanted to be a police dog, but he hadn't the required height. He's a left-over from the suicide Lodd; must have starved for two or three days. He's perked up quite a bit since then.'

Yeadings had gone down on his hunkers and was scratching behind the basset's ears. 'Which he should do, fed by professionals. Shouldn't you, old chap? Well, I'm off home. You know where I am if anything comes up.'

They watched him retreat. 'What's this about professionals?' Mott demanded.

Beaumont grunted. 'Trust the Boss to sniff out gossip. I know I never told him.'

He grinned at the others. 'Cathy's helping out a buddy who has a catering business. She's started cooking the stuff at home and as family we get the uglies.' He sounded quite chuffed.

'Talking of which,' Mott suggested, squinting at his watch, 'it's rather early, but who fancies the Feathers for a pie and a pint all round?'

MAX HAD SLEPT on the notion, slept *with* it apparently, because when he awoke, Rosemary Zyczynski's face was still freshly printed on his mind. After showering, and before the ritual beefburger and coffee breakfast, he rang the number she had given Annette, and which he'd made a note of.

Z hadn't come in and wasn't expected, he was told. Disappointed, he left a message with switchboard, giving his own number. Later, as Z left with the others for the Feathers, she was handed a note.

'Look, I have to return a phone call,' she told Mott. 'You

others carry on. I'll follow—unless I get caught up.' She went back to the detectives' office to dial Max's number.

'The fact is I'd like your advice on something,' he began, and was slightly put off when he heard her laughing.

'Why the merriment?'

'Joke of the year, surely. That crestfallen tone really doesn't suit you.'

'There's nothing wrong with my crest. It's right up there where it always is. The problem's a should-I-shouldn't-I one.'

'I can't imagine how I could help you with that. Is it a question of expediency or morality?'

'I could explain better face to face. There's some information come my way and I'm not sure if it's relevant. Not knowing the whole of the game, so to speak. I don't like to bother your boss, especially because I rather stepped out of line to get it... Oh, I don't know. Maybe I'd best forget all about it.'

Z considered for a moment. His sudden switch to reluctance didn't fool her for a moment. It was just thrown in to whet her curiosity, make her feel that in turning him down she could be losing something valuable. She'd watched Max closely at Annette's and she could appreciate he was in full charge of his actions, was quite capable of using her for his own ends. Well, two could play at that.

'Do you want to come in and talk to someone?'

'Talk to you. But not officially. Could I pick you up in, say, forty minutes?'

She counted slowly to five before agreeing with apparent reluctance. In fact, although there was no need to advertise it, she *was* intrigued, as he'd intended. Not just by the bait he was ostensibly dangling under her constabular nose, but there was something about the man himself. She could see him quite clearly at the other end of the line, fine-boned, compact, slightly puckish, one finger pushing back the bridge of his spectacles as they threatened to slide down the tip-tilted nose. His mouth twisted with humour. A personality, totally male although by no means a muscle man. He had an appeal that wasn't instantly physical, but promised...

'Are you still there?' It sounded like genuine dismay.

'Sorry, I was thinking. I'm leaving here now. Going for a bite of lunch. Pick me up from the town centre, opposite McDonald's, would you?'

'God forbid! Don't eat. I'll bring something with me. We can picnic when we get there.'

This was getting out of her depth. 'Get where?'

'Deepest Surrey. Sun's coming out. It's a lovely day for a drive into the country. In forty minutes, then.' And he was gone before she could protest.

In the Feathers, where they had caught up with an equally thirsty Mike Yeadings, Beaumont moved along the bench to make room for her. 'No thanks, I'm not staying. Got to get home and change. It seems I'm being taken for a ride, in one or other sense of the expression.'

She met Mott's alerted eyes squarely and explained, 'With Max Harris.'

Angus didn't betray by a flicker that he'd picked up the full significance of this. She meant to let him off any imagined obligation after last night, while demonstrating to the others that her interest lay in someone else.

'Personal or business?' he ventured to ask.

Rosemary smiled. 'It's Saturday. I rather fancy a picnic in the woods, if we don't get rained off.'

'Better be prepared for the worst,' said Beaumont in a voice heavy with suspicion of villainy.

'Yes. Raincoat and wellies,' Yeadings interpreted lightly. 'Well, don't keep the gentleman waiting.'

She was conscious of all three staring after her as she left.

'Max Harris has suggested another angle on the Gregory

hit-and-run,' Yeadings murmured into his lager. 'A bit iffy as yet, but there's a chance he may be going to hand her something we can use.'

MAX HAD ASSEMBLED the makings of his picnic in a traditional wicker hamper. It stood beside a folded plaid rug on the rear seat of the tan Toyota.

'Once my maternal grandmother's,' he claimed when she admired it. 'Willed to me with the command that I should remember her. As if I could do otherwise, the old harridan. Ah, we had some rumbustious times together.'

'In Scotland?'

'Keen ears. I thought my southern schooling had covered up the accent.'

'You told Annette you went abroad too. With your parents.'

'My father was in the Foreign Service; in Egypt, Lebanon and Iran. Where I picked up some Arabic, French and German. I had his knack of mimicry. I wasn't diplomatic enough to follow in his career or teach. Which just left newshounding, first as Middle East staff correspondent. I eventually had enough of in-flight catering and living out of a suitcase, went for a softer option in the UK. I still do freelance foreign news comment as well as my regular general feature. But somehow I've never quite managed to settle in London. Live little better than a squatter. You'd find me rather a squalid fellow, I'm afraid.'

Not a sharp dresser, she'd agree, but he had a certain style. 'And you hung on to Granny's hamper.'

He turned and smiled at her. 'I've a few more treasures squirrelled away. Maybe this evening you'd like to come and see my grotty dray?'

The prospect stayed with her as they travelled out into rural Surrey, bound for Bramley, a name which made her think comfortably of cooking apples.

Their final route took them past a high wall topped by

ancient trees. A modern bungalow had replaced the original lodge, and the iron gates stood permanently open.

They rattled over a cattle grid to enter and passed up a long metalled track with pasture railed off on either side. At the top of the gentle incline the drive curved through a copse into rough grassland, at the centre of which they saw the ruined foundations of a large house, and low farm buildings behind it, at right angles.

'The Feaist-Rivers' homestead,' he explained, 'destroyed some years ago in a disastrous fire. Let me tell you why I'm interested in him.'

'Would it save time if I said I'd seen the account of your interview with Mr Yeadings?'

Max turned to look at her. 'It seems he trusts your discretion as much as I do.'

'He asked me to type his notes out. As yet the information's too sensitive to be put in the computer.'

'I see. What I wanted your advice on was my follow-up at his wife's place down at Datchet.' And quickly he outlined his conversation with Constance Feaist-Rivers.

'So this is where they used to live before they became semi-detached. But I can't see why you think there can be anything here to link with Feaist-Rivers' interest in Miranda Gregory.'

'There isn't, I'm afraid. It's just that the man sticks in my craw somehow. Possibly because I don't know enough about him personally, but I am familiar with the climate he functions in.'

Rosemary nodded. 'He has power, but it makes him vulnerable.'

'Exactly. A prominent man has most to lose. There may have been details Gregory could disclose to make him seem politically untrustworthy. Since he'd sloughed off what family he had, his career would be of first importance to him. He's spent time, labour and money to get where he is now. There are younger, keener men crowding behind him.

If he fell, they'd walk over him. His only chance is to go on and ever upwards, with the tantalizing possibility that some day he'd even make it to the top.'

'And Miranda Gregory was employing a detective from the Midlands to gather certain information in London,' Z added thoughtfully. 'So it wasn't only her personal relationship with Feaist-Rivers that she could have used against him. It's thought that the detective was due to report to her at Matherson and Corby that Friday evening when he was shot dead and all his papers on the case disappeared. Which are what we believe link that murder with the apparent attempt to kill Ms Gregory. Now you're laying both crimes at Feaist-Rivers' door.

'That's nasty,' she said shortly. 'But then, whoever did it, it's nasty. And if your guess is true, he's the only person so far with any known reason to hurt her.'

'I'm glad you see it that way too. I have to go on probing. Anything at all I can learn about the man's past may serve to eliminate him or mark him out for the attempt on her life. Suppose, for example, that she somehow learned he'd fired his own home for the insurance. A charge of arson would destroy him.'

'So what's your next move?'

'Someone else is tackling the Westminster end, but I'd like to prove that at some point Miranda Gregory had come down here.'

'Yes. They had to meet somewhere, and it wasn't at her flat in Beaconsfield. She seems to have become invisible outside her work.'

'As you can see, the old family home was pulled down after the fire, but Feaist-Rivers never sold off the estate. There's bound to be some cottage on it which he could use as a love-nest without causing too much stir.'

Z regarded him sternly. 'You should leave that for us to check on.'

'Superintendent Yeadings will be busy with other angles.

I thought an unofficial visit might stir up a less wary reaction. Anyway, perhaps you'd stay put a moment, while I
root around?'

Max let in the clutch and the car rolled past the ruined
foundations towards the further buildings. He got out, am-
bled across to the farm's open doorway and called in. Z
saw him stand a while talking to someone unseen, then he
came back towards the car followed by a large woman who
continued drying her hands on a kitchen towel.

'Come in, m'dear,' she invited Rosemary. 'Mebbe a cup
of tea wouldn't come amiss?'

The woman's name was Garnet Black. 'All the family's
named after stones,' she said proudly. 'Dad's idea, starting
with Jasper.'

It seemed that Max's fame had already reached her. He
was claiming to be researching an article on Constance
Feaist-Rivers.

'Used to be a lady-in-waiting,' said Garnet, intending
they should be impressed. 'I'm a bit of a one meself, only
the right man don't seem to come along.' And she roared
with fat laughter.

'Sad about the house going,' Z suggested, to get her
started on the required subject.

'Ah, well. We don't talk about that.'

Which had been exactly Mrs F-R's comment, Max remembered. The official handout, then. But with Garnet
Black it was no more than a form of words. She was happy
to discuss all aspects of it.

'Were you around at the time of the fire?' Z pursued.

'Right here, till me mum got us all out of bed and down
by the lake. We could see it through the trees, though,
flaring and crackling. Went up with a great whoosh when
the roof fell in. Real fireworks. Lucky there wasn't no one
inside at the time.'

'Yes, indeed. Were the family away?'

Garnet hesitated. 'Had been, but they'd come back. They

was out. But someone was there in the afternoon, because I saw one of the cars round the back, and it had gone later. Two o'clock next morning it was before they got back, and by then it was well under way. Guildford sent a fire tender and ladders but it was too late to do much more than drench the farmhouse here to stop it spreading.

'Must have started upstairs, they said; then the top floors fell through. Some old electric wiring the mice had been at.

'Us all go to bed early, being busy folk, so we didn't know nothing until me dad was roused by the phone after midnight. It was our neighbours over Wonersh. They'd seen the blaze and wanted to be sure we was safe.'

'It must have been awful,' Z sympathized. 'I bet everything stank of smoke for weeks.'

'Months, more like. Us kids useda go across and pick over what was left of it, and I mind we was always getting our ears boxed for traipsing the mess in. Mum was a right tartar for keeping everything nice. Not like I let it go now.'

'And there'd have been firemen coming to investigate, and police, and insurance people asking questions. They always make such a fuss,' Max mused out loud.

Garnet frowned. 'Not so bad, really. Anyway, there wasn't no inspection by the insurance, because they didn't have none. That's what sent Mr Feaist-Rivers through the roof. Well, he would've if there'd been any roof left to go through.

'He swore he'd kept the premiums up, but it seems he never did. Me dad said he shoulda known better, him a magistrate and all.'

'This was while he was a Member of Parliament?'

'Musta bin. Not that that crowd have a lotta sense. Try some of me jam with that scone, miss.'

Max nodded. 'Does he come back much? To stay in the neighbourhood, I mean?'

'Never. Shook the dust of it off his shoes, like.'

'So after the Hall went, that was when the family began
to break up. Constance found a house back near Eton; her
husband took a flat in London. Young Robin went abroad.'

The cake platter in Garnet's hands slid to the table with
a thump. 'She never told you about all *that!*'

'Not as a subject for writing about,' Max said hastily.

'I should think not!'

Garnet stood, arms akimbo, flushing to the roots of her
hair. 'I never woulda thought it,' she said. 'After he was
sent away, everybody agreed we wouldn't say nothing
about him ever again. Just as if he'd never been. I thought
Mr Feaist-Rivers would go mad. Saw us right about it,
though, paid all me expenses and a bit more, I'll say that
for him.

'Said it had been a crazy fancy, and his wife was feeble-
minded ever to have taken the boy in. But it was his name,
see. She thought it meant he belonged to them. A sign from
God, or something. And she was younger then, musta been
very pretty, if the photos are anything to go by. He'd let
her have her way. Indulged her, like, because she couldn't
have none of her own.'

Max nodded encouragement. So Robin hadn't been a
natural son, just adopted.

'But the lad came from a bad background and he never
brought nothing but grief to them. Poor lady, she couldn't
believe any wrong in him up till then. Well, I s'pose he
had us all fooled for a long time. That little sister of his,
and all.'

'There were two of them, then? He had a sister?' Z was
finding it a little hard to keep up. According to Max's account to the Boss, Constance Feaist-Rivers' gallery had
held no photographs of any small girl but herself.

'Yes. I remember her, because she'd be about my age.
Skinny little thing; wouldn't say boo to a goose. Came to
the boy's birthday party once at the big house, cat's ages
back. I wasn't invited, of course, but they useda send me

some of the goodies down afterwards. *Scrumptious,* that's what! Never tasted anything like it. They musta cooked enough for a regiment.'

'You're a pretty good cook yourself,' Max flattered, brushing imaginary crumbs from his jacket.

Z picked up the changed tone of his voice. 'I guess we ought to be on our way,' she put in. 'Thanks for everything, Miss Black.'

With cheerful good wishes Garnet saw them off, leaning in her doorway, reluctant to lose congenial company.

'H'm,' Z muttered, strapping herself back into the car. 'Did you get what you wanted from all that?'

'Not exactly,' Max said. 'But I did pick up that young Robin had started to exercise seigneurial rights. And somewhere there could even be a chip off the Garnet block. What do you think?'

'Maybe. She was quite put out at mention of him. But if she knew about Mr Feaist-Rivers' extra-marital activities with Miranda Gregory, she wasn't letting on. If there were any, I don't think he operated locally.'

They continued in silence, Max seeming to have much on his mind. Garnet Black's hospitality allowed thoughts of lunch to be temporarily shelved. They drove as far as Windsor Great Park before he stopped the car and suggested they took a walk.

Despite bright sunlight, the wind whipped at their coat ends, stung their faces and blew them towards the cover of giant trees. They made a wide circle and came out above a broad panoramic view of the flat, silver-blue Thames valley. When they reached the car again they were glad of its protection and had worked up their appetites afresh. They did justice to the contents of Max's old hamper, washed down with a good claret. Finally they shook out the crumbs for an insistent crowd of birds.

'Robin,' Max said thoughtfully.

Z screwed up the last foil wrapping and glanced across. 'No, it's a female blackbird.'

'You're right. It is. But I was thinking about the *name* Robin. Garnet said Constance Feaist-Rivers had taken to the boy "because of the name". She had thought it meant he belonged to them. A sign from God or something. Now why should "Robin" mean that to her?'

'Not just to her. To *them*,' Z corrected, proud of her verbatim memory.

'You're right again. So perhaps she was referring to the boy's surname?'

'I suppose it might have been either Feaist or Rivers, but surely not both?'

'The question's hardly germane to what we were trying to find out,' Max regretted, 'but it niggles me. Feaist-Rivers' current *Who's Who* entry makes no mention of any adopted child. I wonder if earlier ones did.'

'It's too late to try for a reference library. They close at midday on Saturdays.'

'Not to worry.' Max had started packing away their picnic remains with a new urgency. 'Back home I have a set going back to the year dot. I did warn you what a collector I am. One wall of my workroom is solid Wisden, the other is packed with other yearbooks. Come on, we'll go and satisfy our curiosity.'

Z was intrigued to find that his 'dray', as he'd called it, was a sunny flat in a crooked lane off John Islip Street in Pimlico, not far from the Tate. As he'd said, one wall was dedicated to cricket, another to a broad selection of information.

He had no success starting with more recent editions of *Who's Who*. They contained lengthy accounts of Feaist-Rivers' activities but, as family, mentioned only Constance his wife. Max walked alongside the shelf to take down one for the year 1975. He riffled through it, stopped to run a finger down a page and gave a satisfied grunt. 'Here we are. "Adopted son, Rodney." And then, in brackets, "Robin". Apparently a pet name.'

'Rodney,' Z echoed, frowning. 'That's a coincidence. Miranda Gregory's half-brother's a Rodney.'

Max was nodding. 'Rodney Fairburn.' He looked up sharply, watching her with a smile on his lips. '*Burn*—a small version of a *river*. And if you're determined to find a connection, a *feast* and a *fair* aren't so very different after all. Fairburn, for Feaist-Rivers.'

Z gave a low whistle. 'So Constance twisted the two surnames together in a sort of word game. That was the connection that made her think the adoption was "meant to be".'

'Exactly. When Annie Gregory went to the Lodds, it must have been Julian and Constance Feaist-Rivers who adopted the older half-brother, Rodney.'

Z's face lit up as she made a leap of supposition. 'And Miranda originally got in touch with the MP for help in tracing her half-brother! Somehow she'd found out that he was back in this country, in London. Could that even be what she employed the detective Collins for?'

Max was rubbing the bridge of his nose, having deliberately removed his spectacles. 'Z,' he said, 'I think I'm going to kiss you. I can feel it coming on.'

Since he was at heart a little old-fashioned, and this was their first date, he might have enjoyed it and left it at that, but by then Z had made up her mind. Max wasn't just the next man along. He had something rather special.

Some time later he murmured into her hair, 'I'll come quietly, officer.'

'Don't you dare,' she warned him, laughing. 'I like a man to show a little fight.'

By the time they considered informing Superintendent Yeadings of their less personal discoveries it was too late to disturb him. It was, however, of sufficient interest for Z to ring him at home after eleven on Sunday morning.

'You've not been called out, I hope?' Nan said accusingly as her husband put down the phone.

'No. Provided with food for thought. I'll take a spade to the vegetable patch and chew things over down there.'

With his gardening gloves on, he changed his mind and rang Angus Mott to inform him of the Fairburn/Feaist-Rivers connection.

Angus responded as expected, and had news of his own to pass on.

'Guessing that Myra Shanks would be flying back from Canada yesterday, I called on her this morning. Shanks claims that Miranda Gregory asked her in person to hire the car from the Slough firm. Gregory explained that she wouldn't use her own car that weekend because she wanted to surprise someone.

'Since Shanks only landed late last night, she hadn't heard about the hit-and-run. I had no doubt it was news to her. The girl was very upset about Gregory's injuries.'

'Gregory wanted to "surprise someone",' Yeadings echoed thoughtfully, 'but in the event it was the other way round. Now just why would she want a different car for this surprise, Angus?'

'Like we'd use an unmarked one? For observation purposes. I'd say she was out to do some spying. Subsequent to whatever Collins had found out. And if she got the information she wanted, the object of it was alerted, and determined she shouldn't live to make use of it.'

'M'm,' Yeadings agreed. 'And how does that fit in with what Z has just found out down in Surrey?'

'It gives us a choice to go after: a junior minister in the government, or possibly a TV director. Which of those two had she used to lead her to the other?

'Or could it be yet another person from her past? Her adoptive father who committed suicide soon after the failed attempt to kill her: an OD called Lodd.'

NINETEEN

SHE HAD BEEN LYING THERE for some seconds with her eyes half open before the constable reading beside her knew. Lowering the magazine slowly, afraid that any sudden movement might startle her, he leaned forward, ready to press the bell, then hesitated.

As soon as the nurses came he'd be hustled away, with no chance to get a word from her. She looked—not well: anything but—a little more alive, but foggy. There was a blankness to her gaze.

He knew Dr Dennis had wanted her family to be with her when she came to. Instead there was only himself, and the uniform might put her right off. But he could speak to her, could try to rouse her as the others would have done.

It was, he saw, a unique chance to get her to remember what had happened. If only a few details of that last scene came back, they might lead to the bastard who'd run her down. And it wouldn't do himself any harm in the promotion stakes if he came up with the bingo score, with the big nobs in the offing and all.

He leaned further forward and whispered, 'Annie.' It was the name she'd reacted to before. He wasn't sure whether her eyes changed ever so slightly. Was she listening?

'The car,' he urged her. 'Can you remember the car?'

Her lips came stickily apart. He wiped them with the damp cloth as he'd seen the nurses do, then dipped it again and squeezed on a little water from the jug.

'The car,' he insisted. 'Remember? It was red, wasn't it? Did you see who was driving?'

Her mouth trembled but no sound came. Her eyes took on a strange urgency. Perhaps it was fear. He knew she wanted to speak and couldn't. She shuddered and the half-dead eyes closed again.

He sat back, disappointed. He'd done all he dared. No point now in calling anyone to come.

THE CAR. It stopped beside her at the lights, a red sports model. With two young men in it; students. You could tell that from the way they wore their big scarves wound round, one maroon and silver, the other navy lined with red. Rod—and he still had that yellow hair—with a friend of his. So now he could drive, had his own car, was grown up. She was little more than thirteen, but had been a woman for over a year.

They didn't see her until she walked out into the road, and then the friend made a noise at her, drooling over the short gymslip and the long, long, opaquely black legs. Which made Rod glance across. And she waved.

It was a bright April day and she'd slipped out from school at lunchtime to buy Mama an Easter card. Uncle Peter had given her the money that morning. She'd carried it tied in a handkerchief in her gymslip pocket. A wonderful day with scudding white clouds and sudden sunshine, much more wonderful when it brought her the boy. The boy, a man.

There was no question of going back to classes. Wedged between the two of them, she was setting off for adventure. Unsuitably dressed to be seen with them in any restaurant, she stayed in the car while they fetched things from a pub, and they picnicked—*al fresco*, Rod called it—on a hillside above a wood, miles from anywhere. Their own desert island.

A sudden shower drove them back to the car, with the men carrying her between them, because the drink had made her wobbly.

She woke up at the house, still just the three of them, Rod's people being on holiday abroad and the servants out.

She felt flushed and strangely excited. She whispered that she wanted to go with him up to the attic.

Although she had seemed to be half asleep, she remembered things he had done. Because he loved her, like she loved him. And again it hurt and hurt. There was blood afterwards, although it wasn't the time for that.

Later she was in an upstairs room with books all up the walls, and one of them—he was called Gobbo—was wearing her black stockings. He had a strange face. The top half was all right, but under his nose—because of some accident, or perhaps an operation—the flesh was crooked and puckered. His upper lip had a sort of join, badly done, and it made him talk awkwardly, through his nose. But although he was ugly and frightened her, Rod seemed fond of him. They were rolling together on the carpet like playful dogs, grunting.

She'd got some blood on her clothes, and from them on to papers on the desk where they'd piled her things. When she tried to dress again she got it all wrong and was suddenly sick, but the others didn't notice. She wrapped everything in her blouse, got herself to a bathroom and lay on the floor until she felt well enough to try rinsing the mess off.

But the papers were pappy and smeared. Two were envelopes left ready to post. Because she didn't dare put them back like that she hid them next to her skin with her clothes on the top.

The rooms with books in looked pretty well wrecked. It was lucky Rod's mother didn't much mind what he did. But later, when it started to get dark, even he seemed upset, sitting moaning with his head in his hands. 'We gotta get her back,' he kept saying, and she cuddled up, trying to comfort him.

Which was how he felt the bundle of papers, lumpy through her clothes, and he made her show him. She thought he'd be angry, but when he'd opened some out and read them he kept laughing and laughing. He dropped them into the waste bin under the desk and used the lighter for their smokes to set the thing on fire.

She could still feel more paper scratchy under her vest. She tried to reach for the ones he was burning but, clutching wildly, caught the edge of the bin and it went over.

It was right near the curtains, and bright tongues leapt up, licking at the brocade. Rod was still howling with laughter as he dragged them down and rolled them to stifle the flames. She thought Gobbo was on the floor at the time, out cold. It wasn't until they'd beaten all the fire out that Rod pulled Gobbo out on to the landing and came back for her.

They sat at the top of the stairs, and he suddenly crumpled. He was crying. 'Look what you've done,' he accused her. 'That's the second bloody time. Why don't you burn the whole bloody house down while you're at it?'

Next, they were outside in the dark, and Rod had started up the car, but it wasn't steering right and it was his turn to be sick. When she said she'd phone Uncle Peter to come out and get her, they seemed relieved. So she'd got one thing right.

Only she wasn't quite sure where she was by then, and it took him a long time finding her, while she sat on the floor of the country phone box, waiting. He was riding his friend's motorbike, and he wrapped her in a rug and sat her on the back. She held on to his belt so tight that she thought her fingernails would come off.

Mama was still out at her evening class, and he looked after her, bathed her gently and put her to bed, then climbed in to comfort her. That was the first time he did that when Mama was out.

They had to tell Mama something, because Uncle Peter had never before put her school clothes through the washing machine. She said she'd been sent home sick, and next morning Mama took one look at her and decided to keep her in bed.

Then some interfering person rang up to say she'd been seen in a car with two wild young men. So she admitted who they were and that she'd gone with them down to Bramley, but not what happened there, and certainly not that she'd come back on the pillion of the despised motor-bike.

So Mama locked her in her room for the rest of the week, on short rations, because she couldn't be trusted. And even then, for a few days afterwards she wouldn't speak a word to her. Which was no punishment anyway.

As in a dream, she saw a policeman leaning over her. His voice came like the sea, in waves of sound. 'An-nie...the...car.' But it was just the start of a nightmare. She knew this had never happened in real life. She could take no notice, and go on sleeping.

DCI MEREDITH GAVE the Met's approval for Z to go through the late Peter Lodd's things. There was only a slim hope of finding some connection with the Gregory hit-and-run, but the two had once been related by adoption, and his death—officially accepted now as suicide—had followed so closely on what appeared an attempt on her life.

The scientific experts had finished in the flat, but nobody had cleaned away the evidence of their work there. Z un-locked the door on to a stale smell that required windows opened in all the rooms. The contents of kitchen cupboards and refrigerator, where she began her search, indicated that for the most part the man had lived simply enough. There were, however, a few exceptional items such as an imported carton of Gewürztraminer with three bottles missing, and several small drums of herb flavourings with writing on in German.

A continental connection, Z told herself drolly. But any-one who took holidays abroad might widen their tastes to such things. She sniffed at the herbs and was satisfied they hid no sinister substances. It was rather sad, though, to think of the man, a declared solitary, bringing such innocent treasures through Customs. Perhaps now and again he had tired enough of a diet of sausages, eggs and oven chips to make a special meal with wine accompaniment.

Or had someone else dined there on occasion? Someone with more spicy tastes?

She remembered the Met's report mentioning a woman's clothes. There were three dresses hanging in plastic covers in a wardrobe of the second bedroom. A small quantity of underwear was folded in a suitcase. Why not in the empty drawers? And why no outer clothing, toiletries, shoes, umbrella?

Either Lodd's woman friend had left some time ago, taking her main wardrobe with her, or she visited briefly. There was yet another possibility: that Lodd had bought these things to wear himself.

Z examined the high neckline of a woollen dress under the kitchen's striplight. Although she could make out faint traces of make-up and caught a hint of perfume, that proved nothing. What she could not find was any plucking of the fine material from being worn close to stubble.

The underwear too, although of good quality, was not flauntingly sexy, as she imagined a transvestite would demand. The overall impression of the clothes was of unremarkable cut and colour, yet with pricey labels. Which seemed to indicate a woman accustomed to quality but not wishing to be noticed. Someone who perhaps visited seldom and then didn't stay long. Coming for what? To consult? For asylum? As a secret lover?

In the bathroom cabinet was a supply of remedies for headache and constipation, disposable razors, soap and talcum. No contraceptives. The only aftershave was an unopened bottle of a very superior brand. Perhaps, Z thought, a present?

The small sitting-room had an old-fashioned desk. Z pulled a chair across and began to go through the contents already examined by the Met. There were several hand-written shopping lists, and only two recent bills, both paid during the week before Lodd died. A Barclays cheque book showed careful entries of quite normal expenses. There was also an Abbey National account showing total savings of a little more than £8,000. He received a small pension from Wandsworth Council. Correspondence showed that he had taken early retirement from a post as school caretaker. A rather humble job for the husband of the efficient Gwen Lodd.

Beyond all that, some library tickets, tax particulars, a few *Reader's Digest* magazines. No personal correspondence of any kind.

Z put the kettle on for some instant coffee. While it came to the boil she went down to talk to the woman in the flat below. When she showed her warrant card, Mrs Goudge was disappointed.

'I thought you might be his lady friend. I heard tell he'd had one but I never saw her myself. She musta slipped in and out ever so quiet like. And if I heard voices, well, natcherly I took it for the telly. Nice man, he was. Quiet. Gawd knows what wild lot we'll get in there now he's gone.'

Z thanked her and returned up the outside stairway. The secrecy of Lodd's visitor intrigued her. How had she arrived so silently? If she'd driven there, so secretive a woman wouldn't leave the car close by. Parked it elsewhere then, and walked the rest of the way. An unremarkable car, because she wasn't inviting attention.

It struck her then, quite physically. A mental connection that went through her spine with a shock of excitement. Perhaps a *hired* car, to ensure anonymity—was that too wild a supposition?

Miranda Gregory had hired a car for the weekend she

was almost killed. Could she be the woman who used to
visit here? The one who'd worn the size 12 dresses from
the guest-room wardrobe?

Z abandoned her coffee. Where else could she look for
proof of the mystery woman's identity? There was no cellar
to an upstairs flat; only a small trapdoor in the passage
ceiling which would give access to the loft, and no obvious
means of reaching it.

She fetched the kitchen stool and could just manage to
raise one side of the unhinged trap to shine her torch in. It
showed only the water tank, lagged pipes and cobwebs.

There had been no hint of drugs, stolen goods or firearms
in this case. With the death accepted as a suicide, the Met
seemingly hadn't bothered to look up there. But she had
to.

A wooden laundry box balanced on top of the stool felt
insecure but gave her height enough to push the lid inside
and pull herself up. She stood crouched under the rafters,
shining her torch round the cramped space. Nothing. Not
even a trunk or suitcases, but behind one corner of the tank
there was a glint of shiny fabric.

Treading from joist to joist, she made her way round.
Something box-shaped appeared to be wrapped in waxed
cloth. She bent and lifted it, felt loose objects slide slightly
inside as it tilted. Under the waterproof wrapping the sides
gave a little, like cardboard.

She knew that she had found what she was looking for.

SERGEANT FOX, summoned by phone, was understandably
upset. 'Let's hope it's got a lot of rubbish inside, so we can
forget about it. If not, you've really set the cat among the
pigeons. Our men are supposed to have done a search job
on that flat.'

He taped the box, still unopened, with his own and Z's
initials on the seal. At the area station it was opened and

the contents listed: letters, photocopies of accounts, and glossy child-porn photographs.

DCI Meredith accepted these as strengthening his belief in the man's killing himself. 'It does look as though he was involved in some nasty business. A paedophile, and most likely a blackmailer too,' he told Z. 'I'll give your super a buzz and you can take him photocopies of all this stuff to see if it squares with your Thames Valley case.'

Which it certainly does, Z decided. All that's missing is a sample of the cord he used to truss Miranda before he faked the road accident.

Miranda: it was clear now where the name came from, and when. The most affectionate of the letters in Lodd's handwriting were dated some ten years back and began, 'My little darling'. And all were signed simply, 'Your own Prospero'.

TWENTY

THE BLACK SALOON TURNED out of Victoria Street into Artillery Row, took a sharp right and braked. The driver stayed with it in case some new face among the traffic wardens failed to recognize its number. DS Fox had Mott with him representing the Thames Valley force interest, and they were taking along a uniformed woman constable.

Gwen Lodd, warned in advance by telephone to expect the visitors, had rung through to Matherson and Corby explaining that she was unavoidably delayed. She let them in silently, white-faced but in perfect control.

In a sitting-room at the rear of the house there was no sound of the rush-hour traffic outside. It was prettily tricked out with Victoriana, the patterned fabrics impeccably fresh, the mahogany richly polished. The woman's family might have broken up, Mott thought, as they all seated themselves, but she was still a houseproud woman.

'You haven't told us all you might have done about your late husband, Mrs Lodd,' Fox accused.

She looked away towards the lace-draped window with a tight little smile. 'He had been my husband, Sergeant. How far do you expect a woman to go to be disloyal?'

He made no answer, watching her.

'I suppose something has—come to the surface.'

'I suppose it has, madam. What, do you think?'

A quick flash of anger crossed the stiff face. 'Really, this is insufferable. If you have no specific questions to put to me, I'm afraid I can't help you.'

There was a short silence. Fox's eyes flicked a request to Mott who stood up again and leaned against the mantelpiece, looking across at her. 'Very well. When did you realize that your husband was sexually interested in young Annie?'

She closed her eyes momentarily, tight-lipped. 'I was afraid it was that. You must give me a little time, Inspector.'

'Would you like the constable to make you some tea?'

'She could do that. I've left everything ready in the kitchen.' Her voice was low; she seemed to make an effort to summon lost dignity.

'You asked when I knew. Not until far too late. Not in fact until the child was pregnant by him.' She watched their consternation. 'Oh yes, my daughter was expecting her father's child.'

'Her adoptive father's.'

'My husband's.' A flash of barely concealed anger.

Ah yes, that hurt. She hadn't been able to conceive a child by him herself.

'And what happened to the baby?'

'I'm not a modernist, Inspector. I don't approve of abortion. Fewer people did in those days. Annie was sixteen, old enough to know it would be a sin. She could pass for eighteen; I arranged for her to go away and have the child. Then it was adopted.'

'As its mother had been.'

'Just the same. The sins of the fathers...'

'But Annie hadn't been illegitimate.'

'No. Far worse: the child of a murderess!'

'It was manslaughter, Mrs Lodd. There was provocation.'

'Bad blood on both sides. The child had a double inheritance of evil.'

'So you blame her for what happened under your roof? There was no corruption by anyone else?'

'My husband was a weak man, Inspector. Kindly, but spineless. She played upon his feelings, heartlessly, and destroyed our marriage.'

The arrival of the WPC with a tray of tea interrupted proceedings. Mott waited until they were all served before continuing.

'Mrs Lodd, I believe Annie Gregory was only four when she first came to live with you. Are you suggesting that the child was a threat to your marriage even then?'

The woman's nostrils flared as she rounded on him, breathless. 'She was never innocent. She had seen too much. She and that brother of hers. But her looks were deceptive, and she took me in completely. I had trusted her, and she betrayed me wickedly.'

'You mentioned her brother. Were they close?'

'I made sure they saw as little as possible of each other. The few times they met were—disastrous.'

'He was older, I think.'

'About six years, yes.'

'So what were these occasions when they did meet?'

'The boy had been adopted by a very well-placed family. When they invited Annie to his fourteenth birthday party I saw no reason why she should not go. We had no car then, so she was to stay overnight and would be brought back next day.'

'Go on.'

'I was horrified afterwards, when they told me how—*abominably* she had repaid their hospitality.'

'In what way?'

'Sneaking about at night, prying into rooms she wasn't supposed to be in, carrying a lighted candle, of all things. And then stealing food from the kitchen to eat alone up in an attic. She'd always had this thing about attics. They seemed to fascinate her. She knocked over her candle and there could have been a terrible fire, but luckily the boy was returning from the bathroom and heard her crying. He went up and found her with her nightie smouldering. He was able to smother the fire before any real damage was done.'

'She must have been terrified.'

Mrs Lodd stared at him. 'You don't know the bold-faced little thing. She denied everything, swore she'd never left her room, slept the whole night through. Of course, when she was asked to show her nightdress she couldn't. She'd got rid of it. Such a pretty one I'd bought for her specially.

'They found it later under a bush near her bedroom window. Naturally the boy's family wanted nothing more to do with her after such behaviour. And I must say I felt much the same myself. I was so ashamed of what she'd done.'

'But they met again?'

'They must have kept in touch somehow. It was years later that I found out. She played truant from school to go off with him in his sports car, came back in a terrible state. Thirteen, she was then. Heaven knows what they'd been up to together. Drink, drugs, everything decadent, I'm sure. I knew then I'd never be able to control her, and I think it was from then that she started working on Peter. He never could believe what a bad girl she was.'

There was a silence in which they could now hear the faint hum of city traffic and the *hooh-hah* of a fire engine emerging from the Horseferry Road station.

'Have you any photographs taken in those early days, Mrs Lodd?'

'I could find some, I think.' She moved across to an ornate piano stool and removed the seat lid. 'There's this album you can look at. I don't want to see it myself; it's too painful.'

'That's all you have?'

'Yes. I had an old Ilford camera but something went wrong with the shutter. After she behaved so badly I no longer felt like taking any snaps.' She went back to her seat.

'Didn't your husband have a camera?'

'No. He wasn't artistic at all. His interest was machines,

bits of old cars and motorbikes. He thought they had a historical value.'

'How did he take the news of Annie's baby?'

Mrs Lodd drew herself up stiffly, kneading her hands in her lap. 'He was quite out of his mind. He even thought we might look after it ourselves. As if we hadn't trouble enough with Annie!

'I came home one day to find he had moved out, without leaving any address. That is when I first thought he might do himself some damage. But it has taken until now, all this time later.

'He had been an accountant, certified not chartered, but it was a respectable position. I heard he had lost his job and was unemployed. By then I was doing secretarial work, part-time, and I was able to support myself and the girl when she came home again. But Peter continued to go downhill. She had ruined him. He seemed to crumple up. All he managed to get for work after that was as caretaker at a secondary school.'

'Not perhaps a safe occupation for a man who was too fond of children?'

'He was perfectly all right with any innocent child. But Annie was corrupted.'

'Yet later you supported her application to join the same firm you worked for.'

'It was *much* later, Inspector. She was a grown woman by then and had good qualifications. We hadn't seen each other for years. I have tried hard to be charitable and forgive. I'm sorry if you think I sounded vindictive, but just at this moment, with Peter's death—'

Her voice was choked. She began to rock silently in her chair, one hand covering her face, the other across her breast. The woman constable went over and knelt beside her, offering comfort. Mott stirred uneasily.

'I'm sorry. So—sorry,' Mrs Lodd said wretchedly. 'What must you think of me? But, you know, even through the horrible business of the divorce, and afterwards, with all that pain and disillusion, I never—stopped—loving him. He was a good man. He hadn't deserved to suffer so.'

'PHEW,' MUTTERED FOX, slamming back into the car, 'the messes some people make of their lives!'

'And of others'. I think she told the truth this time. Earlier she'd said she and Lodd were left together when Miranda walked out on them. Now it's the other way about. Perhaps not an important difference; it just shows she'd been trying to minimize the personal scandal with the odd white lie.'

Fox shrugged. 'Well, that about covers it, as far as I'm concerned. Peter Lodd had reason enough to hate Gregory's guts. We may never get to know where and how they met up that day, but it's obvious enough what happened. In an outburst of anger he attacks the woman, they fight, he ties her up because she's a hellcat. Then he finds she's badly enough hurt for there to be an almighty row, a charge of GBH. So, to cover up, he fakes a road accident to finish her off, drives the car away and abandons it.'

Mott grunted. It sounded pretty wild, but no more so than some scenarios he'd known which later proved to be spot on. 'I'd like some solid evidence to back it up.'

'You've got the man's suicide. The Gregory business provides reason enough for that.'

Which was true. 'Okay,' Mott agreed. 'If you're happy it happened that way, I'll pass it to the Boss. With any luck we'll eventually get the Gregory woman to confirm the story.'

'SHE'S DEVASTATED,' Mott reported back. 'It's not surprising if she's bitter after all she's been through; obviously a strait-laced woman with old-fashioned standards.' They had been discussing Gwen Lodd's reactions to their discovery of Annie's abuse by her ex-husband.

'I'd like more photocopies made of all this stuff,' Yeadings ordered, gesturing towards the papers on his desk. 'I'll
take one set home to study at leisure. And Z should have
a set too. We'll meet and exchange impressions tomorrow
at nine, emergencies permitting.'

Children, he thought, weaving through traffic, a Rhein-
berger sonata rumbling away quietly on disc, children are
a complication because we see them with adult eyes.

An efficient, conforming, seemingly self-sufficient individual, Gwen Lodd had not understood the need for protection of the vulnerable young. Vulnerable and amoral,
because ethics were something you picked up by the way:
no one was born good, any more than born bad. He doubted
she'd done much for little Annie's moral education. The
girl would simply have grown to understand what it was
that worked in the new family, and what she had to keep
dark. Such a lot of the poor little mite's first experiences
had come under that second heading.

The photographs were appalling. He thought he could
just recognize in the drugged features of the lifeless doll
something of the adult Miranda in coma. Both had a fragile
spoilt beauty; both retained a curiously untouchable quality
that was heart-searing. They affected him in much the same
way as the blunt little puppy features of his own daughter
as she slept.

In the early days had Gwen Lodd watched over Annie
in that same way, experiencing her hurts, suffering with
and for her? It was harder for Yeadings, a father, to feel
the woman's part in this. He needed Nan's help. And Rosemary Zyczynski's, once an abused child herself.

Even knowing his wife as well as he did, her instant
reaction surprised him. Of course the photographs shocked
her, but she stayed silent, her eyes hardened and her mouth
became a single tight line.

'Who is the man?' she demanded at length.

'Unknown. Someone the photographer knew perhaps.'

'And who was the *artist* who set all this up?' Her voice was harsh with loathing.

Well, he should have known. Anger and the need for revenge were what came first to a woman's mind. Sorrow later.

'Yes,' he said half aloud. 'We have to find someone to blame.'

When, after supper, he let her read some of the letters the tears began. 'Poor devil. He loved her.'

'Nevertheless…'

'I know. Love and desire. It's a universal muddle we've none of us ever got neatly sorted. Mike, these letters don't go with the photographs. There's no connection. One is tenderness that overstepped the line; the other's obscenity.'

'I'm glad you think that too. You see, the man who wrote the letters had no camera, wasn't interested in that sort of thing. But the photographs are superb, an art form. Technically not quite perfect here and there. The camera hand may have been unsteady, but the intention was undeniable. I could almost believe that the person who took these—' He stopped, staring into the distance.

'What about him?'

'Later went on to perfect his art.'

Abruptly Yeadings got to his feet and made for the hall. Nan heard him at the telephone and listened, guessing who was on the line's other end.

'Angus? Get on to Rodney Fairburn. You know where to find him. Yes, there or at the studios. I want him in for questioning tomorrow, 11.00 a.m. No excuses accepted. In connection with the Gregory case, yes, but a possible charge arising from child-porn.'

TWENTY-ONE

THEY USED THE LARGER interview-room, which was a little less severe. The superintendent came in just as Mott was explaining about the tape-recording. Yeadings gave a low-key greeting to Fairburn and nodded for Mott to switch on. Despite the tape, Z sat alongside the door with a note-pad on her knee.

'I had the impression,' Yeadings opened, 'that you'd gone to Australia to take up sheep-farming.'

'That's the British for you,' said the young man languidly. 'Oz, the land of convicts, sheep and Crocodile Dundee. As it happens, we're quite civilized. In TV circles the world has a lot to learn from us.'

'You went straight into television? At nineteen?' He managed to sound genuinely interested.

'I had what they wanted, once I'd trimmed the Pom accent, learned Strine. I started as a general assistant; a bit of everything; then had a camera test and did some voice-over. Before too long I was doing small-town race commentaries and working up towards the serious stuff.

'My first big chance came with a war epic. I joined Equity, was the dumb Britisher who needed a helping hand from the tough home product. But I was too tall to go on lumbering round with little Nip captors for long, so I got killed off in the serial and transferred to a comedy about class-conscious Pom immigrants.'

'Did that suit you better?'

Fairburn indicated superior amusement. 'Badly enough to make me determined to find something other than acting. I directed some videos and did two films as assistant director, but I wanted creative freedom. I had ideas which I didn't intend offering up for someone else to get the credit. Then Milliken—you must have heard of Milliken—had his breakdown, went for drying-out. *The Walrus* was only a quarter in the can, with over half its budget used up. An unknown replacement would cost less, and I persuaded the money-men I was god-sent. I got it finished on schedule and without running up big debts. Came out little richer myself, but it made my name. I could pick and choose after that.'

'And eventually chose to come back to Britain.'

'Everyone makes mistakes, Superintendent.' He matched the lazy drawl with a big, toothy smile, projecting Role-Model Outdoor Man.

Such insulting confidence asked to be pricked.

'So are you now getting back behind the camera yourself?' Yeadings asked with quiet menace. 'There's a considerable market for the sort of stuff you were producing here before.'

Mott laid out the photographs like the start of a game of Patience on the table between them. 'We know who the girl is,' he said tersely. 'Who's the man?'

There was a rigid silence. After the first alarmed glance Fairburn avoided looking at the glossies. 'She gave you these? She *told* you?' He seemed to find it unbelievable.

'The man, Mr Fairburn.'

'A friend,' he admitted at last.

'He's no friend of hers.'

'Mine. We were at school together. Gobbo.' His voice was barely audible.

'Is that a nickname? What's he properly called?'

'George Bowden.' The man's face was a pale mask as he strove to control his state of shock.

Mott's lips tightened. Yeadings, aware of the strong antipathy sparked between the two men, took up the questioning again, softly, patiently. 'Why?'

The word hung on. Fairburn seemed not to hear at once. His eyes were shadowed. He scarcely seemed to breathe.

Then he frowned, forcing himself back into the immediate present, freshly aware of the investigators facing him. 'You mean—why did I give her to Gobbo?'

He paused. 'I owed him, I suppose. He wanted it. He was curious about girls. He'd never had one.'

'And you had?'

A brief shrug that Yeadings took for indifferent admission. He leaned closer.

'You'd had *her*, your *half-sister*.'

'Annie, yes. A long time back.'

Yeadings nodded. He'd called her Annie; so he meant the child, not the woman. 'And since then?'

An impatient gesture with one hand, dismissive. 'Females, I can take them or leave them.'

'Men, then?'

Again the words hung between them. The silence was answer enough.

There was something more, though. Yeadings watched the haunted eyes avoiding his own. 'And Gobbo?' he asked quietly.

At last the man faced him, in naked pain. 'He died. Two years back. In Oz. We'd gone out together.'

'So that is when you came back to this country.' Yes, he saw it now: Fairburn had returned changed, adult, and Miranda would never have recognized him as the younger 'Robin' Feaist-Rivers. Perhaps she hadn't actually met up with him. But she got to know he was here. Someone had told her, and she'd begun looking for him, through a private detective.

'I—I've changed.' It seemed his mind had been following a similar track to Yeadings'. 'I have my work. That's what really matters. All this'—he waved contemptuously towards the photographs—'is in the past. It doesn't mean anything.'

To him, no. But others hadn't so lightly dismissed it. 'Yet you'd kept the photographs. I'm surprised you didn't destroy them.'

'I would have done long before now, but he found them. He threatened me!'

Patches of bright colour appeared high on the man's cheeks. The flash of anger came as sudden warning of his precarious mental state. Changed, yes—but into what? Chameleon changes, Yeadings guessed. Fairburn hardly knew what he was any more, so easy was it for him to move among optional personalities. Still the actor, and barely controlled by the director part of himself.

Mott invaded the new silence by demanding, 'He? You said "he" found them. Do you mean this Gobbo?'

'Julian, of course. Feaist-Rivers.'

He sounded impatient, as though he found his questioners thick-skulled. 'It was a bad time. There was trouble over a farm girl I'd been having it off with. She got in pod. Julian was on the rampage. He went through my things, and he found these prints.'

'And that was why he packed you off to Australia?'

'He never did. I *went*. Constance scraped me some money together and I—' His mouth snapped shut, his eyes slyly shuttered.

And the fire? Yeadings was wondering. Was that his final vicious adieu to the family that had raised him?

But Fairburn was offering nothing more.

Mott seemed to have come up against a brick wall. 'How did you get in touch again with Miranda?'

But the man had had enough of questions. He closed up. They waited, but it was obvious he wasn't going to speak again. Yeadings put the photographs together, rose, nodding to Mott, who formally closed the interview, took out and pocketed the tape. He followed the Boss outside. A uniformed constable at the door went back into the room and stood guard.

Yeadings waited while Mott was given a label by the duty sergeant, sealed the tape with it and added his signature. They walked on together. 'What do you think?' Mott asked.

'Let's not be judgemental.'

'He corrupted the kid.' The DI spoke roughly. Every instinct in him condemned the man for a hedonist callously indifferent to any destruction his self-indulgences called down. And a queer besides.

'You're just seeing one thing,' Yeadings said mildly, forced into an attitude of tolerance by his inspector's strong prejudice.

'So what do *you* see?' Angrily. *'Sir.'*

'A chain.' He left it at that until they had reached his office. There he flicked on the coffee-maker and seated himself at the desk. He drew a pad of blank paper towards him and rested his elbow on it, watching his inspector.

Homosexuality troubled Mott. He found it incomprehensible because he saw it from the wrong end. The act offended him: it was depraved. He had not considered there might be love.

Love did more than make the world go round. It held it together. In chains.

Love—in all its different versions—was the key to this whole case, Yeadings saw now. Love denied, love frustrated, love betrayed and defiled. And in the destruction of these unhappy people there was still a vicious connection he hadn't grasped yet.

Ignoring Mott's glower, he began to write a list of names, and then the same names in a different order. Until eventually the chain emerged.

While Mott saw to the coffee, Yeadings sat silent, drawing on his tobacco-free pipe. It gave needed comfort. The adult male's dummy, Nan once called it. Until he showed her how grimly his teeth bit into the stem.

As he reached for his steaming mug with one hand, the other crumpled the page he'd been sketching on.

Keeping it to himself, Mott thought resentfully. He watched while the Boss changed his mind, flattening the sheet out and folding it away in an inner pocket.

'Fairburn loved his friend Gobbo,' Yeadings said. 'And Miranda—no, I'm wrong: she was still *Annie*—loved her half-brother Rodney. So who loved Annie/Miranda? Somebody did. That's something we have to know to complete the chain. Who's available?'

'Do you mean the Briers girl?'

Yeadings gave a little *chk* of impatience. 'In a kindly, childish way, I suppose. But not obsessively, like the other links. No; as Nan pointed out, it was Peter Lodd. He knew who was the source of contamination, and it wasn't his little girl. He saw she was the victim.

'If he had any wish for vengeance, he wouldn't have wreaked it on his Miranda. It would have been on Rodney Fairburn. Why do you think he hung on all those years to those photographs? And where would he have got them from? The last we heard of them, they were in Julian Feaist-Rivers' hands.

'Lodd left his wife because of her harshness, not from shame. Read those letters again, Angus. It wasn't Peter Lodd who attacked Ms Gregory and ran her down with the car. Instead he killed himself in despair, believing his Miranda was going to die.'

ROSEMARY ZYCZYNSKI felt wrung out. It wasn't from any physical exertion, but pure emotional wear and tear. The elation of finding Lodd's cache in the loft had been swiftly followed by further doubts as she started reading through the contents.

The letters had been particularly difficult for her, starting as she did with utter contempt for any man who could take advantage of a child. But as she had gone through them, there was no escaping the tone of protectiveness in one set and the childish affection revealed in the other.

She found it hard to believe that, an unwilling voyeur, she could respond with sympathy; but the words on paper, divorced from any face or voice, spoke with an undeniable directness. He had loved the child. It was hard to see which of the two had led astray the other. Both must seem equally innocent.

No, it was wrong. If you started accepting a thing like that you were lost. In self-defence paedophiles often claimed pure motives; but there was a line drawn, and crossing it was unacceptable. Even with love, there had to be self-discipline. Hadn't she told herself that, only a day or so before, when she'd turned away from a full-blown affair with Angus Mott?

And if she could feel any empathy for poor Peter Lodd, shouldn't she re-examine her own experiences as a child? The revulsion she felt for her aunt's husband who had abused her?

Doubts of this kind were distasteful and exhausting. She turned from the photographs and letters to the sheets of accounts.

They appeared to have been removed from a ledger, cut out by a sharp blade. No, *two* ledgers, because the printed lines were of a different colour on some of them. She remembered that Lodd had once been an accountant. This information had come from Mott's interview with the man's ex-wife.

So what significance had these pages, that Lodd should hang on to them, along with such unpleasant matter as the pornographic photos, and his own and the child's letters?

Had he really intended blackmail, as was at first thought? He certainly hadn't made a successful career of it, his possessions and savings being pathetically few and simple.

And who would have been his intended victims? Only Fairburn, because of the photos, surely. Unless he also knew the identity of the schoolfriend Gobbo. The rest of his collection seemed to refer back to himself. He would have made a better victim than mastermind in blackmail.

The thought, lightly conceived, startled her when she looked at it again. Of course he'd not been blackmailed, because he held the stuff himself and his personal moneys showed no evidence of the regular payments you'd expect.

But—suppose it wasn't Lodd at all who'd hidden the box behind the tank in the loft. Suppose it was the woman who sometimes used to visit him secretly; Miranda, whose own home had been curiously empty of mementos and clues to her past.

In which case, Miranda had obtained, by some means, the shaming photographs of her own abuse. She would recognize who the man in them was; and she might well know who had been operating the camera. So what would she have done about it?

The Boss had thought she employed the private investigator to find her lost half-brother. Didn't possession of these prints give her a new and grim motive for running him to earth? And while Collins tried to trace him, she had approached Julian Feaist-Rivers on the offchance that he knew Fairburn's whereabouts in England, although scarcely willing to admit publicly to any connection with him. That had been severed long ago, after the fire.

Fire. Hadn't there been something in among the pages of accounts that rang a bell there? A loose cheque made out to the Sheldrake Fire and Theft Insurance Company.

She scrabbled through her pile of photocopies until it came to light. The signature, like the date, was illegible, but it was a long one. For some reason there were smudges and dark blobs on the copy. She wondered if these had been on the original or come from the photocopier. It was an old cheque, though, from the time before banks printed the drawer's name below the box for the amount.

Whatever the signature, she couldn't be sure where it led.

It was too much to go ploughing through any more. She rose, stretched, groaned when she saw the time, and sneaked off for a quiet shower in the hope that the gurgling cistern wouldn't wake her landlady.

YEADINGS LAY on his back in the dark, beside the humped form that was Nan. Sleep was impossible while his mind raged still on the interview with Fairburn, on his claim, 'It doesn't mean anything!' In his imagination he took the dialogue further.

'To you? No, it never mattered. But to her?

'Without a second thought you grabbed whatever you wanted, corrupted a child for your passing amusement. Worse, betrayed the innocent love she had for you. Substituted this pathetic Gobbo for yourself when she was incapable of knowing the difference!

'And when later your treachery is revealed'—Yeadings doubled his fist and beat at the mattress—'how bitter would she feel? What limits wouldn't she go to in order to bring you low, low as you'd once dragged her, throwing her to your creature?

'"A woman scorned"—you know how it goes. "Hell hath no fury."'

His eyes burned into the darkness as he confronted the man's ghost. 'So did she threaten you with the very photographs you'd taken of her; this proof of your true nature? So you felt compelled to destroy her?'

TWENTY-TWO

WEDNESDAY MORNING DAWNED with fitful showers, but the cloud cover seemed to be wispily pulling apart. As Yeadings shaved by the bathroom window the first direct sunlight shot dazzlingly through. Basking in its warmth, he dared to believe that the Gregory case might also be about to break open.

But there was vital evidence missing; even vital connective assumptions. He needed to talk with Julian Feaist-Rivers, and privately. There were gaps which only he could fill in, yet a junior minister of the government had to be approached with great care. He would be wary of possible scandals arising from whatever information he gave, whether concerning Miranda, or her half-brother. Apart from any implication of recent sexual involvement with the woman, a link with either would certainly bring bad publicity; and in the interest aroused by a subsequent arrest the press would not overlook a VIP's connections.

An application to interview the minister should be made formally through Thames Valley's chief constable; but this could appear accusatory and place the man on the defensive. Better perhaps to use an intermediary who was part of Protective Security. Feaist-Rivers could be as loth as Yeadings to have the approach officially recognized.

So it was through Maybury of SIS that Yeadings decided to gain access: the adept manipulator disguised as a burnt-out alcoholic, to whom he had turned for help a few years ago in the Prague case.*

A phone call brought the expected response that Maybury had been retired some time back: would an alternative

* *Three-Core Lead.*

be acceptable? It wouldn't; and Yeadings sat on at his desk, awaiting the outcome.

Maybury rang at a little after eleven, suggesting time and place for a meeting. Not the previous Dover Street bar, but by the skeletal diplodocus at the Natural History Museum. Yeadings, always delighted to revisit his schoolboy enthusiasms, arrived in advance of the midday rendezvous, hovering in the outer gallery between his favourite ichthyosaurus and the giant turtle shell. It was Hallowe'en half-term and there was a scrum of buzzing children with semidetached parents on hand. He wished he had known of the venue earlier and had Nan bring Sally along.

Maybury silently materialized alongside, little more than skeletal himself, raincoat over one shoulder, earnestly bespectacled, and with guidebook in hand. He made a convincing enough old-fashioned teacher boning up on next half-term's syllabus.

Yeadings said as much, and was rewarded with a wince much like he'd give, himself, in response to Beaumont's abysmal puns.

'Julian Feaist-Rivers,' he murmured, going straight to the matter in hand. 'I want to talk to him.'

'Question him?' Maybury sounded ever so slightly shocked.

'About his sometime adopted son.'

'Rodney Fairburn.'

'You seem to know of him.'

'Even something to his credit. He's doing interesting work.'

'Come off it. Don't pretend you take me for a film buff.'

'Ah, well. We took a look at him ourselves when he first came back. I hope you're not going to say he's returned to the wild ways of his youth.'

'It's partly his youth I'm concerned with,' Yeadings said abruptly.

'Best buried,' Maybury gave as his opinion.

'I'm sure that's what Fairburn thinks himself. But suppose there's someone anxious to dig it all up again? How far would he go to make sure that person didn't succeed?'

'Oh dear.' Maybury walked on and flopped on to a wooden bench. 'How much of his past?'

'Whatever he was sensitive about.'

'Mike, I take it we're talking blackmail here?'

'The materials for it exist. I don't know that we'd want to follow up his misdemeanours after all this time, but the possible blackmailer has been left in a bad way. Fairburn could be guilty of a recent crime: attempted murder.'

'I hope to God not!' Maybury took out a silver cigarette case, looked round, realized where he was and put it away again. 'We are running perilously short of experienced politicians with clean hands, let alone with clean families.' He sighed.

'Ex-family in this case. The public might award Feaist-Rivers brownie points for sending the fellow packing.'

'Mike, you know as well as I do that the great British public relishes only the nastier aspects of the news. It would be sold as the heartless chopping off of a promising young career, hypocritical harshness, breaking the poor adoptive mother's heart, etc. The gutter press would make a meal of it. Anyway, how can an approach to Feaist-Rivers affect your decision on the matter?'

'Frankly, I don't know. But I need the whole picture, not just jigsaw pieces. Fairburn has clammed up; suddenly claims the right to silence.'

'Provokin', ain't it?' Maybury's gaze swung back suddenly from the dinosaur's vertebrae and fixed Yeadings with suspicion. 'You haven't mentioned Miranda Gregory by name. Hope you're not trying to hold out on me.'

'I'm not entirely sure she has much of a connection with Feaist-Rivers. To my mind she contacted him to find out where her half-brother was.'

'Picked him up and laid him.'

'The easiest approach she knew.'

'I take your point. Certainly, after she'd been seen with
him three or four times she broke contact. But then one
can't carry on a torrid affair from a hospital bed. And while
we're on the subject, what's wrong with waiting until she's
in a position to tell all herself?'

'Because she may not pull through. So are you going to
say that that's the cue to brush everything under the carpet?
If so, I'm not with you. In a case of attempted murder I'll
have it *all* out in the open.'

'You know your trouble?' Maybury asked sadly. 'You're
a policeman, that's what. It's a waste of a decent fellow.'

He rose, stretching his lanky frame. 'Well, I was afraid
that was what you were set upon. I've had it set up:
2.30 p.m. in the Commons car park. Just gives you time to
stand me a round and a plate of smoked salmon.'

YEADINGS HANDED OVER the note Maybury had passed to
him and was shown where to leave the car. Not more than
five minutes after he arrived, Julian Feaist-Rivers appeared,
briefcase in hand, and climbed into the driving seat of a
claret-coloured Jaguar. He leaned over to push the passenger door open. The superintendent sauntered across and got
in. Neither spoke until they were at the top of the slope and
out in the open.

'Cleared up nicely,' the minister said then, gazing up at
blue sky.

Yeadings hoped the case might be too. 'A pleasant day,'
he said stolidly.

They went by Whitehall and Cockspur Street to Pall
Mall, then Feaist-Rivers turned into Waterloo Place to park
along Carlton House Terrace. 'Now, Superintendent,' he
invited, 'how can I help you?'

He was too intelligent to play footsie with, Yeadings
decided, and went in at the deep end. 'During the investi-

gation of an apparent road accident we came across a reference to Rodney Fairburn.'

'A *reference*, Superintendent?'

'We hold photographs and documents which lead us to believe that if there had been an attempt on the life of the injured party, he could be the person with the most solid motive.'

The man appeared genuinely shocked. So no one had prepared him for this. He thought a moment, then said, 'I assume it is no news to you that he was formerly known as Robin Feaist-Rivers; my adopted son, in fact.'

'Yes. You were aware he had returned to this country, sir?'

'Of course. I made it my business to follow his career from afar. Not from any remnant of affection, you understand. I wished to be quite certain that he made no approach to my wife. The poor woman has had grief enough from that quarter.'

'I appreciate that, sir. May I ask you to be quite frank with me about the reason for his dismissal from your family?'

Feaist-Rivers clearly found it distasteful. He hesitated, but finally gave in. 'I imagine I know what photographs you are holding, Superintendent. If they are the ones I have kept concealed for more than fifteen years, and recently handed to the young woman who had most right to them, you must know well enough my reason for refusing to harbour the wretch any longer. It was the last of a long series of disgraceful actions. I had endured much because of my wife's obsessive fondness for the boy, but even she finally found him—beyond all tolerance. I arranged for him to fly out to Sydney where he would receive a small monthly sum provided that he found honest employment and stayed in it for a period of two years. With that I washed my hands of him.'

'You say the final straw was the photograph incident? Not the firing of your home, then?'

Feaist-Rivers expelled his breath in a stifled gasp. He shook his head. 'No, that came after his dismissal. I could never prove that he was responsible. He was already forbidden access to the house. I will explain how it all came about.

'We had been abroad at the time of the—the orgy. There had been a small accidental fire in the library which he blamed on a visit from his sister. The girl had a tendency to arson, as we then, quite wrongly, understood. That was bad enough, but our tenant farmer, a man called Black, had come with a serious complaint that his daughter—er—'

'We know about Miss Garnet Black, sir.'

'I was incensed. I asked myself what depths he had sunk to.'

'So you searched his room, and you found the photographs of his sister and the friend Gobbo.'

'It had been staged *in my home*. That was clear from the background of the shots. Despicable in every way, but voyeurism on top of such depravity!'

'I understand, sir. How did the boy react?'

'There was no way he could defend himself. He tried appealing to my wife, but even that was out of the question by then. I insisted he move out while provision was made for his removal abroad. It was on the evening of the day he was due to leave by the night flight that the fire broke out. My wife and I were out of the house at the time.'

Yeadings nodded. 'The official report attributed the fire to an electrical wiring fault.'

'Quite so. Which he would have been more than capable of arranging. And although I had demanded all his keys back, he could have used a second set to get in; I had never changed the locks. There was no way of proving he had caused the fire, but I couldn't overlook the fact that the insurance premium had curiously gone astray.'

'You wrote a cheque for it to the Sheldrake Fire and Theft Insurance Company?'

Feaist-Rivers couldn't hide his start of surprise. 'You appear to have checked my movements minutely, Superintendent.'

Yeadings reached into an inner pocket for an envelope. He let the other man open it. His hands were trembling as he read the photocopied cheque. 'You have the original?'

'Yes. We think the girl was holding it. Miranda Gregory—Annie Lodd as she then was. It has been tested for stains. They were traces of blood and vomit of long standing. The blood was of her group. Somehow she must have taken it away with her—'

'I had written it in advance,' Feaist-Rivers said. 'It was left in the library with other correspondence for my secretary to post at the correct time. I have no doubt that the boy opened it, and I assumed it had been deliberately burnt in the waste bin—together with correspondence concerning Miss Black—while he was in a drug-induced euphoria. Perhaps he remembered something of it later, and that suggested burning down the house as a departing gesture.'

He stared ahead, the lines on his face deeply etched with bitterness. He turned to Yeadings. 'You say the girl had the cheque? Why should she have hung on to it so long?'

Yeadings kept his eyes off the other's face as he answered woodenly. 'Who knows? Perhaps first as a pathetic souvenir, and later for the same reason that you kept the photographs: as a guarantee of Robin's good behaviour from then on. We believe that once she had found out from you where he was to be found, she was starting to blackmail Rodney Fairburn, for revenge. And that was why he decided he had to kill her.'

Feaist-Rivers drummed with the heel of his hand on the steering wheel. 'When we met, some weeks back,' he said sombrely, 'I had no idea who she was. As a child she was so different—scrawny and mouselike, and she had the other name. We were attracted to each other. I believed she felt the same affection for me that I—

'Eventually she told me everything. I was appalled. Particularly because in the past I had totally misjudged her.

'She knew her brother had returned to this country but not where to find him. I'm afraid that, unintentionally, I let slip enough for her to know where to look. She seemed obsessed by him. She told me of her earliest memories, how brutally her father had used him. She had seen him as a martyr, even a fallen angel.'

'I should like to hear everything she told you, Mr Feaist-Rivers. Right from those earliest memories.'

The man was silent a moment, then in a shaken voice told the superintendent of the vicious canings she had overheard as a child, her own experience with the boy in the attic of the Surrey house, her complex involvement with him as both reached puberty.

'Her impressions of his conduct towards herself were extremely confused. I was strongly against their meeting again, and to ensure this I'm afraid I showed her the photographs.'

'What effect did they have?'

'She was horribly shocked. Not so much at sight of herself. Whatever memories of the incident remained, she had contrived to find an excuse for it. What appalled her was the identity of the man she was photographed with. In her drugged state she hadn't realized which of the two was ravishing her, and even as a child she'd found this Gobbo revolting.'

'Yet you gave her the photographs?'

'She wouldn't hand them back. She said something that seemed to make sense then: that she must keep them as part of the cure.'

'And you thought she meant her own?'

'Yes. There had certainly been trauma.'

'You were no longer using them as a threat yourself?'

Feaist-Rivers shook his head. 'Fairburn appeared to have changed—and society had changed—enough for his present behaviour to seem almost the norm.'

The man sounded cynical but not vindictive. There was another short silence.

'After that, you broke the association with Ms Gregory?'

'It was entirely her doing, as though the truth of Robin's treachery was too much to lie between us. I admit now I misjudged the depth of her feelings. I should have known there was more than enough cause for her to feel rancour, and that our relationship must suffer because of it.'

Yeadings watched him with a kind of pity. Feaist-Rivers still believed that she had cared for him, not merely used him.

And yet—the man was a skilled political animal. How could one ever be sure he hadn't deliberately presented her with means and motive to avenge them both?

TWENTY-THREE

ROSEMARY ZYCZYNSKI felt restless and unsatisfied. The almost springlike sky and gentle sunshine mocked her. Of late she had felt increasingly impatient with herself and determined to tackle her personal hang-up. But consideration for the job, and the thought of Paula, had forced her to break off the budding affair with Angus Mott. Then, scarcely drawing breath, she'd turned to Max Harris. Not tentatively or submissive, she acknowledged, but with a quite fierce possessiveness.

She had amazed herself. Now, in the aftermath, she was left to puzzle out just where they stood, because Max wasn't an object, an old dog's bone to pick up, gnaw at and discard again. She wasn't sure she could just say thanks for the therapy and walk away. Yet she wanted that option left open.

Admittedly there were other things in life than bed and breakfast. She played with the idea of applying for a transfer, even going back into uniform to face the challenge of promotion. But if her feeling for the Yeadings team was too strong to put it at risk in one way, defection was also out of the question.

Today Angus and the Boss were both in London, Mott at Scotland Yard about the Collins shooting, Yeadings busy on some unspecified chore of his own. Z finished typing her reports and took a call from Wycombe Hospital.

Miranda Gregory had died in the night.

It depressed her further. This evening she should visit Annette Briers and sympathize. There was Gwen Lodd too, but she hoped that the task of comforting her would fall to someone else. In the meantime...

They still held the keys to the Gregory apartment. On an impulse Z went to sign for them and collected her car.

On the drive to Beaconsfield she questioned her motives. Perhaps she was moved by a kind of respect for the dead, a wish to tidy up and leave things seemly.

THE APARTMENT WAS full of sunshine, painfully welcoming. Z walked from room to room, picturing the elegant woman in her home, rising from bed, showering, making her meals, writing her shopping lists, binning the trash: alive. In the kitchen she opened cupboard doors and surveyed the contents: packets and tins of every imaginable delicacy; asparagus tips, game soup, celery hearts, cat food.

Cat food? Nobody had ever mentioned that Miranda Gregory had a pet. There was no entry flap to the front or balcony doors.

Z went through to look at the tubs of evergreens and saw a small green china bowl upturned by one of them.

'Hallo there!' a cheerful voice from the neighbouring balcony called. 'Isn't the sunshine lovely? Are you a friend of Ms Gregory?'

The amiable greeting didn't mask that the building housed a Neighbourhood Watch conscience. Z leaned across and flashed her warrant card. 'WDC Zyczynski, Thames Valley Police,' she told the woman. 'I was wondering about Ms Gregory's cat.'

'Cat? She never had a cat. Unless you mean poor little Minou? She belonged at number five, but she visited us all for what she could get. She thought milk wasn't good enough; it had to be cream. Siamese can be funny that way.'

All in the past tense. 'What happened to her?'

'Oh, it was horrible. Some yobbo got in. People don't always make sure the outer door shuts properly after them. She was literally carved up. Quite disgusting. Everyone was most upset. The body was left out on the landing near Ms

Gregory's door. It must have been a terrible shock for her, coming home and finding it.'

'Dreadful.' Z shuddered theatrically and withdrew. As she re-entered the kitchen she was suddenly aware of the irregular outline of a rack above the working surface. It held five excellent Sabatier knives with black handles. But it was made for six. She went across to examine them. They were inserted in order of size. The missing one would have been a meat cleaver.

Miranda Gregory must have been out of her mind to attack so savagely a pet she normally gave food to. Yet the connection with the bloody cleaver found wrapped in a tea towel in Lodd's Wandsworth kitchen was undeniable. The cat had been killed here, and the weapon later taken elsewhere. Why? When it could have been disposed of in so many other ways.

Perhaps it wasn't Gregory who'd killed the cat, but, as the neighbour said, some outsider who had managed to get in. Had got inside Gregory's flat and taken one of her Sabatier knives to do it!

Lodd himself? Had she given him a set of keys to her apartment? But if they were so close, wouldn't he have known that the cat wasn't hers in any case? And Miranda had reputedly never received visitors here.

It was more likely that an intruder in the apartment had found the cat on the balcony and assumed it belonged there. Maybe Gregory had wrapped the bloody knife and taken it to Lodd to show him how vindictive someone had been.

And then he'd kept it. He must have had some reason to do that. But what? Reason seemed to be lacking all round.

Still pondering their mental states, Z let herself out, taking due care shutting the outer door, and returned to her car. By the time she had lunched, written up her notes on the morning and checked up what was waiting for her at the office, it would be time to set out for Wembley to break the news of Ms Gregory's death.

ANNETTE, having gone off for a quiet weep in her room, came back insisting that Z should share a bottle of wine with them in an effort to raise their spirits. It was a rosé, like Max had brought on the evening they all had a meal together.

Z, short of a subject that didn't involve him or the recent crimes, asked, 'Did Ms Gregory ever mention a cat?'

'Minou,' Annette said. 'A neighbour's beautiful Siamese which insisted on cream. She seemed really fond of it.'

Clearing the table to lay the cloth, Annette removed a stack of papers. Z put out a steadying hand as they seemed about to spill. 'What are those?'

'Estimates. When we set up an operation at M and C we make out a menu of different options. These are the primaries. When the client has selected one scheme we transfer the details to differently printed sheets. See? Green lines instead of blue.' She pulled one out. 'That one's an authorized operation, ready to send to the client.'

'I've seen sheets like this before,' Z said faintly. 'I thought they were accounts.'

'They are, in a way. We start off like this before the final entries go into the company computer.'

'I see.' She hoped she did. 'And you bring them home to make them up?'

'Well, I shouldn't really, but I do when I'm pressed. It saves office time. They aren't really supposed to go out of the building.'

Z nodded, regarding the girl with fresh interest. As soon as she could politely get away she would be haring back to her own office to take another long look at the 'accounts' from the box in Lodd's loft.

YEADINGS CAME IN LATE and caught her frowning over the entries. 'Have you got something interesting there?'

'I think so. It's difficult because they use a code of abbreviations and serial numbers which I haven't access to, but comparing the blue entries with the green—'

'Show me.'

'—it looks as though there are two sets of accounts. The same figures aren't copied through identically because changes are made as the plans are considered. See this pair. They're for the same operation, but added items have sent the total up by several thousand.'

'Have you come up with any idea why Miranda Gregory should have held on to these particular sheets?'

'Not unless— We did decide, didn't we, that she was at least considering blackmail of Rodney Fairburn. Suppose she was holding these figures as evidence against someone else. Evidence of cooking the books.'

'But you explained that the difference in totals on each pair of forms was legitimate.'

'Yes. But which set of figures went into the company computer? If it was the first, lesser amount, then the final settlement would have been for more than shows up on company accounts. Auditors aren't going to inspect every cancelled cheque alongside those figures.'

'But the cheques had to be payable to Matherson and Corby. How could the difference be fraudulently diverted to someone's pocket?'

They pored over the figures together, then called in one of the uniformed inspectors who was notoriously numerate.

'No doubt about it,' he gave as his final opinion. 'If the same department issuing the estimates has control of its own expenses, one could arrange a nice little scam with the computer entries. All one would need to fix it would be a fictional outside company being paid irregular fees. Call yourself Ditchem Factors, or whatever you like; make yourself the owner-director. A bit risky, though, if you've given anyone working alongside cause to think you're up to some dodgy business.'

'And the dates on these estimates,' Yeadings said heavily, 'refer to a couple of years back. The clients being Farringdon Bell and Winter on this set and Fuller Thorburn on the other.'

'Files from the F drawer,' Z said. 'These could be the firms Mrs Lodd was checking on the other night, when I went back and caught her.'

'Checking? Or making sure all the records were still there?'

'She could have discovered these had gone missing, having been removed by Miranda Gregory.'

Yeadings sat and made a steeple of his hands, resting his head on them. 'I think,' he murmured, 'we'll have Mott in. He should be back from London. Ring him, Z.'

'Did you hear, sir, that Ms Gregory died in the night?' she asked, when she had phoned through to the DI.

'No. Poor lass. But just as well, perhaps. Now we don't have to charge her.'

'With fraud?' Not so nice to have that as the source of that elegant living, she thought.

'No; blackmail. Don't you remember Annette mentioning how Mrs Lodd had disappeared from Matherson and Corby in the course of an afternoon? That would have been Miranda's doing. If it had been the firm that forced her out, they would never have recalled her when Gregory went absent. Gwen Lodd's dismissal was a private and personal arrangement between the two women. Lodd "applied for early retirement for health reasons", rather than face the music.

'Look at the dates again, Z. They're from a period when Lodd was still in charge, and Gregory hadn't overtaken her in the Matherson and Corby hierarchy.

'As a new broom Gregory proved so efficient that she backtracked, and discovered Gwen's habit of compensating herself for all her frustrations. And what's sauce for the goose... Our Miranda decided she'd profit from putting pressure on wherever she felt a need for personal revenge. She was going into the blackmail racket with relish, punishing her half-brother for past abuse, along with her adoptive mother for harshness to herself and to poor Peter Lodd, her only friend in need.

'An avenging fury, provoking an equal fury in return. As Gwen saw it, Miranda had already brought disgrace on her while still a child, had depraved and stolen her husband, wrecked her home life, and now ruined her remaining career. She was driven into a corner where the only escape was to get rid of Miranda by any means to hand.

'Z, I want you with Angus when he goes to bring her in.'

AS GWEN LODD OPENED the door and saw the three of them—Fox had come along for the ride—she fell back in dismay. It was clear she had been drinking. Something dark had spilled down the front of her housecoat, and her normally neat hair was disordered.

'Shall we go through?' Mott suggested as she seemed to bar their way.

In the little back parlour, dark now that the sun had long passed over, she sank into a chair under the single light. It made her face more sallow, its hollows brutally shadowed. 'Annie...' she said hoarsely.

'Your daughter is dead, Mrs Lodd. She died in the night, quite peacefully.'

'I went—I went to see her. This afternoon. They told me.'

It seemed to have blown her mind. She couldn't get past it.

'Mrs Lodd,' Mott asked, 'can you drive?'

She nodded.

'Did Ms Gregory come to visit you the Saturday night before she was found injured?'

The woman seemed to be considering this. 'What if she did?'

'Did you have words?'

'About what?' Her eyes had taken on the sly look of the insane.

'About the cat?' Z said quietly. 'The little Siamese cat you'd attacked with a meat cleaver.'

'Horrid little thing,' she muttered. 'It scratched me.'

'How did you get into the apartment?'

Gwen Lodd smiled distantly at her remembered cunning. 'I'd taken her keys at the office, and got them all copied.'

'And why did you go there?'

No answer.

'Was it,' Z suggested, 'to get back some papers she'd taken from the office? Did you think she had them at her flat?'

'They weren't there.' There were desperate tears in her voice.

'Let's go back to her visit to you here,' Mott insisted. 'She came by car, a red one which you wouldn't recognize when it pulled up outside, so you opened the door when she knocked and she came in.'

'Pushed in. She was rough with me. I—I hit her with the brass lamp, and I thought when she woke up she'd do me some damage. I was scared.'

'So you tied her up. How did you get her into the car?'

'I made her walk. She managed all right.'

'And so on and so on,' Mott said as if to himself. He looked at Fox and shrugged. The woman must already have been out of her mind over killing Collins the previous day.

'Z, put some things together for her. Mrs Lodd, I'm arresting you for the murder of Miranda Gregory, and I have to caution you that you have the right to remain silent, but anything you do say...'

YEADINGS STAYED ON until Mott radioed in that they were on their way back with the woman. Although the Collins killing was the earlier crime, he'd beaten the Met to the arrest. They'd later need access to question the prisoner on the London case. 'Good,' said Yeadings. 'They will have every facility.' He was just reaching for his hat when a call came through from DCI Meredith.

'I thought you'd like to know our men have found the

.38 revolver at Gwen Lodd's house, a Smith and Wesson belonging to her sometime husband.

'It seems Lodd had been an officer in the Royal Signals TA unit at Hammersmith. Probably had used the thing for his small-arms practice and left it behind when he quitted the family home. They also turned up Miranda Gregory's crocodile-skin handbag with various contents now being listed. One item was Collins' visiting card with a scribbled note: "Your office sevenish for delivery," and the date he was shot. He must have been lurking in the building somewhere waiting for her to get free.'

Yeadings grunted. 'God knows how Gwen Lodd got wise to him. Perhaps his shadowing wasn't so good. We have to assume she noticed him watching her at some time, reversed the order and started shadowing him, ready armed in case of trouble, hoping to find what further evidence he'd unearthed about her money dealings. He led her into Matherson and Corby, then his luck ran out,' he suggested.

'Something of the sort. Fox says she's cracked up completely. He thinks we'll have no trouble getting her to talk, but she may be found unfit to plead. We'd need to question her on the Collins death while you're holding her for Miranda Gregory's. Congratulations anyway; it's a statistic cleared for us both.'

YEADINGS HAD NO FEELING of elation. Only part of the effort was over; next would come the assembling of their case for the Crown Prosecution Office. Mott and Z would be recording the questioning, which would take them well into the night. Later the wretched woman would be officially charged. For himself, he was going home.

Arrived there, Yeadings went straight through to the lounge where Luke, retrieved from his cot after a bawling session, was sitting on the floor dozily sucking the ear of a stuffed rabbit. He lifted him up, ruffled his hair and set him on his knee.

In a few moments Nan came in with Mike's tea and a

wholemeal biscuit. 'I just heard on the local news that your hit-and-run victim has died.'

'I'm afraid so.'

'So now it'll be a murder or manslaughter charge. The newspapers called her the Limbo Lady. A mystery woman without any past, you said. That's going to be a teaser for you.'

Yeadings leaned back wearily. 'I think we've got it sorted. Finally it turned out that she'd more past than most of us. Up in the loft and the attic.'

Murder at St. Adelaide's

A FRANCES FINN MYSTERY

First Time In Paperback

Kansas City private detective Frances Finn
returns to her alma mater at the request
of dying Mother Celeste, who claims that a
young nun who died thirty years earlier was
actually murdered. The Mother Superior knows
who the killer is, but refuses to point the finger,
insisting that there is no danger. But when
Mother Celeste is found brutally murdered,
Frances knows that there is indeed a great deal
of danger at hand and that someone has a
secret they want kept…at any cost.

GERELYN HOLLINGSWORTH

"A good debut." –Armchair Detective

Available in November 1997
at your favorite retail outlet.

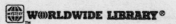 **WORLDWIDE LIBRARY®**

WGH255

Just the Fax, Ma'am

First Time in Paperback

A MOLLY MASTERS MYSTERY

To Molly Masters, the whole situation was absurd. As a cartoonist and mother of two, she was surprised—and a little angry—to find that the only risqué drawing she'd ever done has appeared in the pages of a porn magazine. Not quite surprising was the fact that Preston Saunders, the husband of her arch rival, had stolen the drawing and submitted it to the magazine.

Molly begins receiving hate mail from antiporn groups, then Preston is found dead. In search of a killer, Molly goes undercover—posing as a high school student—and is forced to dodge a hail of bullets. But it's only a matter of time before she finds the killer...or the killer finds her....

Leslie O'Kane

"Excellent." —*Poisoned Pen*

Available in November 1997 at your favorite retail outlet.

 WORLDWIDE LIBRARY®

WLOK254

From the author of THE GIRL WITH THE PHONY NAME

Charles Mathes

"...a real page-turner with a
genuinely surprising ending."
—*Booklist*

Emma Passant is a professional magician who knows that the hand is
often quicker than the eye. But when her grandfather is murdered and
soon afterward a friend is killed by the same gun, Emma puts her act
on hold and sets out to find some answers. With only a smattering of
clues, she follows a trail of cryptic words, rumors of stolen treasure
and her own snow-shrouded memories, where she discovers
shattering deceptions—and the shocking truth about her own past....

The Girl Who Remembered Snow

First Time in Paperback

Available in December 1997 at your favorite retail outlet.

To order your copy, please send your name, address, zip or postal code along with a
check or money order (please do not send cash) for $4.99 for each book ordered ($5.99
in Canada), plus 75¢ postage and handling ($1.00 in Canada), payable to Worldwide
Mystery, to:

In the U.S.
Worldwide Mystery
3010 Walden Avenue
P.O. Box 1325
Buffalo, NY 14269-1325

In Canada
Worldwide Mystery
P.O. Box 609
Fort Erie, Ontario
L2A 5X3

Please specify book title with your order.
Canadian residents add applicable federal and provincial taxes.

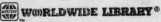 WORLDWIDE LIBRARY®

WSNOW